# THE LADY ⊕F S⊕RR⊕WS

# THE LADY
# OF
# SORROWS

## A SEVEN DEADLY SINS
## MYSTERY

### ANNE ZOUROUDI

Little, Brown and Company
*New York  Boston  London*

Copyright © 2010 by Anne Zouroudi
Map © 2010 by John Gilkes

Little, Brown and Company
Hachette Book Group
237 Park Avenue, New York, NY 10017
littlebrown.com

First North American Edition: March 2014
Originally published in Great Britain by Bloomsbury Publishing, 2010

Little, Brown and Company is a division of Hachette Book Group, Inc. The Little, Brown name and logo are trademarks of Hachette Book Group, Inc.

The publisher is not responsible for websites (or their content) that are not owned by the publisher.

ISBN 978-0-316-21784-2
LCCN: 2014930472

10 9 8 7 6 5 4 3 2 1

RRD-C

Printed in the United States of America

For Kate

Island of Kalkos

Gypsy camp

Bishop's House

Church of the
Lady of Sorrows

Cemetery

Port

Navayo Bay

"She harbors in her heart a furious hate,
And thou shalt find the dire effects too late;
Fix'd on revenge, and obstinate to die.
Haste swiftly hence, while thou hast pow'r to fly.
The sea with ships will soon be cover'd o'er,
And blazing firebrands kindle all the shore.
Prevent her rage, while night obscures the skies,
And sail before the purple morn arise.
Who knows what hazards thy delay may bring?
Woman's a various and a changeful thing."
Thus Hermes in the dream; then took his flight
Aloft in air unseen, and mix'd with night.

Virgil, *The Aeneid*
Book IV

# DRAMATIS PERSONAE

Hermes Diaktoros – the fat man, an investigator
Father Linos Egiotis – a priest
Sambeca – a church custodian
Agiris – Sambeca's brother, a gardener
Nassia – mother of Sambeca and Agiris
Kara Athaniti – an art historian, an old friend of Hermes
Kostas & Kostakis – a pair of elderly twins
Apostolis – proprietor of a harbor-front *kafenion*
Sotiris – an icon painter
Sammy – Sotiris's grandson
Mercuris – Sotiris's son-in-law
Tina – Sotiris's daughter
Pavlos – a gypsy

# THE LADY OF SORROWS

# Prologue

### Spring, 1863

In favorable conditions, the crossing from mainland to island was short: with a moderate southwesterly, half a day, or less. And, when the *Constantinos* sailed from the mainland port, the captain judged the weather pretty fair, though the wind was a little more westerly than was ideal, and fresh enough to put foam crests on the waves.

The cabin boy was the captain's nephew, and too young to take work seriously; instead, he played a game, picking out images in the white clouds overhead.

"Look!" he shouted, pointing upwards. "An old man's face!"

But the mate and the crewman were busy hoisting the sails; by the time they'd looked up to indulge him, the clouds had shifted in the wind, and the cabin boy's old man was dissolving.

"That's no old man," said the crewman, head tilted back to see the sky. "Any fool can see it's a ram's head!"

"Ram's head, my backside," said the mate. "Look at the

breadth in that beam! It's the rear view of my mother-in-law, is that!"

The game passed time; they played on as they coiled ropes on the boat's deck, as they set the sails and the captain steered his course beyond the harbor. The crew was cheerful; they'd been away from home for several weeks, ferrying cargo between the islands, traveling wherever the work took them: maize from Gallipoli to Chios, mastic from Chios down to Crete, citrus fruits from Crete back up to Naxos. Boat and crew were for hire, their destination always in the hirer's hands. Now, at last, they'd picked up a shipment for home, and all their spirits were high.

Except, it seemed, for their passenger's.

This stranger watched the horizon and smoked his pipe. Black-bearded and heavyset, with a nose which had been broken more than once, and a scar across his scalp where no hair grew, he was silent and unsmiling. His clothes were in the Cretan style—wide trousers tucked into broad-topped, mud-caked boots—and, even though the sun (when not behind the shifting clouds) was warm, he kept his leather coat fastened tight around his body with an ornate-buckled belt.

He sat where he had chosen, on a barrel of Naxos wine, his feet resting on a box of Turkish apricots. His accent suggested origins in the Baltic; he'd claimed to have no Greek currency, and paid his fare with a silver bangle engraved in Cyrillic script. The crew's island wasn't his final destination, so he said; he was traveling north, to Italy, but their home, he told them, was another step on his way. When the captain asked why he didn't take the packet—the fast mail boat that left each week for Athens—he shrugged, and said that he preferred the slower route. At his insistence, his bags were in the wheelhouse, out of the spray; he'd brought aboard a sailor's canvas sack, and an alligator-skin suitcase with brass fastenings, more suited to a gentleman than this man. In curiosity, the captain looked them over, but found neither bag was marked: no name, no place of origin, only outlines on the suitcase where all past carriers' labels had been removed.

An hour from port, when the hills of the mainland were fading behind them and the coast of remote Kalkos was to the east, the weather worsened. The fresh breeze which had been in their favor strengthened, and veered; the spring sky reverted to wintry gray, its benign white clouds darkening, and swelling with rain. With the sun hidden and the wind rising, it grew cold. The cabin boy fetched a blanket from the hold, and, draping it round his shoulders, took a seat close to the stranger on the wine barrels.

As the waves increased, the boat was lifted higher, pitching and rolling like a rocking cradle. The stranger placed his feet on the wooden deck, bracing his legs to hold himself steady, and stared back across the sea towards the land they had just left.

"Are you seasick, *kyrie?*" asked the cabin boy.

The stranger turned his dark eyes on the boy. The wind blew the stranger's long hair across his face; with that and his heavy beard, it was impossible to tell if he were ill or not.

"It never bothers me," said the boy, "no matter how heavy the sea. Never been seasick in my life."

The stranger looked away and hooked his hair behind his ear, as if a clear view of the disappearing mainland were important. His earlobe was pierced by a gold hoop, in the fashion of the gypsies the boy had been raised to mistrust.

"Where're you from, *kyrie?*" asked the boy. He dipped his head to admire the stranger's belt buckle; it was a craftsman's work, an airborne eagle gripping a writhing snake.

The stranger's eyes turned once more to the boy; then his attention switched back to the fading landmass.

"You ask too many questions," he said, at last. "Where I come from, they cut the tongues from lads who prattle."

The boy looked into the stranger's face, expecting a smile at what must be a joke, but no smile came. Alarmed, he slipped down from the barrels and, clutching his blanket around himself, made his barefoot way to the wheelhouse.

Ahead, through the wheelhouse window, high banks of dark clouds signaled the approach of a storm. The boat rolled to port, and the boy, stumbling, grabbed his uncle's jacket to keep himself upright. The captain was fighting the wheel, endeavoring to stay on their homeward course; in his wrists, raised veins showed the tightness of his grip.

"Tell the men to shorten sail, fast as they can," ordered the captain, "then go below, and lie yourself down. This storm can't miss us, no matter what. And tell our passenger he'd better join you below. He's sitting in the way of a soaking where he is now."

The boat rolled to starboard, more heavily than before. Above the wind and the flapping of sailcloth, both mate and crewman shouted as they struggled to reduce sail. With the rolling, the boy stumbled again, and dropped his blanket on the stranger's luggage.

The lashings on the cargo were frayed and half-rotted, and as the *Constantinos* rolled, the cargo shifted, snapping one of its bindings. Crates, boxes and barrels slipped, shifting a foot or two across the deck and causing the boat to list to starboard.

Hand over hand along the deck rails, the boy made his way back to where the stranger still sat, facing the land they had left. The stranger seemed not to notice the boy's approach, and started when the boy's hand touched his shoulder.

"Captain says to come below, or you'll get wet," said the boy, raising his voice over the wind and the flap of the lowering sails. He pointed to the wheelhouse.

The stranger's feet were braced now on the deck, his body rigid against the wine barrel. It was this stance, the boy observed, which gave the man his steadiness.

"Leave me be," said the stranger, roughly; but as he spoke, more of the cargo slipped, shifting farther towards the deck edge, and the stranger kept his place only by splaying his feet wider to hold the barrel's weight. Cold spray hit the boy's face, and spattered the leather of the stranger's coat.

"You'd better come below," urged the boy. "You'll get the worst of it, here."

"I've paid my fare," said the stranger, brushing down his coat, "so you can tell your captain to let me choose my own seat."

The boy started back towards the wheelhouse; but as he moved, the boat suddenly dipped, and the peak of the wave that had hit her ran up over the side, sluicing the deck boards with seawater which covered the boy's ankles before running out through the scuppers. Beneath his bare feet, the boards were slippery, and the boy moved on in tiny steps, his anxious eyes on the crew still struggling with the sails.

"Lash it down, lash it down your end!" shouted the mate, but the crewman shook his head as the sailcloth billowed and thrashed, resisting his efforts to roll it tight enough to throw a rope around.

The first drops of rain fell, driving hard as pellets in the wind. Another great wave struck the port side, causing the boat to heel so far that the whole cargo—easily mobile on the now-slippery deck—shifted under its own momentum to the starboard railing, leaving only the stranger's barrel held in place by his braced feet.

Now hopelessly unstable, with an increasing list to starboard, the *Constantinos* failed to right herself, but lay with her decks dangerously close to the water and vulnerable to the sea. The rain began to fall heavily, forming a mist as thick as fog, through which wind and waves moved them farther and farther off their intended course, closer and closer to Kalkos's treacherous lee shore.

The mate and the crewman left their fight with the sails, and instead turned their efforts to the cargo, attempting to right the caïque by maneuvering the heaviest of the load back to midships; but the angle of the deck was against them, and their feet could find no purchase on the slippery boards. Heaving on an unmovable crate, they caught each other's eyes. They knew what they must do; they knew too that the captain would never give permission.

But the mate shouted anyway to the boy.

"Tell your uncle we must jettison some cargo," he yelled, "or else we'll all go down!"

Hand over hand on the deck rail, the boy at last reached the wheelhouse.

The captain wasn't there.

"Uncle!" shouted the boy. "Where are you?"

He shivered from cold and apprehension. Crouching, he peered down the ladder into the hold, where the captain, red-faced with effort, struggled to close an open porthole half-submerged by the caïque's list. Seawater poured into the hold, drenching the captain; around him, floating objects—the mate's going-ashore hat, a nautical chart, the bailing bucket—bobbed on rising water which had already reached the captain's thighs.

"Uncle!" yelled the boy. "They're asking should they jettison some cargo?"

"Jettison cargo be damned!" the captain shouted back. "We'll jettison whatever's cursed us with this storm!"

With some violence, another wave hit; the boat heaved, the hold timbers creaked, and overhead more slipping cargo scraped across the deck. The captain moved one foot in an attempt to keep his balance, but slipped, and went down on his backside, up to his chest in water as the porthole cover swung free, and through it the sea ran in like an open tap.

Shaking water from his hair, spitting water from his mouth, the captain pulled himself to his feet. Water streamed off him, from his sleeve ends and the hem of his jacket. Angrily, he faced the frightened boy.

"There's something foul aboard with us," said the captain,

wagging a finger at the boy, as if he were to blame. "Someone's brought bad luck aboard my boat."

Another wave hit, and the caïque seemed perceptibly to sink several more inches. In the wheelhouse, the mate grabbed the boy's arm, pulling him from the doorway to look down the hold ladder at the captain.

The sight of the rising water made him pale.

"God save us," he said, and crossed himself.

"God may save us, if he wishes," shouted the captain, "but your job is to save this boat! Get forward, where you should be!"

"The cargo must go!" the mate shouted back, crossing himself again. "It's all slipped, and it's taking us down!"

The captain gave no answer, but moved back to the porthole, and tried again to force it shut with his elbow, his cold-stiffened fingers ready to turn the fastening screw; but the pressure of the incoming water defeated him.

"What do you say, captain?" persisted the mate. "Yes or no?"

"Jettison the cargo and you'll go in after it!" yelled the captain. "The pair of you are no more use than women! Get it midships and lash it down, for Christ's sake! The boy'll help you. Go!"

But as the mate turned, cursing, from the hold, a crate splashed overboard.

In fury, the captain left the porthole, waded through the water to the ladder and climbed it in two strides. As he rounded the wheelhouse, a second crate hit the sea.

Less afraid of the danger in the hold than of his uncle's

rage, the boy didn't follow the captain, but instead descended the ladder and lowered himself into the water, which on his small body was to his waist. Half swimming, half wading, he reached the porthole, and leaned all his slight weight against it, attempting to accomplish what the captain had failed to do.

The captain was on the deck directly over his head, and above the noise of the boy's own struggle—his splashing and the rush of water, his cursing of the sea and the obstinate porthole—came unmistakably the sounds of argument, though over the running-in of water and the wind, the angry words were lost, and the subject of the argument was unclear. Another jettisoned crate plunged into the sea; a moment later, a fist smacked a jaw, and a heavy object dropped onto the deck.

Three minutes of effort showed the boy that his task was impossible. Tired and chilled, he forced his way back to the ladder, up onto the deck, and around the wheelhouse.

On deck, the stranger lay on his back, arms splayed. A little blood ran from a cut on his cheekbone; from the back of his head, where it had struck the boards, more blood ran in the wet.

The mate, the crewman and the captain all stood in silence, looking down at the stranger.

"Is he dead?" asked the cabin boy.

"Not likely," said the captain roughly, "but out cold enough to stop him ditching any more of my load." He kicked the sole of the stranger's boot. "Bastard's cost me a small fortune already. If we lose this cargo, I'll lose this boat and we'll all be out of a job. You," he said, laying his hand on the boy's head, "go and take the helm! Bring her round to port if you can; bring her round hard, and we'll do all right."

But as if to prove him wrong, a wave caught the stern, and swung the *Constantinos*'s prow towards the sharp rocks and shallow waters of Kalkos's shoreline.

And as the boy made his way back to the wheel, the mate raised his objections.

"The stranger was right to do what he did!" he shouted. "She's going down anyway, now! Lighten the load, and she might at least take us within swimming distance!"

"I've paid you to crew this boat, and if you don't, I'll lay you out like him!" yelled the captain. He jerked his thumb towards the stranger on the deck, whose eyelids flickered briefly to show the whites of his eyes, then closed again.

"You go down with her if you like," shouted the mate, "but I'll not be joining you." He glanced across at the island's shoreline, now less than a kilometer away, though the sea was high and rough, and the water would be cold and life-sapping. He took off his jacket and threw it aside, then sat down on the deck planks by the unconscious stranger's feet and pulled off his boots.

The crewman crouched beside him and grasped his shoulder.

"Don't leave us!" he begged. "We'll never get through this without you! There's the boy, remember—think about the boy!"

The mate shook off the crewman's hand and got to his feet, shirt-sleeved and barefoot. Through the wheelhouse window, pale-faced and white-knuckled, the boy watched the men whose words he couldn't hear.

In the hold, seawater was halfway up the ladder.

"Let him decide," said the mate, hands on his hips, facing the captain. "The cargo goes, or I do. Choose! Can you swim, from here to there? Can the boy?"

The captain shook his head.

"The hell with you!" he said. "All right. Ditch half!"

The three men worked together, heaving barrels and boxes over the side, as the boat was blown closer and closer to Kalkos, a trail of floating cargo in its wake; but when half was gone, the *Constantinos*'s prospects were still bleak.

Shaking his head, the captain called out to his men.

"Enough!" he said. "Enough, no more! We're beaten, lads; save your strength for swimming! Prepare yourselves, and say a prayer whilst I fetch the boy."

He hurried to the wheelhouse, where water from the hold tickled the boy's bare toes and the view through the window was of approaching rocks.

The captain grabbed the boy's arm.

"Leave it!" he shouted, pulling him from the wheel. He glanced around, then grabbed the stranger's suitcase. "This'll float," he said, slipping the catches to empty the contents. He raised the lid, expecting clothes and shoes; but the suitcase contained nothing except a single object wrapped in chamois leather. The captain grabbed the object, ready to toss it aside; but in curiosity, and in the hope of recovering losses the stranger had cost him, quickly removed the chamois. The object was a painting, an icon of some age: old gold and the sorrowful features of a red-robed Virgin. "A few drachmas for this, maybe," he said to the boy and, rewrapping it, shut it in the case.

"Now listen to me," he said, bending to the boy and pressing the suitcase on him. "You hold on to this as if your life depended on it. And stay as close to me as you can!" Like the mate, he shrugged off his coat and tugged his boots off his feet. "Keep hold of your float, and swim hard as you can for shore. No matter where; anywhere you can get out of the sea. We'll worry about where we've washed up when the storm passes."

Dragging the frightened boy with him, he joined the crewmen on the starboard side, where with each wave the deck rail touched the water.

"Well, lads," said the captain. "Good luck to us all; St. Nicholas watch over us."

"Swim for the barrels," said the mate. "Get hold of one, and it'll take you in."

The boy looked at the stranger still lying on the deck. The sea had washed the blood from round his head.

"What about him, uncle?" asked the boy.

"He must take care of himself," said the captain. "If the *Constantinos* doesn't go down, we'll come and find him, later. For now, you think about yourself. Keep hold of that suitcase, and stay close; stay close to me, for God's sake. Are we ready then, lads? Abandon ship!"

# One

The work was laborious; the task was always long. The icon painter's art required silence and solitude, and he preferred the late hours of the night, those quiet, hallowed hours whilst others slept. Each time he sat down in the lamplight at the bench, he bowed his head to ask a blessing through prayer, so that the image he created should be worthy of the venerated saint.

He followed the steps laid down by the ancient masters, giving to each meticulous process its necessary time and care. The seasoned oak panel was sized with rabbit-skin glue, covered with fine linen and sized again. Coat by coat, he built the plasterlike base of whitest gesso, sanding the flaws from each dried layer until the finish was smooth as glass. With compasses and ruler, he traced the design's sacred geometry—the underlying cross, the squares, circles and triangles—painstakingly checking measurements and the calculated proportions: four nose-lengths in the figure's face, two nose-lengths from nose tip to chin.

The gold leaf for the background was too delicate for fingers. Instead, he ran a squirrel-hair brush through his own hair, giving the bristles the trace of oil they needed to lift the precious tissue. On the glue-soaked polished surface, he lay down overlapping leaves until the base was covered and, with the agate-tipped burnisher inherited from his father, spent hours coaxing the gold into a rich glow.

Then, to painting. Night after night, he mixed the tempera as his father had taught him, breaking an egg and straining white from yolk. With care, he rolled the soft yolk ball from palm to palm, passing it from hand to hand until its skin was dry; then, pinching the sac over a porcelain bowl, he pricked it, and let the yolk run from the sac as his emulsion. He ground the pigments finely on a marble slab, and mixed the prescribed colors—vermilion, raw sienna, titanium white—with the egg yolk, adding vinegar and water to the right consistency. He applied the paint in the required symbolic order, working from dark to light—robes and hair, then flesh tones, then the highlights which made the holy figure radiate its sacred light. And, when all was done and dry, he mixed his varnish to the secret recipe, and glazed the icon to enhance its mystical glow.

His eyes, as they reflected on the painting, were reddened with fatigue. But the work was good, near perfect, and the icon painter was pleased. He'd studied his craft diligently, over the years, and put heart and soul into mastering the family knowledge.

Time, then, to put that knowledge to good use.

Experience had taught the travelers many lessons; the most important was *Better to stay away from others if you can.*

They arrived on a morning ferry, then bided their time; they wanted no trouble with policemen, or landowners, or stone-slinging brats.

The people called them dirty. Grime filled the creases of their palms, and the children's broken fingernails were black from playing in campfire ashes, but the travelers were not dirty; it was the odor of their way of life—of clothes washed in muddy rivers and the fishy sea, of woodsmoke and of the chickens, dogs and goats that traveled with them—some found offensive.

All day, they kept themselves to themselves. They got in no one's way, and waited for dusk.

Then, like fugitives, in the half-light of evening they took the back roads, and drove over the hill, straight for the place they'd camped before: a piece of flat land out of town, with trees to keep them private, a spring nearby, and plentiful dry wood for them to burn. Despite the years since they'd been here, Nana remembered the way; though the names of her own grandchildren confused her, her memory for places was still sharp.

The camp was quickly pitched. They rigged tarpaulins over frames, and weighted the edges with gathered stones. They fetched water from the spring, tethered the goats and gave them hay to nibble. The children were sent for firewood, and came back arms full of sticks and branches, with pinecones and twigs to use as kindling.

The dogs sniffed round the tree trunks, and cocked their legs.

The women hiked their long skirts over their knees and

squatted to light the fire. When the blaze died down, they raked hot embers to one side and put potatoes on to boil. The bread they had was stale, so the children toasted it on long sticks over the fire. They ate together, seated on the ground: potatoes, cheese made from the goats' milk, a few cans of mackerel, leftover stew.

When it grew fully dark they lit the oil lamps, though lamps and fire together seemed to make the darkness deeper. The women sipped cups of chamomile; the men opened a few shop-bought beers, and gave the children chocolate they had pinched from the same store. The men drank more beer, and turned on a radio for music, and as they drank, they sang along, and the women, catching the spirit, began to dance. The women whooped, the men laughed and clapped, and turned the music up louder.

When the fire burned low and the little ones yawned, they made up the children's beds in the flatbed truck. The adults shared three tents.

The fire and the lamps went out; the dogs curled up together beside the ashes. The smallest baby cried; his sleepy mother soothed him with her nipple. Drifting into sleep, the children watched the sky for shooting stars, whilst an owl settled in the high branches of the pine trees, and searched with hooded eyes for moving prey.

The night had brought coolness with it, sending the people indoors to the comfortable sleep which had eluded them through the season's worst heat. High above the port, a floodlit church shone white over the black rocks of the promontory, the steep steps which were the church's only access descending into the dark.

Long after midnight, when the alleyways between the houses were abandoned to the foraging rats and to the cats that hunted them, an oceangoing cruiser moved over the sea, rounding the headland into Kalkos's harbor bay. By starlight and the glow of a half-full moon, subtle bands of gold and navy picked out the curves of her white hull; navigation lamps showed the gold-lettered name on her stern: *Aphrodite*.

Maneuvering around the craft moored in the bay, she came to rest between two yachts, one flying a tattered Danish flag, the other the distinctive cross of Malta. On the *Aphrodite*'s deck, a crewman in white uniform signaled to his colleague in the wheelhouse, who lowered the two anchors at the bows. The chains ran out fast and loud, their rattling breaking the quiet of the night, until she was made secure and her engines were cut. The crewmen went below, and the bay was still, all other craft asleep.

Only aboard the *Aphrodite* was someone wakeful. Through the porthole of a cabin near the stern, a light burned on, going out only with the first brightening of dawn.

# Two

W elcome," said Father Linos, in English (though his command of the language—beyond this script he recited, in summer, up to four times every day—was poor). "Welcome to Kalkos, and the Holy Church of the Lady of Sorrows."

As Sambeca had said to him that morning, it was the beginning of summer's end. The hard light of midsummer—the light whose brittle brilliance created diamonds on the wave peaks and gave taut edges to every shadow right up until dusk—was perceptibly softened, and the sky's blue had inarguably paled. Though the day's heat was intense enough to warrant shade-seeking, and the old women still carried umbrellas as their parasols, the thermometer had dropped by five degrees, compared with yesterday.

Inside the church, those at the front were pressed close to Father Linos, forced forward by those at the back of the crowd who couldn't hear. The smokiness of incense mingled with coconut-scented sun lotion and the tang of fresh sweat; the visitors' breath carried nicotine and beer, ouzo's aniseed and spearmint gum.

The low-wattage bulbs in the brass chandeliers lit up the ceiling's sky-blue dome, where gold stars circled a painting of a benevolent Christ. Beside the offertory box, Sambeca handed out wallet-sized photographs of the famous icon and tiny, cork-stoppered bottles of holy oil, presenting the gifts only to those she judged Orthodox.

Father Linos stood with his back to the icon and wiped the sweat from his forehead. In the sandboxes, scores of burning candles added to the heat, but Sambeca ignored his requests to snuff them until all visitors had left. Sambeca had many superstitions; a snuffed candle, she said, invalidated the supplicant's prayers. Father Linos's gray summer robes were stifling, his black hat a tight fit around his crown. He envied the visitors their shorts and T-shirts, their feet cool in sandals, and their bare arms and legs.

"You see behind me," he went on, "our miraculous icon of the Virgin, which has made its home here since 1863. The icon is, of course, much older than that. It is believed to have been painted in the fourteenth century, though the place of its origin is disputed."

He stepped to one side and held out his hand, presenting the Lady of Sorrows to the crowd. Secured behind a glass panel, the icon itself was small, both frame and painted panel formed from a single plank of oak; the Lady's expression was unhappy, but might be read as frowning more than sorrow. For a work of such age, the icon's condition seemed excellent; the colors in the robes and flesh tones were still vibrant and intense, and the gold leaf was still lustrous, reflecting the light of the candles in its burnished glow. Around the edges of the glass which protected the image hung dozens of offerings: withered posies and roses; necklaces, rings and bracelets in silver and gold; and *tamata*—aluminum votives shaped as arms, babies, men in hats—to plead for intercession, or give thanks.

"The story of the icon's arrival in Kalkos shows the Lady's determination to make her home here, and to bring her holy blessings to the faithful of these islands," said Father Linos. "During the winter of 1863, four men were caught in a terrible storm at sea. Their boat went down, and they were forced to abandon ship, in rough seas and with little hope of reaching safety. But as they were struggling in the water, the Lady herself appeared to the men, shining her holy light towards them like a beacon."

Outside, in the courtyard, a child shouted; to Father Linos's left, a smirking teenager whispered in another's ear. Near the open door, Sambeca picked up her broom, and swept the intricately tiled floor in rhythmic strokes, catching the heels of the back-most in the crowd.

"The men were afraid when they saw the shining figure beckoning to them across the water," continued Father Linos. "But by keeping their eyes on her, they were able to follow her to this island's shores. When she was sure all four men were safe, the Lady left them on a rocky beach, blessing them with a deep, refreshing sleep. When dawn broke and they awoke, they found their clothes quite dry, and gifts from the Lady to hand—a barrel of water, two loaves of bread, and in her place this beautiful and ancient icon, lying on a rock by their heads. The men were amazed, having no idea how this wondrous icon came to be in that barren place. It came, of course, by a miracle. The men understood immediately that the Lady wished them to build a church here in her honor, and three of them swore there and then to dedicate themselves to the construction of the splendid and imposing church you stand in now. The fourth—just a young man at the time—decided he wished to honor the Lady in a different way, by becoming a painter of her icons. And when he sat down to try this holy labor, even though he had never painted in his life before, the Lady gave him the gift of the art, which is a difficult craft, normally taking years of apprenticeship. This man quickly became famous for his skill, and for many years his icons were carried all over the world, and placed in churches everywhere the Virgin is honored. When this man was on his deathbed, she appeared to him again in a dream, saying it was time to pass on his gift to his son, and she told him to take his son's hands in his own, and the gift would pass. And so it did; and in this way the gift of painting Kalkos's famous icons has been passed to the eldest son of each generation in this same family for over a hundred years—but never until the moment of the outgoing painter's death."

At the back of the crowd, a man taller than most listened closely to Father Linos's words. He wore a linen suit, Italian in its cut and tailored to disguise a generous stomach, and beneath the suit, a polo shirt with a small crocodile on the breast. His graying curls required a barber's attention, and on his nose were owlish glasses which gave him an air of academia. On his feet, he wore white canvas shoes in the old-fashioned style once worn for tennis.

Growing enthusiastic in her sweeping, Sambeca let her broom's bristles catch the toe of the man's left shoe, leaving a smudge of dust on its white toecap. He, with a frown of annoyance, asked her in a whisper to take more care.

"The icon is most famous for its miracles," said Father Linos, raising his voice a little to be heard over noise from the back. "Each year, the Pure, All Holy One—the Panayia, our Lady—gives on the feast of the Dormition a gift of healing, and for that reason several thousand people gather here, bringing their sick and afflicted with them. From all these people, the Lady chooses one to be healed. Sometimes the healing is public—a deaf man who can hear, a cripple who can walk—and sometimes we simply do not know who has been healed: it is a private matter between the Lady and the one she has chosen. She does not favor the rich or the powerful; she chooses from amongst all equally; all who come here with their hearts open have an equal chance of being healed. But her miracles do not stop there. The Lady has answered the prayers of countless faithful over the years. Most miraculous of all, from time to time the icon weeps tears of holy oil, and many of the faithful come to be blessed with the touch of this rare gift. Ladies and gentlemen, thank you for your time. When you have viewed the icon, please make your way through the rear door to our small museum, where there are many fascinating items of ecclesiastical history and fine examples of our icon painters' work."

The visitors pressed forward, some merely curious, others anxious to receive the Lady's blessing. The Orthodox stepped confidently up to the glass and kissed it, making the triple cross over their hearts; believers of other denominations placed their hands on the glass, and whispered personal prayers. The dubious and the doubting were less interested in the icon than in the trappings of the faith, and pointed at the offerings made to the Lady, speculating on the value of the jewelry.

Anxious to be gone, Father Linos stood impatiently, answering the questions they always asked.

"Why are there images of babies?"

"To ask the Lady's intervention for sick children."

"Who brings the flowers?"

"Those who are grateful for answered prayers."

"What happens to the offerings when they get too many?"

"They stay here in the church, but after a time some are moved to a special sanctuary. For how are we to know when prayers have been answered? The Lady answers in her own time. To remove these offerings from the church would be to interfere in her work."

"How much is the icon worth?"

The question, both inevitable and crass, was put by an Englishman whose skin was pallid as a plucked chicken's, and whose balding scalp was showing signs of sunburn.

"You cannot put a value on the icon," said Father Linos. "Its value to members of our church cannot be calculated. Quite simply, it is priceless. If it were just a simple painting, of a dog, or a horse, or a tree, even then it would be difficult to say; but as a piece of art alone, its age and the quality of its craftsmanship would make it worth well over 500 million drachma."

"What's that in pounds?"

Father Linos shrugged.

"I don't know, my friend," he said. "I suppose a million, a million and a half."

"That's a lot of money," said the Englishman, "especially in a little place like this."

"Be assured, we take good care of her," said the priest.

The Englishman gave no "thank you" for his answer, but walked away from the priest and the icon, and followed his obese wife through the rear door.

Outside, the clock on the campanile—three-tiered and many-arched, with the sky showing through the arches a perfect match to the campanile dome's blue—struck one. Before the icon, a gray-haired woman knelt, mouthing prayers with tears in her sad eyes. Father Linos went out into the sunlit courtyard and, ignoring protocol, removed his tight-fitting hat. Pushing his way between the chattering tourists, he left the church, and headed down the steps towards home.

Sambeca had left Father Linos's lunch on the kitchen table, the plate covered with aluminum foil and four slices of bread wrapped in a paper napkin. She had laid out his knife, fork and spoon, and a clean glass, inverted to keep out the droning flies. She cared for him like a child or an invalid, and he had never, in all these years, voiced any objection to her coddling.

He carried his food outside, to the table under the almond trees, where he removed the foil from his plate and folded it for her to reuse. Sambeca's repertoire was limited, and the menu varied little, regardless of the season. Today being Tuesday, she had made spaghetti; but, though she had cooked the thinner kind that he preferred, and made the Bolognese exactly to his taste—the sauce well spiced with cinnamon and cloves, the onions very finely chopped and the garlic sliced opaque, the grated cheese his favorite *kefalotyri,* melted into the stove-hot sauce when she plated up his meal—the heat and monotony left him little appetite, and he laid his fork back on the table with the dish untasted.

Wasps buzzed over the lukewarm food, not quite daring to settle. The priest batted them away, and wafted his hand over a housefly crawling on the plate's rim. But in a moment, the insects had returned, joined by a gangly-legged, red-striped hornet, which hovered lazily over the meat sauce, preparing to descend. A hornet's taste was usually for rottenness and carrion, and if the creature touched the food, it wouldn't be fit for supper; so Father Linos stood up from the table, and carried the spaghetti back into the kitchen, covering it with a second plate from the dresser.

In the fridge was a bowl of ripe peaches, picked that morning from the bishop's garden. Father Linos chose the best one of the five, and went back to his chair beneath the almond trees.

With the knife's serrated blade, he cut into the peach's red mottled skin, and the first dribble of chilled juice ran on to the tabletop. He divided the peach into four sections, and teased them from the claret-colored stone, which had split to free the seed-nut from its case. The flesh was creamy orange, bloodshot at the heart close to the stone; firm in the mouth, yet soft enough to be crushed between teeth and tongue, the fruit had the sugary-sour tang of citrus. On the white checks of the plastic tablecloth, the juice was the color of cantaloupes, and its sweetness drew the wasps to drink.

With relish, Father Linos ate the first piece of four, rubbing a dribble of juice into his graying beard. He picked up a second piece of the peach; but as the fruit touched his lips, he heard the yard gate squeal on its hinges, and the slow, tired slide of Sambeca's badly fitting slippers on the path.

He closed his eyes, bidding goodbye to any plans for the afternoon: an hour or two in the coolness of his shuttered room, free of his robes and dozing; or there might have been time to take the boat around the coast, and far from anyone's eyes, strip down to his underpants and plunge into the waters of Navayo Bay; or he might have walked down to the end of the pier, and dropped a line to catch a fish or two.

But time was always short; in the bishop's prolonged absence, all the services fell to him, and he must be back in church to read the evening's service.

And now Sambeca stood before him, fanning herself with the torn flap of a cardboard box, an old woman's shapeless dress hiding her bony body. Father Linos knew Sambeca's age, because they shared a birthday: on the day she was born, he had turned fifteen. How old was he now? He was losing count: the days dragged by, yet the years passed so quickly. Was he forty-five, or forty-six? It didn't matter, if only he didn't look as old as she did.

*"Yassas, Papa."* She spoke, and his spirits sank; her voice— a monotone, and every word a sigh, coming from a mouth so

averse to smiling its corners drooped in mournfulness as perpetual as the Lady's—drained the beauty from the day. "Isn't it hot? So hot! Hotter than yesterday."

Father Linos laid the peach segment back on his plate, and, picking up the end of his beard, scanned it for drips of juice.

"Do you think so?" he asked. "I was just thinking it's a little cooler today. If you're hot, you should take yourself for a swim. It would do you a power of good: seawater, and the Lord's own sunshine. I shall be going myself, later."

With lackluster eyes, she regarded him. Sambeca avoided the sun; the paleness of her complexion always brought to Father Linos's mind the men he used to meet on prison visits. Deprived of sunlight, the life bled from their skin and left it ashen.

"Cold water isn't good for you," she said. "And anyway, I don't know how to swim."

"It's not cold," said the priest. "Warm as a bath, it'll be."

"If God had meant us to swim, he'd have given us fins instead of feet. That's what my mother says."

"God is more clever than that," said Father Linos. He picked up his knife, and began to cut what remained of the peach into bite-size pieces. "He gave us legs, and thus the ability to walk *and* swim. Or paddle. Kick your shoes off, dip your toes in the water. It'll make a new woman of you."

"I've brasses to polish, this afternoon. And there's a bulb needs replacing in one of the candelabras. Have you finished with that plate?"

Compelled by the habit of serving, she leaned across him

29

to take away what remained of his peach. On her dress, he smelled the smoke of holy incense.

"No, no," he said, putting out his hands to cover the plate. "I shall sit and finish my lunch, before I do anything else. Go, now, and get your own lunch."

"I can't eat, in this heat," she said. "It turns my stomach to eat when it's so hot."

"Was there something you wanted?" he asked. A wasp landed on the tablecloth. Father Linos watched the creature closely, wondering at its ability to circle its antennae in opposite directions. "Because I thought I might take a nap for an hour or two, before my swim."

"You must," said Sambeca, firmly. "Swimming on a full stomach gives you cramp. In that cold water, you'd go straight down."

For a moment, he closed his eyes; when he opened them, the wasp was gone.

"So was there anything?" he asked. "Only, the afternoon is getting on. It'll be time for the service before we know it."

"I came to check with you," she said. "I asked him to leave, but he wouldn't go. So I wanted to know if I could leave the church unlocked. I have to get Mama her lunch. She always has a good appetite, whatever the weather."

"Who?" asked the priest. The irritation which he had tried hard to repress had wormed its way regardless into his voice; his jaw was tight, and a vein at his temple pulsed. "Who wouldn't leave?"

"There's a man in the church, looking at the icon. I told him I was closing up, but he asked for a few more minutes.

It's the Lady's house, so I didn't like to insist. I suppose he's entitled to be there, whether it's convenient to me or not. But Mama will be upset if I'm late again. So I wanted to ask you if it was all right to leave the church unlocked."

"For heaven's sake!" said Father Linos. "What man is it?"

Without interest, she shrugged.

"A Greek. But no one we know. He's not from here."

Father Linos sighed.

"All right, I'll see to it. You take yourself home."

From a pocket concealed in the seam of her dress, she withdrew an iron key, dark in color and shiny with use.

"You'd better have this, then," she said, handing it to him. "I expect he's gone by now."

"I expect so too," he said. "You didn't have to bring the key down. You should have just left it in the usual place."

"But what if he'd seen me?" she asked. "If he'd seen where I put it, he might come back when he feels like it and get up to who-knows-what. I'd better get on, or I won't be back in time to open up for the service. I'll go up at half past, in case they're early. I suppose all this trouble means you won't have time for a swim. By the time you've been back up there and locked up, there won't be much time left, will there?"

"There won't be much time, no," said Father Linos, shortly. "But it's surprising how much we can get out of the hours God gives us, if we put our minds to it. Go and see to your mother, and I'll make sure all's secure up at the church."

In his right hand, Father Linos carried the key to the church, in his left a shopping bag Sambeca had made from some threadbare skirt. The bag—in faded, floral cotton, cut out and stitched by hand—held a towel and swimming trunks, and a small flask of well-water. It was the priest's intention, once the church was locked, to follow the path beyond the church's lower steps as far as his favorite beach, where the water was so clear the fish seemed to swim in air, and there was shade beneath the olive trees where he could sleep.

The waterfront, in siesta, was quiet. The boats which brought the daily tourists had moved on, and the doors to the *kafenion,* to the travel agent's and the *periptero* were all closed; the house doors were shut too, though many windows were fastened open to draw in any breath of breeze coming off the sea. But there was no breeze, and sweat ran from under Father Linos's hat, trickling down the back of his neck and dampening his hair.

Out on the bay, the visiting craft were unmoving on a calm sea. As he walked, he admired an oceangoing cruiser (whose name—*Aphrodite*—was drawn on her hull in curling script, and whose flags at mast and stern shone with a gloss, as if made not of cotton but of silk), until he noticed on an Italian yacht a girl in a scanty bikini, who lay stretched out on the deck, her face covered with a paperback book, one long leg drawn up so tight her heel almost touched her half-seen buttock. He watched her; and from a chair in the shade of a plane tree, a scowling old woman watched him, her arthritic hands folded in her lap, her legs crossed demurely at the ankles. Beneath her chair, a black cat stretched a rear leg up into the air, and lovingly licked its own thigh.

At the harbor end, the stony path to the beach lay before

him; one hundred and fifteen steps led upwards to the church. In any weather, the climb was long, but the heat added to his discouragement. The sunlight created glitter on the sea; on the unshaded promontory, it reflected off the cement steps as dazzling glare. Squinting, he gazed up at the church, and considered forgetting his duty and carrying on along the pathway to the beach. But Sambeca was worse than any conscience, and she would neither forget his carelessness nor forgive it; and so, for the second time that day, he picked up the hem of his robes and began slowly to climb.

The courtyard door, when he reached it, stood open, though the courtyard was deserted. Beyond its white walls, he heard the sea break on the rocks at the promontory foot; above him, the campanile clock struck the half hour.

The church door, too, stood open. Father Linos left his cotton bag at the doorway and stepped inside the church.

The church was dark. Sambeca had blown out all the candles and switched off the overhead lights, so only a single lamp was lit, the eternal flame before the Lady of Sorrows. Around the walls, more images of the Virgin looked out sadly from their frames; without the light of candles, their paint was dull, their silverwork and gilding without luster.

Before the miraculous icon was a man. His light-colored suit stood out from the shadows thrown by the wavering lamp's flame, and Father Linos saw immediately that the visitor was no pilgrim, nor any penitent on his knees at the Lady's feet. Instead, he was standing disrespectfully close to the icon, peering at the image through its protective glass. One hand was held behind his back; in the other, he had a torch little bigger than a pencil, whose beam was narrow but exceptionally bright; and the beam was trained on to the icon, which the visitor was examining in its light.

Disturbed by the man's close scrutiny of the icon, the priest omitted his obligations to the Virgin's images around the walls, and immediately stepped forward to challenge the stranger. Disbelieving Sambeca's assertion that the visitor was a Greek—his disrespect for the Lady made that impossible—Father Linos addressed him in English, which would, he hoped, be understood by a Frenchman, or an Italian, which the cut of the stranger's suit suggested he might be.

"Sorry, closed," he announced. *"Chiuso."*

The stranger clicked off his torch, and turned to the priest with a smile.

"Church closed," said Father Linos, again in his bad English. "After five, again."

*"Yassas, Papa,"* said the stranger. "I'm glad to see you. I have one or two questions to ask you about your work of art here." The stranger's Greek was perfect, the beautifully enunciated Greek of TV newscasters. He took a step away from the icon, towards the priest, and showed himself to be both tall and overweight. "If you wish to lock up, I won't keep you long. But there's something here I really think you should see."

The priest hesitated.

"Forgive me," he said. "I took you for a foreigner."

The fat man smiled.

"No, no, indeed," he said, "though you aren't the first to assume it. Which goes to show, doesn't it, how outward appearances may deceive?" On his feet, Father Linos noticed, the fat man wore white tennis shoes. He came lightly down the three stone steps before the icon, and joined the priest where he stood beside the candle boxes. The fat man's clothes carried the scent of laundry dried in fresh air. "Allow me to introduce myself. I am Hermes Diaktoros, of Athens. Diaktoros being, as you may know, an ancient word for messenger. My father has a strange idea of humor. He's something of a scholar of the classical world."

Politely, the priest took the fat man's offered hand, which was, in spite of the day's heat, quite cool to touch.

"Father Linos Egiotis," said the priest.

"A pleasure," said the fat man. "Now, I know you must be anxious to close up for siesta, and I won't keep you."

He turned back to the icon.

"She's very lovely, isn't she?" he said. "I have been wanting to make her acquaintance for many years. Quite by chance we were passing within a few miles, and had time enough before my next engagement to make the detour. She has quite a reputation, I believe, for performing magic tricks. Magic tricks are a particular interest of mine."

"Magic tricks?" queried the priest, with annoyance. "The Lady occasionally sees fit to grant miracles. They are acts of divine grace, not magic tricks."

The fat man smiled again.

"Forgive my turn of phrase," he said. "The truth is, I am not a religious man. But I am still intrigued by this lovely lady, and her special reputation. An object such as this is very vulnerable, surely? She seems so little protected, and we are infested, these days, with people of no scruples. To a collector, or a fanatic, I imagine she would have a very high value. You have heard, I am sure, of the audacious icon theft at Elona, which was only the most recent amongst many. If you lose your Lady, your island's livelihood will go with her, and yet she seems defenseless. I have been here, alone with her, for quite some time—quite long enough to remove her from the wall, and be gone. She's smaller than I expected, and would be easy to transport; she would fit quite easily into my bag here." He indicated on the floor a red leather holdall of the type favored by athletes, somewhat worn and battered from use.

"Yet there she is, still in her place with us," said the priest. "We must show our visitors some level of trust, *kyrie*. And might I point out that those icons which do go missing have a habit of returning home, even if many years—or many decades—go by before they do so. You mentioned Elona, but the Lady there was brought home very quickly, within the month, I think. And the Serres icon of Christ being taken down from His cross was recently returned after thirty years abroad. They find their way home, *kyrie*. And believe me, I would never be careless of our Lady. Her well-being is my primary concern."

For a moment, the fat man regarded the priest.

"I believe it is," he said, and turned again towards the icon. "You know, I am most impressed by the quality of this work. The craftsmanship is faultless. Or should I say, it would seem faultless to most observers. Please, step up here with me just for a moment."

Touching the priest's elbow, the fat man led him up the three steps to the icon, where he held up his pencil-sized torch to show it to Father Linos.

"This is a wonderful gadget," he said. "It slips into any pocket, but is as powerful as a torch ten times its size. My uncle bought it for me in Germany. It's a lovely little thing, isn't it? In this environment—why do you Orthodox like to keep your temples so dark?—it lights up what you want to see as bright as day. Here, look." He switched on the torch, and pointed its beam at the Virgin's face, leaning towards the flesh-colored cheek. "You see this glaze here?"

With some reluctance, the priest focused on the Virgin's face. The painted skin was coated in brittle, discolored varnish whose fine cracks formed a distorted honeycomb.

"Do you see it?" asked the fat man. "My father has a fine collection of antiquities, and he has taught me to recognize the good from what we might call the not-so-good. But this is as fine an example as I have seen. It really is quite remarkable. So I was wondering if you knew how it was done. My father would be most interested to know."

The priest frowned.

"I'm sorry," said the priest, "but I'm really not sure what you're asking me. I'm no icon painter. If you have questions about technique, you should talk to Sotiris. He's our current incumbent."

"I shall indeed talk to him," said the fat man. "It's superb work, really very special. And I have an acquaintance who would love to see this. It's such an excellent example of its kind."

"I must close up now," said the priest. "You're welcome back in the church again this evening, for the service. Sambeca opens up at half past five."

"Oh, I shall definitely be back," said the fat man, picking up his holdall from the floor. "I have a little time still to spare before we have to leave, so it's entirely possible our paths may cross again."

Father Linos watched him go; the fat man went unhurriedly, humming under his breath a traditional song, of a boy riding on a dolphin. When the priest was sure he was gone, he turned again to the icon. To his eye, there was nothing remarkable in its appearance beyond its obvious beauty. The Lady of Sorrows seemed as she had always seemed: splendid, severe, sullen.

He pulled the church door closed, turned the key in the lock and hid the key in its usual place, above the doorframe to the right, where a hole in the mortar concealed it from visitors' eyes.

The afternoon had grown still; the cicadas had stopped singing. Puzzled by the unnatural silence, Father Linos listened. No goat bells jangled; no dogs barked, and no children shouted on the town's far beach. There was nothing to hear but waves breaking on the shoreline rocks.

Then, low-pitched and distant, from far below his feet came a rumbling like the growl of a drowsy dog, and as the rumbling grew louder, the ground trembled, shaking his body and rattling the church door in its frame.

Instinctively, the priest ran several steps from the church building, and looked up anxiously for falling roof tiles. But the earthquake was no more than a tremor, and had already passed. For a few moments, the silence which had preceded it persisted, until the cicadas could resist their urge no longer, and burst back into song.

Father Linos picked up his cotton bag, and brushed from it the dust that wasn't there. With the bag on his arm, he went through the courtyard door, expecting to see the stranger somewhere ahead of him; but the long run of steps and the waterfront were both deserted, and of the man in the linen suit there was no sign.

# *Three*

The fat man had taken a detour, drawn away from the steps by a path through the low-growing bushes which, though poorly defined and probably used only by goats, seemed to lead down to the sea. As he followed the path downwards and around the promontory, dry, twiggy shrubs caught at his trousers, and gave off, as his legs brushed their leaves, sharp scents of thyme and sage. Camouflage-brown crickets jumped to avoid his feet; where stones lay in his way, he kicked them forward to warn sleeping snakes and scorpions of his approach, marking his shoes brick-red with the dust of clay.

Where the hillside scrub merged with the shoreline rocks, the path came to an end. High above him rose the church's blank rear wall; the steps and its courtyard entrance were hidden from view. The rocks he faced—volcanic matter not yet worn smooth by time—were jagged and split by fissures, and seemed, at first, to present a barrier he could not cross; but carrying his holdall in his left hand and using his right for leverage, the fat man pulled himself up to stand on the first rock's flanks.

There seemed, from where he now stood, to be a way down to the sea requiring only a few bold strides from rock to rock. With his hand above his eyes to block the glare, he looked across the bay towards the *Aphrodite*. A crewman in white uniform leaned on the deck rails, holding a fishing rod whose orange float was bobbing on calm water. The fat man placed his holdall by his feet, put both his little fingers under his tongue, and blew a piercing whistle. The crewman—a stately, blue-eyed youth with an air of innocence—lifted his head and scanned the waterfront, searching for the whistle's source. The fat man waved both arms above his head until the crewman, having seen him, wound his line back onto the reel and laid the rod down on the deck. Moving at a jog to the *Aphrodite*'s stern, he stepped into a small dinghy tied to her steps, turned the key to start the outboard motor and cast off.

When the dinghy reached the shore, the fat man was already at the water's edge. The crewman brought the dinghy in close, and the fat man stepped into the prow and took a seat.

As they sped over the water towards the *Aphrodite,* the fat man didn't speak. The dinghy's wake was white on the cobalt sea; but moments after they had passed, their track was gone, melted into the ever-moving water as if it had never been.

Beneath the navy-and-white-striped canopy over the *Aphrodite*'s rear deck, the cedarwood table had chairs for eight. A white cloth covered the table end which faced the view, and there a place was laid for one with glasses, napkin and cutlery.

As the young crewman tied the dinghy to the stern, the fat man climbed the steps on to the deck.

"Is lunch ready, Ilias?" the fat man asked the crewman.

"At your convenience, *kyrie*."

"Tell Enrico to bring it up. Did you have any luck with the fishing?"

"Not a bite, *kyrie*," said Ilias, dejectedly.

The fat man laughed.

"You need to change your bait again," he said. "All your experimentation has given no improvement in your catches. May I assume there's no fish for lunch today, then?"

"I'm afraid not, *kyrie*. I believe Enrico has prepared something with aubergines."

"Again?" asked the fat man. "His love of aubergines will turn us all purple."

He made his way below deck, and entered a cabin kept cool by unseen and noiseless air-conditioning. There was plush carpet on the floor; the oval window was darkened with smoked glass which dimmed the view of the church and promontory. Against the wall was a bookcase with one shelf filled with telephone directories, a full and up-to-date set covering both the mainland and the islands. A swivel chair stood behind a desk which held the barely used effects of a businessman: a pen in a stand, a leather-framed blotter, a page-a-day calendar still open at January, a Rolodex file.

The fat man sat down in the swivel chair and pulled it up close to the desk. Reaching for the Rolodex, he flipped backwards through its cards to the letter "A." Having found the right entry, he tore off the calendar page for the twelfth of January, copied onto it the phone number he had found in the Rolodex and added a name. He folded the paper in half and tucked it into his trouser pocket, and closed the cabin door behind him as he left.

Back on deck, the fat man sat down at the place set for him and looked out at the other boats moored on the bay. On board the Italian yacht, the girl in her skimpy bikini stretched languidly, closed the book she had been reading and lay down to sleep in the sun.

From the galley, Enrico approached the table with a tray of dishes. He was a dark man, and balding, with the lascivious mouth and eyebrows of a satyr; over his white uniform, he wore an apron stained with the bright red of tomatoes, and the darker red of blood. Resting the tray's corner on the table edge, he began to lay the food before the fat man, but his eyes were on the girl—her tanned limbs glistening with oil, her long hair streaked blond from the sun, the curve of her breasts barely hidden by her tiny top—and the beginning of a smile was on his lips.

"Are you thinking of getting to know the neighbors?" asked the fat man, watching him.

"I was considering it," said Enrico, placing a carafe of chilled water on the table and allowing his smile to grow. "A friendly invitation for a drink aboard, maybe?"

The fat man wagged a finger at his crewman, and shook his head.

"You leave her alone," he said. "The boyfriend—or husband, whatever he is—isn't young, but he looks healthy, and he's big enough to deliver a punch that'd break your nose.

I think on this occasion you should make a gesture towards improving international relations, and stay away."

As Enrico took a last look at the Italian girl, the fat man gave his full attention to the food. Enrico had prepared *papoutsakia,* little shoes—aubergines filled with garlic-rich meat sauce, baked with a cheese-topped béchamel. A salad of tomatoes and red onions was dressed with virgin oil and sprinkled with ferns of fresh dill. There was half a loaf of still-warm bread, and, from a Santorini vineyard, a bottle of cold rosé.

"This looks excellent," said the fat man. "But when will Ilias catch us some fish? Surely his luck must change, eventually?"

Enrico laughed.

"Luck be damned," he said. "The boy's all posture and pose. He's only got that rod out in the hope our neighbor there might take an interest in his other one!"

"Well," said the fat man, picking up his fork, "since we're agreed that the neighbors are more sensibly placed off limits, he had better spend his time baiting his fish hooks, and earn his keep."

Enrico tucked the empty tray under his arm and turned to go, but the fat man stopped him.

"I almost forgot," he said, reaching into his trouser pocket. "I have a job for you, once siesta is over. I want you to go ashore, and make a phone call for me. Call Miss Athaniti—I've written down her number—and ask her to be so good as to join me here. Ask her to come as soon as possible, as I cannot stay much longer. Invite her as my guest, and arrange some suitable transport, at my expense. Find her a decent room somewhere in the town. And if she wants to know why I'm asking for her, tell her I need the benefit of her expertise, and that I have found something here which I think she will find of interest."

Enrico raised his eyebrows.

"Something of interest?" he asked. "This doesn't seem the kind of place that has much to interest anyone."

The fat man took a sip of cold wine.

"Appearances deceive," he said, "and someone's gone to a great deal of trouble to deceive the people here. But intriguing though this little mystery is, it's not one that we have time for, and Kara is quite capable of handling it by herself. So call her, and tell her to come quickly, or I shall be gone before she arrives."

Enrico took the phone number, and gave a small bow of his head.

"And, Enrico," went on the fat man, holding up an admonishing finger once again, "Miss Athaniti is to be treated at all times like the lady she is. No overfamiliarity there; you understand me?"

For the briefest of moments, a light of defiance showed in Enrico's eyes. But the fat man's expression was stern, and with a smile of acquiescence, Enrico left the fat man to his lunch.

When he had eaten, the fat man slipped off his shoes, sat back in his chair and slowly sipped a second glass of wine. The afternoon drifted into its stillest time; only the shouts of children on the far beach disturbed the quiet.

Yawning, he brushed the bread crumbs from his shirt-front, and walked up to the prow, where a hammock was stretched beneath a canvas awning. The deck boards were hot to his feet; the *Aphrodite* rocked lazily on the swell of some distant ship.

As the fat man climbed into the hammock and closed his eyes, the first breath of a breeze set the mast flags fluttering. Through the open galley window, Enrico, washing dishes, whistled a bawdy seaman's song; but the fat man by now was dozing, and did not hear.

The evening service was over, and Father Linos had already headed home. Hands on hips and weary, Sambeca watched the last of the women worshippers start down the steps. Down below, the dust cart moved slowly along the harbor front, stopping to empty every litter bin; out on the bay, on the deck of an oceangoing cruiser, a white-uniformed crewman held a fishing rod over the side. The sinking sun had lost its heat; in the courtyard, the cicadas had stopped singing.

Inside, the church was dark, and silent; the oil lamp before the icon was burning low. Sambeca chose a candle from the few left on the silver plate, and lit it from one burning in the sandbox. Cupping a hand around the flame to protect it, she carried her candle to the icon, where she made the triple cross over her heart, and knelt down on the steps before the Lady.

Eyes closed, head bowed, hands clasped, like a child she prayed; the more she prayed, the tighter she squeezed her eyes, the firmer she clasped her hands, the lower she bowed her head, as if the degree of tightness, firmness and lowness enhanced her prayer, and so improved her chances of an answer.

But no answer seemed to come.

So after a while she rose, and once more made the crosses over her heart. She blew out the candles in the candle box, and pulled them from the sand, replacing them with her own solitary flame.

There was still light to see by; if she cleaned the choir stalls now, there would be one less chore tomorrow. The tools for her work—brushes and pans, mops and buckets, dusters and polishes—were kept in the courtyard outbuildings. She filled an aluminum bucket at the well; she poured a splash of bleach into the water, dropped in a floor cloth and a scrubbing brush and carried the bucket and her broom back into the church.

She swept methodically and efficiently, progressing from the church walls to its center, collecting the sweepings in a pan. Before the iconostasis—the painted screen beyond which she, as a woman, was prohibited to go—she hesitated. The responsibility for cleaning the sanctuary lay with her brother, as altar assistant; but Agiris was slack in this duty, as he was in many others. He had no conscience; if the altar cloth was dirty or the crucifix was finger-marked, it wouldn't trouble him. On his own initiative, Agiris could be trusted to do nothing; yet she dared not press the point, because his anger, if she nagged him, made her afraid.

So the temptation to disobey the prohibition was strong, and on several secret occasions she had broken the rule and gone behind the screen. God knew she meant well, surely; the Lady knew she had Her interests at heart, but still it was a sin she had committed. To repeat the sin was to double it. Agiris must be pushed to do the job.

In the choir stalls, the tall, wooden half-seats were soon polished, and she knelt down to wash the floor between the rows. The stalls obstructed her view of the church, and hid her from anyone's sight; but as she worked, over the scrubbing of her brush and the dribbling of water in the bucket, she heard the squeal of the church door opening. A breath of air set the chandeliers tinkling, and tickled the hairs on her neck.

Someone was there. Though there was no footstep, no cough or sigh to give anyone away, yet she was sure someone had joined her in the church. But who would come here at this time? Uneasiness stole over her, and she stayed silent, though the faint rustle and dropping of paper, the light knocking together of candles as one was taken from the plate, the striking of a match reassured her that the visitor was a supplicant.

From where she knelt, she dropped on to all fours, and, face close to the wet tiles, peeped through the narrow gap between stalls and floor. Her view was restricted, giving sight only of the visitor's feet: a man's feet, naked in sandals below the hems of cotton trousers.

The feet moved to stand before the icon, where their owner dropped to his knees; now she could see his sandals' soles, his lower legs and thighs; but, even craning her neck, she could see no more.

Now, she was in a dilemma. It was too late to move, or speak—the supplicant would know he had been spied on—and so she settled on her haunches to wait.

Minutes passed, but slowly; the time until the figure rose seemed long. He crossed the floor in front of her, and the hinges squealed with the door's closing, the chandelier tinkling in its draft. Then, silence.

She got to her feet. A glance around the church confirmed she was alone. In the sandbox where her single candle had burned, now two were lit.

The offertory box was closed with a small padlock, to which Agiris had the only key. Sambeca picked up the box and held the slit in its lid up to her eye. She could see nothing. She shook the box; no coins rattled, but there were notes inside.

Inverting the box, she prized off the base with little difficulty; it was her habit to check the contents, to ensure Agiris handed over all the money he should. The box contained three banknotes: two 10,000-drachma notes, and a 5,000.

Puzzled, Sambeca frowned. Who would leave such a large gift at this quiet time, without an audience to admire his generosity? And what high-priced favor had he asked of the Lady?

Certain that the cash would not be safe if Agiris found it, she lifted the collar of her dress and slipped the notes inside her underwear. With a slam of her palm, she secured the base back on the box, and replaced the box beside the plate of offertory candles. Moving quickly, she left the church and crossed the courtyard to its open door, where she looked

down the steps, following with her eyes the route the supplicant must have taken.

He was already halfway down, his back to her as he descended; yet she believed she knew him. She squinted, not
quite sure; but his build, the way he moved, convinced her.

Without a doubt, she knew him; and whatever outcome
his generous donation brought for him, his presence here was
an answer to her own prayers.

# *Four*

S hortly after dawn, the fat man rose naked from his bed.
Through the open porthole, the air was fresh with the
cold scent of the sea; as feeding fish rose, soft circles of ripples
broke the water's oil-smooth surface, splitting the reflections
of moored boats. On the headland, the church's walls were
coral in the first red rays of sunlight.

The fat man stretched—arms high, then from the waist
to left and right—before touching his toes a dozen times.
Lifting his elbows, he pulled them back to stretch his chest.
The muscles of his limbs were well defined, his skin evenly
tanned; and, satisfied with his own suppleness, he slapped his
generous belly with both hands and stepped into the shower.

In the bathroom, he dried himself and wrapped a white
towel around his waist. Using a badger-hair brush, he spread
shaving cream over his face, and shaved with a silver-handled
razor. From a bottle of his favorite cologne (the creation
of a renowned French *parfumier:* a blend of bitter-orange
neroli, the honey notes of immortelle and the earthy tang of
vetiver), he splashed a few drops into his palms and patted it
on to his cheeks. With a fingerful of pomade from a small

jar, he smoothed his damp curls, then cleaned his teeth with powder flavored with cloves and wintergreen, ran the tip of a steel file behind his fingernails and polished each one with a chamois buffer.

From the bedroom closet, he picked out a polo shirt in palest rose-pink, slipped on a pair of shorts (flatteringly cut in navy twill), and threaded a crocodile-skin belt through the waist loops, leaving himself plenty of breathing room when he fastened the buckle. Then he sat down on the bed and took a bottle of shoe whitener from his holdall.

He gave both of his tennis shoes a full coat of whitener, paying particular attention to the rubber toe caps and heels, and holding the shoes up to the porthole's light as he worked to check no spot was missed; but when he had finished, the brilliance of the shoes showed the griminess of the laces. From a drawer in his bedside cabinet, he took out a pair of new laces, removed their paper band and laid them full length beside him on the bed. Having pulled the old laces from both shoes, he deftly threaded in the new, creating on the uppers a neat ladder of lines.

As he was threading the lace through the right shoe's last eyelets, a knock came at the door, and Enrico entered. His white uniform was freshly pressed, and crisp with starch; he carried a brass tray of antique Turkish design, which held a cup of Greek coffee, a glass of iced water and, propped upright by the glass, an envelope addressed with a single word.

He gave a slight bow of the head and stood the tray on the bedside cabinet.

*"Kali mera, kyrie,"* he said. "I trust you slept well."

"Excellently, thank you, Enrico," said the fat man. "I shall be ready for breakfast in ten minutes."

"Very good, *kyrie,*" said Enrico. "A message was delivered for you, last night. It was very late, so I didn't disturb you."

The fat man glanced at the envelope on the tray.

"Who brought it?" he asked.

"A boy, *kyrie*. He rowed across."

"I trust you gave him something for his trouble?"

"Five hundred drachmas, *kyrie.*"

"You should have given him more. It's a fair distance for young arms, here and back again. I shall be going ashore myself, shortly. Will you take me, or will Ilias?"

"Ilias is still sleeping. The boy's plain idle."

Enrico spoke with annoyance, and the fat man sighed in sympathy.

"I agree he's idle," he said, "but we have short memories if we can't remember the time when we were the same. We came here for relaxation, so whilst there's opportunity, let him sleep. When he needs to work, he'll work; I shall make sure of it. Have breakfast ready, and I'll let you know what time I want to leave." He picked up the discarded shoelaces and held them out to Enrico. "And be kind enough, would you, to dispose of these for me."

As Enrico closed the door, the fat man took his first sip of coffee and picked up the envelope from the tray. He ran his finger under the flap to break the seal and took out a single sheet of paper. The paper held only a line or two of writing; but when he read the words, the fat man smiled.

★　　　★　　　★

The fat man had breakfasted on purple figs, on yogurt and honey and a slice of moist almond cake. Now, he sat at the prow of the *Aphrodite*'s dinghy, his holdall at his feet. At the stern, Enrico's hand rested on the tiller; the outboard engine echoed off the seafront buildings as the propeller churned the sea to creamy foam. At the commercial quay, a small ferry prepared to dock, and the dinghy's prow smacked the water as it rode the swell of the ferry's wash.

As they reached the harbor front Enrico slowed the engine, and ran the dinghy along the line of craft moored at the quay. The ferry's wash hit the harbor wall, gurgling in wall cavities and lifting the moored boats' hulls, jangling the stays at the top of a yacht's high mast. Between the *Ayia Varvara* and the *Doukissa*—both elderly fishing boats, whose primary-colored paint was cracked from salt water, sun and wind—Enrico guided the dinghy into a narrow gap. As the dinghy closed in on the harbor side, the fat man stood up on his seat; and as the prow bumped the harbor wall, he stepped ashore.

"Come back in two hours," he said to Enrico. "If I'm a little late, be good enough to wait for me. If I'm much delayed, I shall send word."

Enrico nodded his acknowledgment, and leaned forward to push off from the harbor side. On the headland, the campanile clock struck eight, and the fat man set off towards the harbor-front *kafenion*.

The *kafenion* had excellent views of the bay, and the fat

man took a seat near two old men who shared a table but stared moodily in opposite directions, as if forced to sit together by obligation rather than by choice. In facing away from each other, they emphasized their profiles, which were as similar in outline as a pair of bookends, and confirmed them as identical twins. Time, however, had altered them in different degrees. Though both had noble noses, and ears with hairy orifices and age-lengthened, drooping lobes, one twin had suffered far more wrinkling than the other; his nose was reddened by a sprawl of broken veins, and at the outer corner of one eye was a cluster of pendulous skin tags.

The fat man wished both men *kali mera*. One returned his greeting, and turned his eyes back to the sea. The more wrinkled twin gave no reply, but looked the fat man up and down as if assessing his dress, and finding it inferior to his own scruffy trousers, his misbuttoned shirt and salt-stained sandals.

The wooden-slatted chair was uncomfortable, and the tabletop was leveled by a folded beer mat placed under one leg. A board nailed to the window shutter displayed the *kafenion's* menu—coffee and beer, omelettes and *mezedes*—painted in green with a brush too thick for the job; last season's prices had been blanked out with white paint, and higher prices roughly penciled in.

The fat man reached into his pocket and took out a pack of cigarettes—an old-fashioned box whose lift-up lid bore the head and naked shoulders of a 1940s starlet, her softly permed platinum hair curling around a coy smile. Beneath the maker's name ran a slogan in an antique hand: *The cigarette for the man who knows a real smoke.* The fat man knocked the tip of a cigarette on the table and lit it with a slender, gold lighter. As he replaced both cigarettes and lighter in his pocket, the *kafenion's* patron appeared at his side.

"Yes please," he said, in English, and slammed a tin ashtray onto the table. He was a tall man, whose gut overhung his trouser belt; his voluminous moustache was in need of trimming, and he brushed its hairs from between his lips when he had spoken. The bags under his eyes were dark and swollen, suggesting he and sleep had been strangers for many months, or years.

*"Kali mera sas,"* said the fat man, politely. "Greek coffee, if you please, no sugar. And an iced coffee for my companion, with a little milk and sugar."

At the mention of a companion he couldn't see, the patron lifted a questioning eyebrow, but made no comment and turned his back to go inside.

As he passed through the doorway, the wrinkled twin called out to him.

"Eh, Apostolis! Pour me a little ouzo whilst you're there!" Addressing himself to no one in particular, and to anyone but his brother, he added, "My stomach's not right. All night, it bothered me."

"What do you think," said his twin, to the view in the opposite direction, "you think more ouzo will fix it? It's the ouzo you drank last night that's troubling you now."

"What do you think," called Apostolis from the kitchen, "you think I have four hands? You tell your brother, Kostakis, to pay his bill from last night before he runs up a new one this morning."

"For God's sake," moaned the wrinkled twin, turning at last to his brother. "Pay the man, will you?"

Kostakis reached into his trouser pocket and withdrew several crumpled notes.

"What did you spend?" he asked, sourly. "I suppose you were the last to leave, as usual."

"What's the point in coming home early?" asked his twin. "No man could sleep with your snoring. Pay the man, for God's sake. You act as if the money is yours alone. Pay him, or he'll bellyache all morning, and make mine worse."

The fat man gave a light cough.

"Gentlemen," he said, "excuse me." In a movement accidently synchronized, the twins both turned to face him. "Perhaps you'll allow me to buy you both a drink?"

The old men eyed him with suspicion.

"I'm a stranger here, as you'll see," went on the fat man, "and I'm assuming—forgive me if I'm wrong—you are both long-term residents of this island."

"Born and raised here," said one of them.

"Lived here man and boy," said the other.

"Please, have a drink with me then," said the fat man. "I'd like to ask some questions about your icon. What will you have?"

"An ouzo, thank you, friend," said the wrinkled twin. He leaned towards the fat man, offering his bony hand, which the fat man shook. "They call me Kostas; my brother here's Kostakis. We had the same names as children, because our father couldn't tell us apart. Kostas or little Kostas, both names fitted. My brother had his own name, once, but no one uses it now. We stick with little Kostas, because he's younger by an hour. If you're buying, I'll have an ouzo. My stomach plagues me. A drop of ouzo may settle it."

"Hermes Diaktoros, of Athens," said the fat man. "An ouzo, then. And for your brother?"

"Nothing, thank you," said Kostakis. "I've drunk my coffee for this morning."

"Please, have another," said the fat man.

"One is enough," said Kostakis, and turned his face back to the familiar view.

"So you're here to see our icon, are you?" asked Kostas.

The patron carried out a tray, and placed a cup and saucer before the fat man and an iced coffee at the empty place beside him. Crossing to the brothers' table, he put one glass with a measure of clear ouzo and a second of water before Kostas, tucked the tray under his arm and stood by the brothers' table, waiting.

"How much?" asked Kostakis, grudgingly.

"Two and a half."

Kostakis handed over notes to cover his brother's outstanding debt, and the patron left them.

"Everything she saved, you'll drink," said Kostakis, to himself. "What Mother would have said, I do not know."

Kostas added water to his ouzo, turning the liquid opaque. The fat man drew deeply on his cigarette, and knocked its ashy end into the ashtray.

"I've wanted to see your Lady for many years," he said,

taking the first sip of his coffee, "but circumstances did not allow it, until yesterday."

"You've seen her, then?" asked Kostas, his glass raised to his lips. *"Yammas."* He took a drink of ouzo. "She's a treasure not matched within a hundred miles of here."

"She has a reputation, I know," said the fat man. "Is it true that she works miracles?"

"Oh, regularly, friend, regularly," said Kostas.

Kostakis was looking to the horizon, where out at sea a large boat was approaching.

"Here comes one now," he said. "Tourists by the hundred, all summer long. Our Lady's an economic miracle, if nothing else."

The fat man smiled, and ground out his cigarette.

"My brother's a cynic," said Kostas. "She draws the faithful to her. They say if she leaves the island, disaster will follow."

"Financial disaster is what they mean," said Kostakis.

"You have faith in her powers, then?" asked the fat man of Kostas.

"Oh, every faith, every faith." With three fingertips, he drew a triple cross over his heart.

"Do you not think the power is in the faith, rather than the Lady?" asked the fat man. "Might this coffee cup not grant a miracle, or this ashtray, if faith was strong enough?"

Kostas frowned.

"The Lady is an object of veneration, and has been for generations," he said, "and the icon has great power. You can't expect that from an ashtray."

"I meant no offense," said the fat man. "Perhaps the ashtray was too flippant an example. Let me ask my question another way. If I made a perfect copy of the icon, and what you saw was, in your eyes, still the Lady, would the faithful still see miracles happen then?"

"You ask deep questions for so early in the morning," said Kostakis, turning to the fat man. "What did you say your name was?"

"They call me Hermes," he said.

"Well, Kyrie Hermes," he said, "I say it would make damn all difference if it were an ashtray, or an icon, or a picture of my backside. There are plenty who are gullible. My brother, as you'll have gathered, is the best of them. It's one big racket to make money for the church."

Spots of anger rose to Kostas's cheeks. With a swollen-knuckled finger, he pointed at the fat man.

"Let me tell you, it's no racket," he said. "Our Lady has special powers, and she acts for those who believe. No substitute could have those powers. She's a gift from God, and she's unique. Nothing on this earth could replace her. Nothing."

His brother gave a quiet snort of laughter, and Kostas in his anger turned in his chair to emphasize his point with more words.

But Kostakis had lost interest in the argument; his attention was taken by a woman. Straight-backed with confidence and smiling, she wore a dress of citrus yellow cut just low enough to show a little cleavage; on her bare feet were gold sandals which showed long toes with nails painted a soft pink. Her face was past the age of conventional beauty, and amongst the black of her long hair were many strands of silver-gray; but the smile she was directing at the fat man made her lovely.

Kostakis—alert, suddenly, as a greyhound spotting prey—wiped a little spittle from his mouth's corner, whilst Kostas removed his cap and smoothed his oily hair. As she passed them, the woman murmured *"Yassas,"* and both twins returned her greeting with enthusiasm. She gave them not a glance; her eyes were on the fat man, who rose widely smiling from his chair, and greeted her with a faint blush coloring his face. She held out her hand to him, as his was extended to her; but instead of shaking the hand, he clasped it and drew her to him, holding her close as he brushed her cheeks with his lips, first the right, then the left; then he gripped her by her upper arms, and held her away from himself, still smiling.

"Kara *mou*," he said, "Kara, Kara, Kara! How are you, my beauty? Look at you, just look at you!"

The old men needed no instruction, and were already looking.

"Sit," said the fat man, "sit." He pulled a chair out from the table, brushing its seat free of dust which might mark her dress. "How are you?" he asked again, as she sat. "It's been too long, too long, and here you are more beautiful, far more beautiful than ever! How long has it been, *koukla mou?*"

"Five years, Hermes," she said. "In fact I think now it's nearer six."

"So long?" he said, shaking his head in disbelief. "My fault, of course; always my fault." He reached out, and, grasping her right hand, studied the backs of her fingers. She wore a single ring: on the middle finger, a silver band set with gold-flecked lapis lazuli.

The fat man frowned.

"What happened?" he asked.

"I left him," she said, and withdrew her hand. She glanced at the twins, whose eyes were on her. "Don't ask me now."

"Later, then," he said. "We'll talk later, over lunch."

"And you, of course, are still not married?"

She looked into his eyes, and gave him a smile which lit both their eyes.

"I? No."

"You haven't changed, Hermes," she said. "You'll never marry. You're no more the marrying kind than I am."

He watched her closely as she sipped at her iced coffee through a straw.

"How is it?" he asked.

She smiled again.

"You remembered," she said.

"A little milk, a little sugar. How could I forget?"

"I came as quickly as I could," she said, putting down the glass. "The message I received sounded urgent."

The fat man sighed.

"Urgent because my time here is short. I myself must leave." She gave him a look of reproach, and he closed his eyes beneath it. "I know, I know. The work is always there, always in the way. This was a detour only; I had a desire to see the miraculous Lady up there in the church. Do you know her?"

"I know her, of course. But I have never seen her in the

flesh, as it were. So I was glad to come." She leaned close to him; he caught her perfume, the heavy floral of Chanel, "And not, if I am honest, for her sake only. When do you leave?"

"I had intended to go this evening. But, under the circumstances, I might delay my departure until tomorrow."

"Circumstances?"

"If I find anything which persuades me to stay."

"What might persuade you?"

"I was hoping, to be truthful, that you might. Is your room comfortable, by the way?"

"As you'd expect, in these islands. They are not people who expect life's luxuries, and they don't provide them for others. But it seems adequate. My flight was late, so I've seen little of it; I slept in the bed, and then came to find you."

"And now you're here, we must attend to our business. Finish your coffee, and then we'll get to work."

He left money for their coffee and one ouzo, and included a generous tip, in case he might return. As he and Kara left the *kafenion,* the fat man called out goodbye to the patron, who sat reading a tattered newspaper whose headline was old news. But the patron gave no reply to his goodbye; the old men offered a subdued *Sto kalo,* and watched in sullen silence as the fat man led Kara away. Along the harbor front, where a pair of fishermen spreading nets looked Kara up and down with covetous eyes, the fat man placed a hand under her elbow to keep her close.

They climbed the long stairway together, and found the church quiet. The early service was over, and there was no sign of the priest. On the harbor side below, the first of the day's tourist boats was lowering its gangplank to the quay.

"We've done well to get here early," said the fat man. "Later on, when the hordes have climbed up here, we would never get near the icon."

"If I tell them who I am," she said, "we can surely have special privileges. I have my museum pass in my handbag."

The fat man's expression was doubtful.

"I'm sure we could. But I think, just at the moment, you should stay incognito. We don't want to tip anyone off too soon."

"Tip anyone off?" Kara took his arm, and made him stand still. "What's going on, Hermes? Why am I here, so urgently?"

"Perhaps I just wanted to see you," he said. "Maybe I brought you here on false pretenses, just on a whim."

"A whim?" She placed her hands on her hips, and glared, half seriously. "I hope you would never insult me by calling me a whim!"

He smiled, and shook his head.

"You're not a whim, no," he agreed. "Quite simply, your company is a pleasure."

From the brightness of the courtyard they stepped into the dim coolness of the church. By the candle box, a plain woman in a cotton housecoat spat on her fingertips, and pinched out the flames of the burned-down candles. Another woman, more smartly dressed, spread the legs of a long stepladder under a chandelier, and climbed cautiously high enough to change an unlit lightbulb whilst a third held the ladder and urged her upwards: *Go higher,* kalé; *go on, go on.* In the choir stalls, a man counted the money in an open offertory box, smiling with sly amusement as the fearful woman climbed.

Kara left the fat man to admire the ceiling paintings and crossed the nave, the heels of her sandals clicking on the intricate tiled floor. By the sandbox, she wished the plain woman snuffing out candles *kali mera,* took several coins from her handbag and looked around for the offertory box.

From behind, someone grasped her arm and, startled, Kara turned.

"Over there, *kalé,*" said the plain woman. The grip of her fingers was tight; with her free hand, she pointed towards the choir stalls. "You can pay my brother, over there."

As she approached the stalls, the man there stopped his counting, and watched her.

"*Yassas,*" she said, when she was close enough to speak. "I want to make an offering for a candle."

He stood; the crown of his head was below her own. His denim jeans, though held up around his waist by a heavy belt, were too long in the leg, and fell in swathes and creases around his ankles, whilst his checked shirt—too long from shoulder to waist—billowed with spare cloth above his belt. But his appearance was made distinctive not by his lack of height, but by his ugliness. His face had the flattened, broad dimensions of a bulldog, and the sagging skin of approaching middle age built on that effect, as did his lower lip, which turned out on itself to show its slippery inner surface. When Kara drew close, the man, as if conscious of this defect, pulled up his lower lip, and held it against his gum, so he appeared, like the aged, to be lacking teeth; and as his eyes traveled over her—hair to legs, returning upwards to remain on her breasts—he ran the tip of his tongue backwards and forwards along the inside of his drawn-up lip and into his cheeks, so it seemed as if something alive was sealed inside his mouth, seeking an exit.

"An offering, yes," he said. "I'm the man, young lady, I'm the man. Give it to me, give it to me."

The corners of his mouth lifted in a smile; but in the act of smiling, he lost control of his lip, which slid outwards like a child's pout.

He held out his hand, and she placed her coins in his palm, half expecting his fingers to close on hers. But instead he looked down at the coins, silently counting them, and his shoulders twitched in what she read as a shrug of disparagement at their sum.

By the sandbox, she took a candle from the plate, and as she lit the wick, the fat man came to her side.

"Ready?" he asked.

"Ready. I feel quite excited," she said. "The thrill of seeing a masterpiece for the first time never leaves me."

The fat man's eyebrows rose by the smallest degree, but without speaking, he extended his arm to guide her towards the Lady. At the bottom of the shrine's three steps they looked up at the icon, and Kara drew three crosses over her heart. In the glow of many lamps, the gilding on the painting was iridescent, the tempera colors fluid in light which brought life to the Lady's unhappy features.

"She's very lovely," said Kara. She made more crosses, and for a moment bowed her head in reverence. Then, she stepped up closer to the painting. "She must be homesick," she said.

Behind them, the women changing the lightbulb were arguing. The plain woman was removing bundles of fresh candles from brown paper wrapping. The ugly man who had been counting the takings was nowhere to be seen.

"Homesick?" asked the fat man. "Why should she be homesick? Does she not have a good home here? This place is a palace built just for her, and filled with her attendants and her worshippers. Any lady would appreciate what she has here."

"Maybe so. But she does not belong here. I thought you would know all this, Hermes."

"Orthodox art is not a great favorite of mine, though my father—as I think I told you—has a small collection. I find all the misery and severity unattractive. Our Lady here is an excellent example. She'd be much prettier if she would smile."

"The faces are miserable for good reason," said Kara. "In this case, she is reflecting on the fate which is to come to her son. So she has very little to smile about."

"Her son's fate was to found a religion which usurped centuries of belief in older gods, and put a whole panoply of deities out of work. Isn't that something to smile about?"

She nudged him with her elbow.

"Sshh," she said, "don't be disrespectful. Someone will hear you."

She turned to see if he might have been overheard. All the women still seemed occupied, and she saw neither the ugly man, nor any priest.

"If you're right about her homesickness, that might account in some degree for her frowning," said the fat man, indifferent to whether he might have given offense. "If this isn't her home, where is?"

"Our poor Lady has traveled a very long way," said Kara, turning back to the icon. "She's not Greek at all. She's Russian."

"Russian? So what's she doing here?"

"She was undoubtedly stolen, and washed up here—I believe the legend is that that's literally the case—on her way, most likely, to be sold in the lucrative markets of Italy or France, maybe even England. There is a record of an icon which was probably this one being stolen from a church in Kiev at the beginning of the nineteenth century."

"So what about the story they tell here? Didn't she appear to sailors as they were shipwrecked? Did she not emerge miraculously from the waves, as your priests would have us believe?"

She gave a shrug of doubt.

"Quite likely, then, that our devout, heroic sailors were thieves?" he asked.

She shook her head.

"I don't think so. Thieves wouldn't have founded a church for her. They would have sold her. For some reason, she was kept here."

"Thieves turned to the good by her intervention?"

"Who knows?"

"When I was here yesterday, I spoke with the priest, who told me stolen icons have a habit of finding their way home."

"That's true. There are some wonderful stories like that."

"So, what if the story here might be another one?"

"What do you mean?"

"What if the Lady who was here has gone on her way, wherever she was going—Italy, or home? Let me show you what I mean." Taking the high-beam German torch from his pocket, the fat man stepped right up to the icon, and shone the torch's light through the protective glass.

"Hermes!" Kara touched his arm to make him step back to a respectful distance, and once again looked round to make sure his behavior was not observed. The fat man, however, did not step back, but took her hand to pull her nearer to him.

"Come closer," he said, "where you can see what a true masterpiece she is."

Baffled, Kara held her candle up to the Lady's face, seeing nothing she did not expect to see: paint that showed its age, worn away in spots, in places flaked away. But the fat man trained the sharp beam of his torch into the painting's bottom corner, illuminating every flaw in paint and varnish.

"Look here," he said in a low voice. He himself now turned to make sure they weren't overheard. No one appeared to be listening. "You'll see it here best."

Puzzled, she bent close to look into the section of the icon lit by his torch. She looked, and then looked up at him.

"I need a magnifying glass," she said. "I know you must have one in that bag of yours."

"As I matter of fact, I do," he said, with a smile, reaching into his holdall.

In the courtyard beyond the open church door, the voices of the day's first visitors could be heard. With the glass in her hand, Kara asked him to stand between herself and anyone's view of her. For a long minute, she held the magnifier to the glass, and bent to examine the painting.

She stood up straight, and he clicked off the torch.

"My God," she said, quietly.

"So? What do you think? Am I right?" he asked. His expression now was serious.

"I think you have uncovered a scandal, Hermes," she said. "Because you know what I'm going to say. It's very, very good, almost impossible to spot—but this Lady of Sorrows is, beyond any doubt, a fake."

Outside, the courtyard was crowded. An Italian tour group waited noisily for their guide; those who had found the climb challenging had taken seats on benches, whilst others photographed the view, or shouted down encouragement to those still climbing.

The fat man and Kara stood at the courtyard's center. The fat man took a cigarette from his pocket, and lit it with the blue flame of his lighter.

"What will you do?" he asked, slipping the lighter back into his pocket.

She spread her hands to show her indecision.

"It's what's best to do first; there seems so much to do. Of course the police must be called, but I think I should speak to the museum before the police are involved. The director will need to be informed. And I should let the church authorities know, too—maybe the priest here before anybody."

"My regret is that I'm unable to stay here to help you; but my visit here was simply a diversion. There's somewhere else I have to be, tomorrow. Yet I feel guilty; I brought you this burden, and now I'm leaving it on your shoulders."

She smiled.

"Don't worry about me," she said. "It's my job to worry about the nation's works of art. And what can you do that the police can't?"

"What, indeed?" he asked.

There was a moment of silence between them, until she said, "I can always rely on you, Hermes, to provide the most interesting diversions. Though this is hardly a diversion. This is likely to be national news."

"What may make it even more newsworthy," he said, "is that I suspect the theft of the Lady may not be recent. The painting that we saw there—the original's replacement—I think has been there for some time. Those offerings on the frame were not placed there recently, unless they were hung with extreme care. But they keep the place so clean; it's impossible to judge from dust deposits or lack of them how long the offerings have been there. I fear that the Lady's been gone some considerable time, maybe even years, in which case the trail will be very cold indeed. And with so many possible culprits..." He gestured at the foreigners milling around them. "Where will you start? Which makes me think—because the colder the trail, the harder it is to follow—whether it might be a better approach, on your part, to keep her disappearance quiet for a while, and make your inquiries discreetly. Your office no doubt knows the right people in Florence, and in Rome; they'll know who'd like to acquire an item like the Lady and have the cash to pay for her. Maybe you should talk to them quietly, without alerting the thief—or the buyer—that you're coming after them."

"You may be right," she said. "Maybe I should just return to Athens, and discuss it with the director."

"Perhaps you should."

"Where are you going now, Hermes?"

"South. There's an island where there's trouble brewing."

"Once again, then, our time together is short."

He hesitated.

"It should be short." At the quay below, another boat of visitors had docked, and pilgrims and tourists spilled on to the harbor front, cameras pointing up at where they stood. "Listen," he said, grasping her arm. "Do you think we might cheat our responsibilities, this once, and get lost together? My island could wait a little while, and a few hours will make no difference to the Lady. What do you say? We could take the launch, and find a little beach all to ourselves, and you can tell me all your news. Enrico shall make us lunch. A bottle of cold wine, and all the blue sea to swim in—how can we not? I promise to have you home by nightfall. Or if not nightfall, tomorrow daybreak."

"That's a lovely plan," she said, "except I thought this was to be all business. I brought no swimsuit."

"There are places in the town that will sell us swimsuits."

"Sometimes, Hermes, you're a very bad influence on me. Don't you think we're a little old to be playing truant?"

He brought his face close to hers.

"I'm going to tell you now one of life's great secrets," he said. He moved closer still, and placing his mouth to her ear, spoke very low to avoid being overheard. "The secret to a long and happy life is to regularly, as often as you can, play truant."

# Five

With the expertise of a long-term sailor, the fat man steered the dinghy away from the *Aphrodite* and around the headland, keeping the boat close to the shoreline. The shallow water was clear as glass, rippling turquoise over the unexplored landscapes of the seabed, which—though similar, in truth, for mile on mile—were made intriguing by the water's magnifying distortion. Each meter of rock or sand seemed to demand the engine's cutting and a dive over the side; each meter promised to be that perfect stretch of ocean, where its hidden life—the fish and flora, the mollusks and crustaceans—would be the ocean's most fascinating, the temperature of the water the most sublime, the view of the matchless blue sky as seen floating on one's back the most inspiring.

Kara sat in the boat's prow, trailing her fingers in the water to make ripples. The land rose from the sea in moderate slopes, marked with the lines of fallen walls where fields had once been cultivated or grazed. They passed a grove of olives—old trees within a circular wall—and an abandoned farmstead where a fig tree grew through a collapsed roof, where the windows had no panes and the door hung crooked on one hinge, and yet the footpath from house to shore was still well worn, leading to a cove where a rowing boat had been hauled across a stony beach, and laid up beneath a rocky overhang.

On this side of the island a south wind blew, and, where depth changed the water's color from turquoise to ultramarine, was strong enough to raise whitecaps on the swell. To make use of the land's shelter, the fat man steered still closer to the shoreline, and followed its curve into the bay marked on the *Aphrodite*'s nautical charts as Navayo Bay.

The bay was a crescent with a broad pebbled beach made inaccessible on foot by steep slopes of scrub and scree. At the beach's far end was a jetty, whose cement had cracked and half fallen into the sea, and as they approached, the fat man slowed the dinghy, and cut the engine. In the moment before the boat touched land, he sprang ashore and maneuvered the craft alongside the jetty with the lightest of bumps.

The fat man tied up, and he and Kara made their way on to the deserted beach. So late in the afternoon was it, the sun had lost the burn of its midday heat, though the pebbles underfoot were still warm through their shoe soles. Close to the water's edge where the pebbles gave way to shingle, Kara spread out the navy-blue towels Enrico had provided. The fat man lay down his red holdall, and the cooler Enrico had filled.

The fat man removed his shirt, and lay back on a towel, his hands behind his head, his eyes hidden behind tortoiseshell-framed sunglasses. Kara stripped down to a black swimsuit, folding her clothes item by item. Her skin was tanned to a soft brown, except for the pale outline of a watch she wasn't wearing now.

"Are you coming for a swim, Hermes?" she asked.

The beginnings of a suppressed smile touched the corners of his mouth, and he wafted a hand towards her.

"Swim away, mermaid," he said. "But make sure you swim fast. There are stories of monsters in these waters who seem to come from nowhere, and spirit careless women away to the cold, blue depths."

"Monsters?" She smiled down at him. "Or only you?"

"If you're brave enough, swim out there and find out," he said.

"They'd never catch me," she said. She crossed the shingle to the water's edge and faced the sea, her hand above her eyes to reduce the glare. For a few moments, she looked out to where a speedboat lay at anchor, then she plunged into the water, slipping below the surface like a seabird, and glided away before reappearing a short distance away, kicking her legs to stay afloat, running her fingers through her wet hair and wiping away the salt water dripping from her face.

"No monsters here," she called.

"You're lucky, then," he said. "If they catch you, I might be sleeping, so don't expect any help from me."

The afternoon moved into early evening as they swam, and talked, and ate slices of red watermelon, rinsing the juice from their hands in the incoming waves, until the fat man glanced up at the sun, now low in the sky.

"Time for an aperitif," he said.

From the cooler, he took a bottle of Attican retsina wrapped in a napkin to keep it cold, and found the corkscrew Enrico had hidden in the linen's folds.

The fat man poured the wine into paper cups decorated with colorful balloons, and they knocked their cups together in a toast.

"*Yammas,*" he said.

"*Yammas.*" She took a sip of the wine, then held up the cup to examine it.

"Is it your birthday, Hermes?" she asked. "Is this another of those secrets you like to keep?"

He gave a noncommittal shrug, and smiled.

"Maybe, maybe not," he said. "At my age, the celebration of birthdays palls. The trick is, of course, to live every day as if it were your birthday, though few of us have enough good humor for that. But don't read too much into the cups. Enrico has a housewife's sense of *economia*. Any bargain, he must buy, wanted or not. No doubt we needed paper cups, and these were the cheapest he could find. We end up with all kinds of unwanted articles, bought because they were bargains. I remember once he bought a case of bottled cherries, and at every meal, at every breakfast and for every dessert, he brought out those damned cherries, extolling their healthy virtues and trying to persuade me they weren't sour."

She smiled, and looked out to sea; crystals of dried salt gave a sheen to her sun-warmed skin. The boat moored on the bay was preparing to move; an anchor's chain rattled as it was raised, and the water carried the throb of a running engine.

"Time to get dressed, I think," she said. "It looks as if we might have company."

The speedboat carried two men. They moored behind the fat man's dinghy, and cut their engine.

"I wonder," said the fat man, "if they might have caught anything they're prepared to sell. With Ilias's dreadful record, it might be wise to use an alternative supplier if we want fish for dinner."

They shook the last drops of retsina from their cups, and draped their damp towels over their shoulders. The fat man replaced the half-full wine bottle in the cooler and, slipping on their shoes, they picked their way along the pebbled beach.

*"Kali spera sas!"*

The fat man called out the greeting as they drew close to the speedboat. One of the men raised a hand in reply; the other was on the jetty, peeling a wetsuit from his tanned limbs.

The fat man looked hopefully into the speedboat's stern, but there were no lines or harpoons, no nets or buckets, only the oxygen tanks, flippers and masks of professional divers.

"No fish," he said, in disappointment. "Did you have no luck?"

"We weren't fishing, friend," said the man in the boat, cheerfully. He was the older of the two, by a number of years. The red outline of a diving mask marked his forehead and cheekbones; the upper of his wetsuit hung stripped and limp from his waist, showing a well-muscled torso. "We were just doing a bit of sightseeing."

"Sightseeing?" asked the fat man. "What's to see out there?"

"My boy wanted to have a look at the wreck," said the diver. "He's got the idea there's undiscovered treasure out there. Haven't you, son?"

The young man gave no answer, but smiled shyly and bent to unzip his wetsuit at the ankles.

His father's expression suddenly showed suspicion.

"You're not from the Archaeology Department, are you?" he asked.

The fat man stood close enough to Kara to give her an unseen nudge.

"I? Certainly not," he said. "Don't worry; we're not here to check your permit. But I've an interest in old wrecks; tell us, what's out there?"

"The bay is named 'Wreck Bay' with very good reason," said the diver. "Three wrecks lie in the waters hereabouts. The closest one, where we were, is an old caïque, the very one—so folks will tell you—that carried the sailors who the Lady rescued from drowning."

"Really?" said Kara. "How do they know that?"

The diver shrugged.

"The same way they know everything: my father tells me the story, I tell it to my son. There's not much to see these days but a few old timbers. But my grandfather told me they took a skeleton from there, when he was a youth."

Kara raised her eyebrows, and returned the fat man's nudge.

"Can I," said the fat man, smiling, "offer you gentlemen a glass of retsina?"

The diver smiled.

"That's very courteous of you," he said. "Please, step aboard."

The diver handed Kara into the speedboat, and she and the fat man took seats on the stern benches with diving gear around their feet; on the jetty, the diver's son laid out his suit to dry, and joined them in the boat. The fat man handed out balloon-decorated cups and poured the wine. On the mild swell, the boat rose and fell, rocking gently.

"*Yammas,*" said the diver, holding up his cup. "Is someone celebrating?"

"Last week," said the fat man.

"May you live to be a hundred," said the diver in the traditional greeting, and the fat man thanked him, and raised his cup to the diver's.

"So, tell us about the skeleton," said Kara as they drank.

"Not much to tell," said the diver. The younger man sat quietly opposite Kara; his eyes were on the brown skin of her feet. "It was many years ago now, before the war, certainly. Before then, they had no gear to get down so deep. They were after treasure, of course. Men always think that where there's a wreck, there's treasure—don't they, son?" He prodded his son playfully, and the young man smiled, and glanced at Kara's face before lowering his eyes back to her feet. "But what do I care if he wants to go treasure hunting? I'm always ready for a day out, a few hours away from the shop."

"You have a business here?"

"By profession, I'm a butcher; I have a shop in town. My wife looks after it whilst I'm gone."

"It must have been exciting, to find a skeleton," said Kara. "What did they do with it?"

The diver shrugged once more, and drained his cup.

"Laid the bones in the ossuary, I expect. Or maybe not; they'd worry about its origins. What if it were some Turk, or Jew? They wouldn't want their Orthodox bones polluted. So the truth is, I don't know. And, do you know, before today, I never thought to ask."

The fat man opened the cooler, where a second bottle of retsina was wrapped in linen.

"Did they find nothing else?" he asked, twisting the cork from the bottle.

"Not that I'm allowed to say."

"Oh come," said the fat man, refilling their cups with cold wine. "Tell us what there was! It's so long ago; there'd be no consequences for anyone now, even if we were a pair of blab-bermouths."

Kara leaned across and lightly touched the diver's knee, showing the tempting cleavage at her dress neck.

"Please, do tell us," she said. "It's such a fascinating story; please, do go on."

"Well, the way my grandfather told it to me was like this," said the butcher, his eyes flickering over Kara's chest, "but take it with a pinch of salt, or better yet a sackful, for tales grow horns and feet here, as they go round. *Pappou* swore he was there, and that might be true; he was a strong swimmer, right up until he died. I'll tell you what he said they found: a bag of gold! Well, it was gold by the end of his life, God rest him. When I first heard the story, there was no mention of gold. It was just a plain old bag of coins. How could it have been gold, anyway? No one would throw gold away, would they?"

"Throw it away?"

"Take off the frills and laces, they found a bag of coins. But the money was useless to them, so they threw it back over the side. They must have been disappointed men, thinking they'd found treasure, and finding it to be worthless."

"Why was it worthless?" asked the fat man.

The butcher looked at him as if amused by the fat man's stupidity.

"Foreign," he said. "The coins were foreign."

"Foreign from where?" asked Kara.

"From somewhere not here," said the butcher, "and that was foreign enough. *Pappou* kept one coin, as a souvenir, and I'm sure one or two others did as well. It's in the house still, I expect; my grandmother's not one to throw anything away. He carried it for many years as his lucky coin, and let me have a look at it, from time to time. But I don't suppose you've ever seen it, have you, lad?"

The young man shook his head, and looked down into his wine.

"If you've seen it," said the fat man to the butcher, "what did you make of it?"

"It's been years," said the butcher, "and when I saw it, I was looking through a young boy's eyes. I expect I was thinking pirates, and treasure, as young lads do. But I can tell you it wasn't from Turkey, or anywhere like that, not Italy or Germany. It didn't have their kind of lettering. Some of the lettering was like our own, or like the script you see in church. It was just a small coin, silver, most likely, under the tarnish. You could read the date—don't ask me what it was, I don't remember—and some of the lettering, in parts. *Pappou* reckoned he could read the letters perfectly, though they didn't make any sense to me; he'd been a seaman, and traveled all over, in his time. So he might have been right, and he might have been wrong; but *Pappou* always thought his coin was Russian."

# *Six*

In the hour before sundown, Sotiris left the workshop couch where he had slept away another afternoon. With the street door closed, the workshop had become airless, the heat soft and smothering; his mouth was dry from snoring, and the wrinkles in the cushion cover had left red ridges down one side of his face.

He took his shirt from the back of his work chair, and shook out the worst of the creases before he pulled it on; because he didn't button it beyond the sternum, the loose neckline of his old vest and his gray chest hair showed between the shirt's front panels. Hitching his jeans up to his waist, he thought he might have lost more weight; when he went home, he should look again for that belt he used to wear. His leather slip-ons were by the sofa, and he slid them on, indifferent to the dirtiness of his feet.

At the sink in the corner, he ran the single tap until the water was cool, and filled a glass. On the shelf under the workbench, hidden behind the paraphernalia of his art, was a paper bag from the pharmacy, from which he took a bottle, and a box. Unscrewing the bottle cap, he tipped a large, pink pill into his hand; opening the box, he punched a red and yellow capsule from the blister pack. He swallowed the medication, and drank down the water before hiding bottle, box and paper bag at the back of the shelf.

On the bench, the work-in-progress—an icon of St. Panteleimon, holding his box of medicines—was barely begun: though the outline was drawn and the gold leaf had been laid, only the dark base colors were painted in.

A light covering of dust had settled on the panel. Sotiris looked down at the icon, then held out his right hand. Its tremor, though slight, would ruin the fine work of the detail. In an hour or two, the medication would reduce the shaking; but the price he paid was drowsiness, and a disinclination to do anything but sleep.

Sotiris opened the street door, and sunlight lit the glistening dust motes, which fell around the room like tumbling stars. His pace down the alley was slow, his walk along the harbor front unhurried. At Apostolis's *kafenion,* he took a seat in the shade of the awning that served, in winter, to keep off rain; above his head, the canvas was discolored with the stains of mildew.

Apostolis had no other customers; he sat at one of his own tables, yawning as he scratched at a mosquito bite on his forearm.

"It's hot," said Sotiris, with a sigh. "There's no wind to cool us down. All summer, there's been no *Meltemi,* none worth a damn."

He looked along the seafront, to the tiny beach where the bay's wing turned out towards open sea. On the narrow strip of sand, four boys played. Amongst the moorings, a man stood at the stern of a small fishing boat whose engine was running; as he poured diesel through a funnel to fill the boat's tanks, his ugly bulldog's face was creased with concentration.

"He's away, already," said Sotiris, nodding in the direction of the fishing boat. "Much too early. What does he think he's going to catch, before sundown? Waste of time, going out now. It wants a good hour yet."

"Who is it?" Apostolis squinted towards the boat, as if to force it into focus. "Agiris? Ach, you know what he's like. He's wanting to set himself up in prime position before anyone else gets out there. Are you going out yourself this evening?"

"I was thinking of it, if I can stir myself. Fetch me a Greek coffee, Apostolis. Make it a double. I need something to clear my head."

Still scratching at the bite on his forearm, Apostolis left him. In the fishing boat, Agiris untied his mooring ropes, and tossed their ends back onto the harbor front.

Hiding his hands under the table, Sotiris gripped his right wrist with his left hand, and stopped the right hand's shaking. On the beach, one of the boys had left the others and was walking back towards the harbor. Passing a garden where the branches of a lemon tree overhung a wall, he reached up and plucked an under-ripe, green lemon. Above them all, on the headland, the campanile clock struck five.

Apostolis brought a glass of water with Sotiris's coffee, and sat back down at a table, his eyes following Agiris's boat as it motored slowly away from its mooring. Sotiris picked up his cup; before he drank, he surreptitiously sniffed the coffee. The water, when he sipped it, had a hint of sourness from the whitewash which fell occasionally into the *cisterna;* bottled and chilled in Apostolis's fridge, its coldness brought an aching to his gums.

As he reached the coffee's dregs—dark, powdery slump, which filled one third of the cup—the boy who had left the others reached his side. Sotiris, lost in thought, hadn't noticed him draw close; he was watching his rival's fishing boat out on the water, and taking note of the direction he was heading.

The boy sprawled in a chair at Sotiris's table; the movement of the chair's feet on the stones as he sat down caused Sotiris, startled, to turn.

*"Yassou, Pappou,"* said the boy. He was underweight, with legs too long for his body and a home haircut; deeply tanned, he was naked except for a pair of maroon swimming trunks, which, stretched by the weight of seawater, bagged over his skinny buttocks.

Sotiris gave his grandson a half-smile, and patted his naked thigh. On the beach, two of the three boys remaining were dunking the spluttering third in the shallow water.

"Why aren't you playing?" asked Sotiris. "You're missing out. Look what a great time they're having."

"They nearly drowned me," said the boy, glumly. "It's Vasso. He spoils everything."

"You want to give as good as you get," said Sotiris. "If he gives you a pasting, get him back."

"I'm too small. They all pick on me."

"Well, stay out of their way then, son." The coffee, or the

medication, had left a bad taste in Sotiris's mouth. He sipped more water to dispel it.

"Here," said the boy, laying the green fruit on the table. "I brought you a lemon."

"A lemon?" Sotiris held the fruit between finger and thumb; its skin was hard, like leather. "Why have you brought me a lemon?"

"You like lemons, these days," said the boy, shyly. "You like the smell of them."

Sotiris put the lemon to his nose, and sniffed; its scent was citrus sharp and fresh.

He smiled.

"You're right," he said, "I do like lemons."

In the doorway, Apostolis frowned.

*"Vre, mikre!"* he called to the boy. "Sammy! Get off that chair in those wet trunks!"

The boy stood.

"Can I have some money, *Pappou?*" he asked Sotiris.

"What on earth do you want money for, now?" asked the old man, wearily.

Sammy gave no answer, but raised his eyebrows, appealing.

His grandfather sighed.

"Not more ice cream, surely? How many have you had today, already? Apostolis, how many ice creams has this boy had off you today?"

Apostolis shook his head.

"I can't answer that," he said. "What goes on between me and my customers is privileged information. Isn't that right, *mikre?*"

Vigorously, Sammy nodded, as Sotiris dug in the pocket of his jeans for change.

"Get yourself whatever you want," he said. "You could do with putting some weight on. Thin as you are, a strong wind would carry you away. Here, see what you can make out of that."

Not noticing the tremor, the boy took the few coins from the palm of his grandfather's hand and ran past Apostolis, into the *kafenion*. In a few moments he emerged, digging a plastic spoon into a tub of pink and white ice cream. He held out his coins to Apostolis, who made a show of counting them.

"You're five drachmas short," said Apostolis.

Doubtfully, Sammy looked at him.

"Mother of God!" said Sotiris, irritably. "It's five drachmas! Put it on my bill, if it bothers you."

"It mounts up," said Apostolis, defensively. "Five drachmas on that ice cream is half my profit."

"As for you, young man," said Sotiris to Sammy, "you'll bankrupt me if you carry on like this. If you're going to be running up my bar bill, you'll have to pay me back. I think you'll have to come and crew for me, tonight." In delight, the boy beamed. "Go and ask your mother if that's OK with her. Then run to the kiosk and get us some bait. Tell him to put it in the book. And if you're back in fifteen minutes, you can have a lemonade to wash down that ice cream."

Still holding his ice cream, the boy ran off, not noticing the heat of the road or the sharpness of stones on his bare feet. Sotiris watched him go; the boy ran like a wild creature, fleet and lithe, his body working perfectly, as it should do: as Sotiris's had worked for him in decades past.

Apostolis went inside; Sotiris heard the ring of the till bell, and the clatter of coins dropped in the drawer. Believing there might be a last swallow of coffee in his cup now the dregs had had time to settle, he put the cup to his lips; but the trembling of his hand caused a dribble of liquid down his chin. Irritated, embarrassed, he wiped it away with the back of his left hand.

He put a banknote on the table to pay his bill.

"I'm off," he said, when Apostolis came to take his cup. "Keep the change."

He rose from his chair.

"Good fishing," said Apostolis, and Sotiris raised his left hand in goodbye.

At the waterside, the departure of Agiris's *Ayia Varvara* had left a vacant mooring next to Sotiris's *Doukissa*. Sotiris shielded his eyes from the dropping sun and looked out across the water, where Agiris's boat was rounding the headland, steering for Navayo Bay.

Sotiris pulled on the mooring rope to bring the boat in close, and stepped aboard. Taking out his keys, he unlocked the padlock which secured the cabin doorway. Out on the bay, Agiris had rounded the headland and moved out of sight, his boat's wake already assimilated by the sea.

Entering the cabin, Sotiris caught his forehead on the doorframe, and swore. From the quayside, Sammy called to his grandfather. The boy had put on a pair of shorts over his swimming trunks, and a T-shirt; he carried a plastic bag of frozen prawns for bait, and a foil-wrapped parcel.

"Mama sent you something to eat," he said, "in case you hadn't had anything. It's milk pie. If you've already eaten, I don't mind having it."

"Your mother's milk pie is better even than your grandmother's used to be," said Sotiris, "so if you want it, you're going to have to earn it with your fishing. I'll make a deal with you; if you can catch three fish before supper, the milk pie's all yours. Did she send anything to eat it with? I don't suppose she thought to send a fork."

From his shorts pocket, Sammy pulled out two forks, and two dessert spoons.

"She thinks of everything," said Sotiris, turning on the magnetos. "Just like your grandma. Now be ready to cast off that line, soon as this engine's warm. You'll have to be quick, then, getting in the boat, or I'll be going without you, after all."

With some coaxing and small adjustments under its cover, Sotiris fired the old engine. Walking briskly along the harbor front, Sambeca was approaching the moorings; when she heard the engine fire, she broke into a slow run.

"Wait, *kalé!*" she called. "Wait!"

"For God's sake," said Sotiris, under his breath. "What the hell does she want?"

Sambeca stood beside the *Doukissa,* panting from her short run.

"*Kali spera,* Sotiris," she said. Turning to Sammy, she ruffled his hair. "*Kamari mou,*" she said, in a childish tone. "How are you, Sammy? Are you well?"

"I'm well," said the boy, embarrassed; he crouched to fiddle with the mooring ropes, his back to her.

"Has Agiris left?" Sambeca asked Sotiris. "Has my brother already gone?"

"Half an hour ago," said Sotiris, roughly. "Always in a hurry to get out there, is your brother."

She sighed.

"I brought his supper," she said, holding up the lidded stoneware pot she was carrying. "I fetched it from Father Linos's. He hasn't touched his food again today. I think he's ailing. But I thought since it wasn't touched, Agiris might as well have it. He told me to bring him supper, and now I'm late. He won't be happy with me. How was I to know he'd go so early?"

"I could have told you," said Sotiris. "Sammy, loose that rope."

The boy's fingers tugged at the line, unfastening the knot.

"Someone should eat it," said Sambeca. "It's a sin to waste good food. But boys won't eat soup. I don't suppose you like avgolemono, do you, *kamari mou?*"

She looked expectantly at Sammy, who shook his head without a glance in her direction.

"I didn't think you would," she said. "You boys never like what's good for you. You're all the same: a sweet tooth and no sense. Your grandpa would enjoy it, though. Here, take it." She offered the pot to Sotiris. "Father Linos says the weather's too hot for soup. But it's not too hot if you let it cool, is it? I made it myself this morning, and it'd be a shame to throw it away."

Reluctantly, Sotiris took the pot and lifted the edge of the lid. The avgolemono was thin and a little greasy, only slightly thickened by the addition of egg yolks; small, gray meatballs and grains of swollen white rice had sunk to the bottom. But the soup was flavored generously with lemon juice; Sotiris sniffed, enjoying its scent.

"Be careful with that lid," said Sambeca. "Don't take it off until you're ready to eat. It's easy enough to spill. I had mother spill a bowlful, just this lunchtime."

Sotiris replaced the lid, and put the pot on the bench beside him.

"Thank you," he said.

*"Kali orexi,"* said Sambeca, wishing him good digestion as she walked away. "Good fishing, Sammy."

The boy, unknotting a second rope, ignored her.

"Cast her off, then," Sotiris called to Sammy.

"She's a witch," said Sammy, as he jumped aboard. "I'll bet her mother spilled her soup on purpose. It's made with frogs, I'll bet. You shouldn't eat it, Grandpa."

Sotiris smiled.

"On the contrary, my boy, I shall eat it with great relish," he said. "What could make a meal taste finer than knowing you're taking the food from Agiris's mouth?"

For a moment, the boy was thoughtful.

"If you're going to eat all that," he said, "perhaps you won't have room for much milk pie."

Sotiris smiled.

"Perhaps I won't," he said. "Now, come back here to this tiller, and you be captain whilst I sit down a while. Steer her straight, and watch for other vessels. And set her on a heading for Navayo Bay."

Evening moved into night, and night into the earliest hour of morning. As the church clock struck one, the *kafenions* were closed; at the empty tavernas, the staff were eating suppers made up of what was left over, drinking cold beer from the bottle and smoking as they talked.

At the moorings from where the *Doukissa* had left, Mercuris, Sammy's father, ground out a cigarette beneath his foot. Agiris's *Ayia Varvara* had tied up hours ago; of Sammy and his grandfather, there was no sign. As the last balcony light went out, Mercuris yawned.

It wouldn't be the first time the old man had kept the boy out there till morning, coming home for breakfast with a good catch taken at dawn. Mercuris looked out once more across the black water; a shooting star streaked briefly across the sky. On the sea, there was nothing to be seen, no red or green of navigation lights; no engine's throb broke the silence which underwrote the water's slip and slide.

Then, from all around came a deep, low rumble. In the tavernas, the staff stopped talking as the ground shook back and forth like a palsied hand, rattling the cutlery and bouncing the ashtrays on the tables.

The waiters jumped to their feet, and ran out from under the canopy where they had sat; but by the time they reached the harbor side, the tremor had passed.

For a few moments, Mercuris stood alert, in case another tremor should strike; but the night remained quiet, the ground still. Laughing, the waiters returned to their seats and their cigarettes.

Still Mercuris hesitated. With the boy not back, Tina would worry, and not sleep all night. But Sotiris knew his way, and Mercuris had an early start tomorrow. With one last look across the empty sea, he shrugged, and headed down the alleyway towards home.

On board the *Aphrodite,* a light burned in a cabin; the dinghy was safely tied up at her stern.

On the narrow beach where Sammy had played that day, seawater black as ink lapped at the sand; and, despite the darkness, children played there now. By the light of a street-lamp, a boy and a girl searched out flat pebbles, and skimmed them across the surface of water they couldn't see.

No one watched over them; they were alone, wide-eyed and wakeful despite the hour. They ran barefoot along the sand, as if it were midday; bare-legged and solemn-faced, they rested at the water's edge, their hair in rats' tails from the salt of bathing, their skin reflecting the weak light like old bones.

Until someone called. Pebble in hand, the girl froze, and listened, like a dog picking up a sound no human could hear. Dropping the pebble to the sand, she took the boy by the hand, and followed the call, leading him in silence from the beach. They took the path which would lead them to the mountains, and disappeared like phantoms in the dark.

# *Seven*

At sunrise, the mooring alongside the *Ayia Varvara* was still vacant.

With fresh bait and a flask of coffee, Agiris chose the same course he had taken the previous evening, steering between a yacht flying the flag of Denmark and a French catamaran, running close to the *Aphrodite*. Aboard the foreign craft, the crews still slept, but at the *Aphrodite*'s prow a man leaned on the railings, watching the sunrise. Tall, somewhat overweight, the curls of his hair damp, he wore a toweling robe and bathing slippers, as if he had taken an early swim in the bay.

He seemed to Agiris somehow familiar. As Agiris passed, the fat man raised a hand as if he knew him; so Agiris raised his hand in salutation, then gave his full attention to the sea.

On the rear deck, breakfast was laid for two: a *cafetière* of Italian coffee, a jug of pomegranate juice, a basket of warm rolls and croissants and a dish of honeycomb.

The fat man poured himself a cup of the fragrant coffee, and from the basket chose a sesame-seeded roll. Enrico filled two glasses from the jug of juice.

"The honeycomb is from Sostis," said Enrico. "He sent it with his compliments; it reached us yesterday."

"Then I shall be very pleased to try it," said the fat man. "Miss Athaniti is leaving us this morning; I believe the ferry goes just after eight, so be ready with the dinghy as soon as she wishes to go."

"I don't wish to go at all."

Kara spoke as she climbed the stairs from below; bowing his head as he left the fat man, Enrico stepped back to let her pass.

The fat man stood up from his seat, took her hand in his and kissed it. He pulled out a chair for her next to his and, having seated her, sat down. He poured her coffee, and passed it to her with a smile.

"You look wonderful this morning," he said. "So lovely, that in your honor I have made a compromise, and indulged your preference for a somewhat weaker brew than I would normally choose."

"You spoil me," she said. "And you didn't have to compromise for me. Enrico would have made your usual coffee, if you had asked him."

"Of course he would. But for you, I am prepared to compromise. I have so enjoyed our time together. As always."

Kara's smile was of regret.

"As always, our time has been too short," she said. "We lead such busy lives, Hermes. We should play truant again, and both stay longer."

He sighed.

"But the work is always there," he said. "I have stretched my time here already, and had my holiday; and even here, I found more than I anticipated. The mystery of what's happened to the Lady is an intriguing one, and if there weren't more serious matters, I'd give it my full attention; but as it is, I leave it in your hands, and in the hands of police detectives. You'll let me know, won't you, what the outcome is? You'll write to me, at the Athens address, and give me a full account?"

"Of course."

He kissed her hand again, and kept it for a moment in his own; his expression showed his own regret, and indecisiveness.

Above them, on the headland, the campanile clock struck seven.

"Time is our enemy," he said, "and you must eat some breakfast before your journey. Please, do try the honeycomb; it's come to us from a very good friend of mine."

As he steered out of the harbor, Agiris made out his sister's form on the waterfront, heading in the direction of the baker's. Even though there was no wind, he kept close to the shelter of the shoreline. The first rays of the sun were growing hot; the sea was almost still, its surface smooth. A container-laden merchant ship moved slowly on the horizon; close by, a gull dipped low to catch a fish, but glided away with its beak empty.

He followed the coastline into Navayo Bay, intending to tie up at the jetty and hunt for octopus in the pools formed by the broken cement; whilst the sea was cool, they would be feeding, and easy targets in the shallow water.

But at the jetty, a boat was already moored: Sotiris's *Doukissa*. Agiris cursed the old man, reduced his speed and leaned hard on the tiller to turn away and try another spot. The prow came round, and as it did so, he sensed a movement in his field of vision transient as the leaping of a fish. Something had moved: not on the open water, but where the sea lapped at the rocks. There was an overhang, and shadow, and something was there, round and dark like the head of a seal. Was it a seal? He knocked the gears into neutral and picked up the binoculars, training them on the shadow to make out what it was. Was it worth a look? If it was something lost overboard from some passing vessel, it might be worth the trouble; once, he'd found a half-full bottle of whisky, bobbing over the waves into his hands, and usable items for the boat—landing nets, and floats especially—were commonplace. But often it was nothing of value: a dead turtle on its back, or a drowned and bloated goat; driftwood, or a skein of seaweed.

He tried the binoculars again, but even their magnification showed no more than a dark sphere on the water. Pushing the gear lever forward with his foot, he opened the throttle to give the boat a little speed and moved the tiller to steer the *Ayia Varvara* towards the rocks.

He steered with care; the water grew shallower with every meter, and there were unseen outcrops of rock which would batter a propeller. The dark sphere stayed where it was, not free floating but attached somehow to the shoreline rocks, rising and falling with the waves.

And then the sphere moved: very slowly it turned, and

showed a face so stricken and so white, Agiris believed he was looking at a corpse. But the face's eyes were open, and its lips were trying to move; and as he drew closer still, he saw small, white fingers gripping onto the rocks. Then the fingers of one small hand loosed their grip, and the hand made a feeble attempt to wave; and in that moment, the face's features made sense to him, and he knew what he had found.

It was Sammy in the water, young Sammy, exhausted, half-frozen and more than half-drowned. But what was he doing here, all alone? And where on earth was that old devil, his grandfather?

As the church clock struck eight, the boy's father was back on the waterfront, at his father-in-law's mooring. Mercuris shaded his eyes from the sun at the eastern horizon, and scanned the harbor bay. A Danish yacht was making for open sea; a youth was fishing from a rowing boat. At the *Aphrodite*'s stern, a tall, fat man was handing a woman into a dinghy whilst a white-uniformed crewman started its outboard. Each minute, Mercuris expected the little *Doukissa* to appear at the horizon; as each minute passed, still she wasn't there.

At the commercial quay, passengers were gathering for the morning ferry, their luggage at their feet. Shopkeepers and tradesmen waiting for incoming cargo stood by their trucks, offering round cigarettes and smoking; they talked of last night's basketball and this week's scandal, embellishing the gossip as they passed it on.

At Apostolis's *kafenion,* Mercuris chose a seat with a good view of the bay. He wished *kali mera* to Father Linos, who was finishing a cup of Lipton tea. Behind him, two shepherds argued loudly about the best treatment for sheep-ticks. A foreign couple shared a German newspaper, and drank Nescafé with their toasted sandwiches.

Mercuris signaled to Apostolis, who approached with a tin tray beneath his arm.

"*Kali mera,*" said Mercuris. "How's it going?"

"Same as always," said Apostolis. "What'll you have?"

"Greek coffee, a double," said Mercuris. "She's sent me on a mission to find our boy, booted me out of the house at the crack of dawn and not even made my coffee. I've told her the old man'll keep him out till lunchtime, but she won't have it. So I'm here on official duty."

As he went inside, Apostolis shook his head in contempt at the ways of women. At the bay's end, a small boat appeared, too far away yet to say if it was the *Doukissa*. Father Linos looked at his watch, and sipped his tea. The shepherds' argument was growing heated, and one of the men brought his fist down on the table, stressing his belief in his point of view. The *Aphrodite*'s dinghy reached the commercial quay; the crewman held the boat close whilst its passengers disembarked, and handed them their bags—an overnight case for the woman, a red holdall for the man—before heading off to find a mooring amongst the fishing boats.

Out on the bay, the approaching boat had moved close enough for Mercuris to see it was not the *Doukissa*. For a small craft, it was moving fast, and its engine was becoming audible, straining to the limits of its power. From some way off, a horn sounded, dismal and deep, and a ferry in blue and orange livery came into view. The waiting passengers picked up their luggage, and began the handshakes and embraces of their long goodbyes. Father Linos considered ordering more tea; but at the waterfront's far end, where the steps to the church began, Sambeca was approaching.

Apostolis brought out Mercuris's cup of coffee and stood at his shoulder.

"Who's this, in a big hurry?" he asked, pointing to the speeding boat. "Looks like Agiris has forgotten his bait again."

"Bait, or breakfast, one of the two," said Mercuris.

"Maybe he's caught a mermaid, and he's rushing her home to bed," said Apostolis.

Mercuris laughed.

"If he'd got that lucky, he wouldn't waste time coming home," he said. "She'd be pinned to the deck and seen to, straightaway!"

Apostolis smiled. At the quay, the fat man put his arms around the woman in yellow and kissed her on both cheeks. Father Linos, an easy target in his robes, sat back in his chair, resigned to being spotted by Sambeca; but her attention was on her brother's boat as it drew close to its mooring.

The ferry docked, dropping anchor with a rattling of the chain; from the decks, her crew bellowed directions as men ashore made her fast. The ramp was lowered, and the waiting tradesmen ran aboard to take off their cargo. Like refugees, the passengers trooped aboard; the woman in yellow turned when she reached the deck, and blew a kiss to the sad-faced fat man.

As the *Ayia Varvara* reached her mooring, Agiris cut the power, and with expert maneuvering drew the boat alongside the quay, throwing a rope to Sambeca who waited, arms folded, for his arrival.

"What's wrong, *kalé?*" she asked; but Agiris, red in the face and yelling, didn't hear her.

"Bring help!" he shouted. "Tell them to call the coast guard! Get them here fast!"

Apostolis went towards him; leaving their chairs, the shepherds and Mercuris followed, whilst the Germans laid down their newspaper and watched them go, bemused. Father Linos drained his cup, and stood to leave, anticipating some overblown drama. At the quay, the ferry's ramp was raised; the ropes were hauled in, and the harbor waters churned. As the vessel moved from the quay, the woman dressed in yellow waved her hand.

"What's happened, *kalé?*" asked Sambeca, peering into the boat. There, on the floor of the stern, Sammy lay motionless.

"Fetch some brandy, woman, to revive him," ordered Agiris. "And fetch the doctor, quick. Use Apostolis's phone and call the coast guard. The boy says his grandfather's sick; he thinks he might be dying. They'll find him in his boat in Navayo Bay."

Apostolis, reaching the *Ayia Varvara* and understanding quickly what was happening, grabbed Mercuris by the arm and pushed him forward.

"Your son," he said. "It's your son."

Ashen-faced, Mercuris leapt into the boat, and lifted Sammy's shoulders to cradle him in his arms. Despite the sun, the boy's body was clammy, and cold as death; with tears in his eyes, his father called for blankets, and patted Sammy's cheeks to rouse him. But the boy seemed to be slipping away; although his eyes flickered open and saw his father's face, they closed without him comprehending that he was home, and safe.

As the ferry headed out across the bay, the fat man watched and waved until Kara was too distant to be seen. When the ferry gave a final blast on its horn, still he was reluctant to turn away; but with that desolate anthem to so many regretted farewells, the point of no return was clearly past.

He picked up his holdall from the quayside, and walked away.

The small crowd gathered by a fishing boat drew his attention. Joining the back of the crowd, he craned his neck to see into the boat's stern. The boy's condition seemed serious. Close by, on the waterfront, the ugly man who had taken Kara's candle money was seated on a bench, a hip flask in his hand.

The fat man approached him.

"What's happened here?" he asked. "What's wrong with the boy?"

"I pulled him from the water," said Agiris, keen to tell his story once again. "He didn't tell me much; you can see the state he's in. I asked him where his grandfather was—they fished together, often—and he only said a word or two, that his grandpa was very sick, and maybe dead. I asked him was the old man in the water, but he said not; he said he'd left him in the boat. He couldn't start the engine—that's no surprise, temperamental as its owner, that engine is—so he thought he'd better swim. I had to make a choice, to get the boy back here or take the time to check their boat, so I brought him home. The coast guard must go and find Sotiris." He shook his head. *"Panayia mou,"* he said. "I was after an octopus or two, and I found this mess."

"It's fortunate that you did," said the fat man. "The boy doesn't look as if he'd have stood much more time in the water."

At a run, a young man with a bag approached the *Ayia Varvara*.

"Here, doctor," called Mercuris. "Thank God. My boy's here."

Apostolis's *kafenion* was empty but for an old man who had taken a seat by the doorway to observe the drama from a distance. The fat man took a table next to him. Under the doctor's direction, Mercuris carried Sammy from the boat, and the physician led him down an alleyway, away from the harbor. With their departure, Agiris reboarded his boat along with Father Linos and the two shepherds; he started the engine and cast off, throwing the rope to Apostolis on the waterfront. Father Linos sat at the prow, watching the horizon for any sign of the coast guard; the two shepherds lit cigarettes and sat down in the stern, smiling at the prospect of adventure.

The old man by the *kafenion's* doorway sat spread-legged,

his liver-spotted hands resting on the head of a cane. He wore a seaman's cap; his face was weathered but not tanned, as if his days of exposure to sun and wind were in the past.

"I hope you're in no hurry for service," he said to the fat man. "There's your host, over there, jumping into the heart of the action." He raised the foot of his cane and pointed with it to the *Ayia Varvara* where, as the boat pulled away, Apostolis leapt aboard to join the shepherds.

The fat man smiled.

"Happily, I've breakfasted already," he said. "Forgive me for asking, but have you no interest in what's going on? The drama seems quite dramatic, as dramas go."

The old man shook his head.

"I'm a man who's learned much patience, over the years," he said. "And I can guarantee you one thing, friend: that if I sit here and wait, the news will come to me. There's no need to go chasing after it. This *kafenion* is its natural home."

"You're right, of course," said the fat man, "and I admire your restraint. Tell me, who is the young man already rescued, and who's the poor soul who has been taken ill?"

"They call the boy Sammy," said the old man. "Sotiris is his baptized name, of course, after his grandfather, but they use the English version, as is the fashion. The one they're saying is sick is his grandfather. Let's hope he isn't dead, or even near it; gossip can put people in cemeteries when they're a long march from the grave. But if he is gone, it'll be a tragedy for us, a big loss for this island. He's been our icon painter for many years."

The fat man's eyebrows lifted.

"He's the icon painter?"

"Yes, friend, he is; he holds that esteemed office. You'll know the legend of our icon painters: when one dies, by God's grace, the gift passes at the point of death to the next generation. If we've lost Sotiris, they'd better make the boy well so he can paint. Sotiris had no sons; the boy will have inherited the job."

"How very interesting," said the fat man.

"Shall I tell you a secret?" The old man leaned close as a conspirator; his eyes were bright with mischief. "There's nothing God-given about it. They train the boys as you'd expect, make them apprentices. It's a craft that isn't learned overnight; it takes great patience, and dedication. And, I venture to say, a certain spiritual commitment. It's more of a calling than a trade. But if old Sotiris is gone . . ." For the first time, the implications of the icon painter's death seemed to strike him. "There'd be a gap in the line, for a few years at least. Young Sammy is only eight, is he, or nine? Who would train him? Would they send him to the monks at Mount Athos? His mother won't like that. Perhaps Mount Athos would send one of their painters to us, to fill the gap."

At the thought of Mount Athos's strict community offering monks on loan, the fat man smiled.

"That seems unlikely," he said. "We must cross our fingers that Sotiris is all right."

"We must. But my gut tells me something might be wrong. Sotiris hasn't been himself for many months."

"Do you mean he's been unwell?"

The old man threw up a hand in a gesture of uncertainty.

"I couldn't say for sure. And I hate to cast aspersions. But he hasn't been putting in the hours on the job that he used to. Time was, he'd work all night on one of his paintings. He was a true master of the art; they say he's one of the best icon painters Kalkos has ever had. These days, he's looking tired, and the man's all skin and bone, though his daughter tries to feed him, as she should. And as for his behavior..." He turned his head to left and right, ensuring there were no eavesdroppers. "I would never repeat this if I hadn't seen it myself—and you must keep this to yourself, of course—but folks are saying he's gone a bit soft in the head."

"Soft in the head?"

"He's developed a passion for lemons. In all my years, I never heard of such a thing as that. Every opportunity, if there's lemons about—a slice for your tea or your glass of water—he's after picking it up and sniffing it. He'll pick one from the tree, and keep it in his pocket like a pet, and then every so often he takes it out and sniffs it! Now, if sniffing lemons isn't a sign of madness, I don't know what is. If he has—you know..." He put a finger to his temple, and twisted it. "Better he goes sooner, rather than later. For the family's sake. They're well thought of, respected. A lunatic in the family would do them no favors, would it? Look, there they go!"

Far out to sea, a coast guard launch swept across the water, throwing up great waves of spray as it sped towards Navayo Bay.

"We'll know soon enough now if we've a body on our hands," said the old man. He made a cross over his chest. "I don't want to think it. I like Sotiris."

"Is he generally liked?" asked the fat man.

The old man considered.

"Oh yes, he's liked well enough," he said. "There's not much about him to dislike."

Within the hour, the coast guard launch retraced its course, heading back to its home port at much reduced speed, moving no faster than the morning ferry. Some minutes later, two small boats appeared on the bay—the *Ayia Varvara* leading the *Doukissa,* their pace steady as they approached their moorings.

The fat man watched as the two shepherds carried the old man's body off the boat, one holding under the arms, the other carrying the feet, the strain of the corpse's weight showing in the shepherds' faces. Rigor mortis had set the body stiff, freezing the pose of Sotiris's dying; he had wrapped his arms around himself in a self-embrace, and drawn his knees some way up to his stomach. Father Linos followed men and corpse onto the harbor side, his face somber; Agiris tied up the *Ayia Varvara* as Apostolis made fast the *Doukissa,* which he had captained home.

The women who had gathered at the waterfront crossed themselves, and whispered to each other. The carpenter and his sons brought a half-finished door to carry the body; as they laid Sotiris down, the carpenter took out his tape measure, and measured him for his coffin. The doctor came, and knelt for a few moments beside the body; he touched the neck and lifted one eyelid, then stood and shook his head. Father Linos said a few words over the corpse, and blessed the men who would carry it to protect them from its taint. The bearers looked serious and troubled; the small crowd that had gathered was quiet.

"Are we ready, then?" Father Linos asked the bearers. "Pick him up."

Sambeca stepped forward from the gathering.

"They don't know you're coming, *Papa,*" she said. "I'll run ahead, shall I, and tell them to expect him?"

Father Linos looked doubtful.

"They should be ready," said Sambeca. "It isn't right if they're not ready to receive him."

"Go quickly, then," he said.

She hurried away; as she passed Sotiris's boat, Apostolis was pocketing the keys.

"You can give those to me," she called out to him. "The priest's asked me to go ahead and break the news; I can give them back the keys. And there, see, give me that pot and the cutlery. The boat should be tidy, under the circumstances. I can drop them off at our house. I'm passing our front door to get to theirs."

Apostolis handed her the keys, along with the stoneware pot of avgolemono, the balled-up foil that had held the milk pie and the spoons and forks from Sotiris's daughter.

"I'd better hurry," she said, more to herself than to him. "I don't want them getting there before me."

Father Linos gave the signal, and the bearers took the strain. In silence, they carried the icon painter away.

The onlookers were reluctant to disperse. The men took out cigarettes, and offered them round; the women stood, arms folded, as one group, and pooled their speculation.

The doctor was talking to the shepherds and Apostolis; the fat man walked across to them.

"Excuse me, gentlemen," he said. The men all looked at him. "I wonder, *yiatre*," he said, addressing the doctor, "what you have to say about this tragedy? What would you say was the cause of death?"

"Heart," said the doctor, without hesitation. "A massive heart attack, in my opinion. Gone like that, I expect." He snapped his fingers, and the men all blinked, as if he'd fired a shot. He seemed to forget the fat man immediately, and excused himself from the men he knew. "I must go," he said, "and do the paperwork."

The fat man considered drinking coffee, but the *kafenion's* tables were all taken, and Apostolis was still talking on the quay.

Agiris had made his boat secure, and was walking away, alone, along the harbor front.

The fat man frowned. He knew his countrymen's character, regarding drama; there would be several hours, now, of discussion and dissection. Yet here was a leading player, leaving the scene.

He watched for a while to see which route the man would choose. Then the fat man picked up his holdall and, at a suitable distance, headed in the direction Agiris had taken.

# *Eight*

The fat man kept Agiris in his sights whilst seeming to take a visitor's interest in the waterfront businesses. A board outside a travel agency advertised ferry tickets on the major routes—Athens, Heraklion, Brindisi—and a poster in the window showed an obsolete Olympic airlines jet angled against a sky of brilliant blue; the woman in the deserted office picked at the lacquer on her nails as she talked on the phone. At the leather shop, tourists browsed through racks of imported belts and wallets, whilst others chose plastic replicas of the Lady from the religious tat displayed on market barrows. In the bank, a cashier doodled idly with a chained-up pen, captive to his colleague's tedious monologue. The proprietor of the souvlaki shop already had customers, and though it was early in the day, the fat man was highly tempted by the smell of spit-roast pork; but Agiris was already well ahead, and the fat man reluctantly went on.

Before he reached the steps up to the church, Agiris took a turning to the left, which the fat man found to be, when he reached it, an upward path of much shallower steps, each one wide enough to take a pace before the next was at his feet. The path ran at first between modern houses, but a little way up from the waterfront it led through an area of abandoned buildings, some with the tumbledown walls of ruins, others still largely complete but with wide and fatal cracks from ground to roof, with glassless windows showing rooms without ceilings and only the rotting crossbeams left of their roofs. Over a doorless doorway, a hook for an oil lamp was still in place; where a door remained, its rusted hinges were elaborate, in the old Venetian style. Thistles and wild grasses overran mosaics in collapsing courtyards, and in the corners of old kitchens, dumped rubbish had become the haunt of rats and cats. Here and there, the walls were daubed with FOR SALE announcements, their contact phone numbers with the dialing codes of distant cities—Thessaloniki, Patras, Sydney.

The route was meandering, winding through the wasteland of abandoned houses, and the fat man now tracked Agiris by his footsteps, though he himself, in his tennis shoes, moved in silence. The steps reached their end at a high wall, and a cast-iron gateway so imposing it seemed to be the steps' destination. Set in a stone arch in the style of the Templar knights, the gateway was built not of local stone but of a rosy-colored sandstone, skillfully cut into close-fitting blocks. The arch was draped in hibiscus, whose blazing trumpets of scarlet flowers hung on weak-stemmed, lime-leaved branches; on the arch's keystone, almost obscured by weathering, was a carved shield cut with a Maltese cross.

Though the steps were at an end, a cobbled lane led away to the left. The fat man listened, but heard no footsteps from that direction. The gate ahead of him rested on its latch, and he pushed it open, and stepped through on to a broad stone path beneath an avenue of lemon trees, whose unripened fruit matched the green of their leaves so exactly, it seemed like deliberate camouflage. The path was made cool by the overhanging branches; recent sweeping had cleared it of debris, so the small object lying ahead of him was out of place, and caused him to pause.

Crouching, he found it to be a tiny mouse, its eyes still open in death. Manic at their discovery, a few ants scurried round the corpse, probing at the ears and the nostrils, some already tracking back to their nest to report the find. The fat man studied the rodent, looking for the puncture marks of a cat's teeth; but though the mouse's own needle teeth seemed bared in threat, he could see no marks on its body.

With finger and thumb, he picked up the creature by its tail and dangled it before his nose, sniffing for the stink of decay. There was no bad odor; but something else was there, unexpected and unusual, like marzipan.

He frowned, and for a moment seemed to think.

Laying the mouse back on the path, he unzipped a front pocket of his holdall, and took out an empty matchbox; he slipped off the cover, picked off an ant emerging from the mouse's ear and placed the mouse in the matchbox, tucking the tail round the curve of its body. He slid the box cover closed, and replaced the matchbox in his holdall.

At its end, the avenue opened into the sunlight of a terrace fronting a graceful house, built of the same mellow sandstone as the gateway arch; this mellowness gave an impression of considerable age, yet there were details in the house's architecture which suggested more contemporary construction. Despite its beauty, the house was not, apparently, occupied; on both upper and lower levels, the window shutters were fastened, and a padlock and chain were looped through the handles of the front door's double panels. Yet the house had no air of neglect, but of expecting an owner about to return, or who had not long been absent. There was no sign of dilapidation; the paintwork was fresh, and free of summer dust; the doorstep, like the pathway, was recently swept. It seemed a loved property reluctantly left, temporarily sealed but ready in a moment to be opened up and lived in once again.

The care given to the house was evident too in its garden, which was the house's glory. The terrace was decorated with pots of plants, some cultivated for their showy blossoms, others for their scent, still others for texture, so roses, stocks and geraniums were mixed with rosemary, soft-headed pampas grass and spiky cacti. All flourished, helped to their best by the grower's attention to their preferences; those that thrived on light were placed in full sun, whilst the shade-lovers were set beneath an elderly vine whose grapes dangled in straggling bunches, the skins not black but darkest purple, dulled with the windblown dust. The vine roots had lifted the flagstones, and even here the gardener had planted alpines, which flourished in the cramped and craggy spaces. At the center of the terrace stood a table and two chairs, all painted in a cerulean blue which glowed against the house walls and the shutters. On the table, an empty beer can lay on its side; the liquid which remained inside a water bottle was condensing on the plastic from the heat.

The fat man moved on from the terrace, into the garden's heart. High walls marked its irregular perimeter, which stretched at one point to a sharp-angled corner, whilst its opposite end swept round in a curve to form the quadrant of a circle. Around the walls grew fruit trees—peach, medlar, pomegranate, fig and cherry—and in front of them, narrow paths wound between beds of vegetables and flowers, from the commonplace to the exotic and the unexpected. At the center of the beds was a pond, where silvery-orange carp rose lazily to the surface, and drifted down again, sinking into the cooler depths. A hosepipe lay coiled under a dripping tap; a wheelbarrow was full of pruned branches, and weeds with soil still in their roots.

For a little while, the fat man took the liberty of wandering through the garden, idling along the paths and stopping to look more closely at what took his eye. He admired the berries on a strawberry tree, and for some minutes studied a large-leafed plant, deciding whether it was tobacco or mandrake. The branches of a peach tree held a heavy, soft-skinned crop; around the roots, wasps fed on the brown-bruised flesh of overripe, fallen fruit.

The fat man bent to sniff at a bush of nicotiana, and mixed with the flowers' scent caught the tang of woodsmoke. Tracing the smoke's source with his nose, he followed paths which led him behind the house; and, between the house's back and the curved wall of the garden, he found the man he had been following, prodding at a bonfire with the tines of a garden fork.

His back was to the fat man, and when the fat man

spoke— *"Kali mera sas"*—he was startled, and turned round, holding the fork before him like a gladiator facing a challenger. The fat man was almost hidden, at first, by smoke billowing from the bonfire, so it seemed his voice had come from nowhere. As a breath of a breeze dispersed the smoke, he was revealed, and Agiris abruptly lowered the fork, as if embarrassed by his overreaction.

"My apologies if I startled you," said the fat man. "Please forgive me for approaching you in this way. Your garden drew me in, and I am guilty of having come the long way round it to find you. And now I have found you, I wonder if you would sell me some of the peaches from your tree?"

The bonfire was of the same pruned wood and wilting weeds he had seen in the wheelbarrow, all far too green to burn; a container of some accelerant—paraffin, or petrol—stood to one side. Agiris dug the fork into the fire, and lifted the top layers of greenery to allow more oxygen at the base; still no flames leapt, but clouds of smoke billowed up, choking him so he coughed and cursed, and wiped his stinging eyes with the back of his hand.

He touched the fat man's arm to move him back.

"Step away from the fire, friend," he said. "This smoke's not healthy."

The fat man did as Agiris suggested, and Agiris stuck the fork into the ground, ramming it as far as he could into the dry dirt with his booted foot.

"I should introduce myself," said the fat man. He held out a hand. "Hermes Diaktoros, of Athens."

Agiris held out his own hand; his grip was firm, but the

skin was ingrained with dirt, and smelled of engine diesel, or perhaps the accelerant he planned to use to boost the fire.

"They call me Agiris," he said. "But the garden isn't mine; I'm only its custodian. You're on church property, friend, property of the Orthodox Church of Greece. It's the bishop's garden, but the bishop isn't here. The bishop's rarely here; the bishop has bigger fish to fry than he finds here."

The fat man narrowed his eyes, pretending to search his memory.

"We've met before," he said. "This morning, down in the harbor. You brought the boy home in your boat."

Agiris pulled up his glistening lower lip and held it against his gum, making himself, quite literally, tight-lipped. His tongue poked at the inner of his cheek and ran along the top line of his gums. From the fire, another cloud of smoke enveloped them, and Agiris wafted his arms in front of himself to disperse it.

"It seems to me," said the fat man, "that what you've put on your fire is too green to burn. Wouldn't you be better to let it dry a week or two, first?"

"A garden this size, it builds up," said Agiris. "What's good clean stuff, I compost. But these weeds, you compost them, the weeds break through and infest the ground again. You water the plants you want to nurture, and you water the weeds at the same time. And their roots go so deep, it's next to impossible to get them out. It'll burn through, by and by. But do you know, breathing in that smoke always makes me crave a cigarette. Where's the logic in that? Just let me find my smokes, and I'll get you some of that fruit. No payment required; what the bishop tells me to say is, make a donation to the Lady. Which comes to the same thing, in the end—money in the church's coffers."

He turned from the fat man and, parting the tendrils of a red-flowered Chinese honeysuckle, revealed a statue almost hidden by the shrub's foliage. The statue was the figure of a bearded man, somewhat smaller than life-size and on a pedestal; the once-white marble was gray with age and lichen. Hanging from the statue's midsection was a canvas satchel, which Agiris opened to find his cigarettes.

Curious, the fat man stepped closer to the statue, holding back the honeysuckle branches to let in sunlight. The bearded figure held a basket of fruit against his round belly; his swollen tongue protruded through lips curved in a lascivious grin. Agiris's satchel hung from the broken stub of the statue's penis.

"Poor Priapus," said the fat man, looking down at the statue's damaged genitalia. "I wonder whether he would be more bothered by the pain of the amputation, or the indignity of your use of what remains to him."

The gardener seemed puzzled, but then laughed; his laughter was high and a little disturbing, as might echo down the halls of a sanatorium.

"You wouldn't care for such surgery yourself, then, friend?" he asked. "The last bishop but one ordered this operation. I remember this gentleman in his prime, when my father used to bring us here, in the time when he was gardener. My sister and I used to come and peep at him. He had a dick this long . . ." He held his hand eight inches apart.

"Which for a man his size was something to brag about, wouldn't you say? My sister didn't understand what she was looking at, but I knew what it was. Then the bishop decided it wasn't a decent thing to have in a churchman's garden, and ordered it be removed." He made a chopping motion with the side of his hand, like a butcher approaching his block; and, as if the action pleased him, he smiled, and did it again.

"The church has strange ideas of decency and indecency," said the fat man. "An image of a thing completely natural and functional—a male erection—it finds offensive. Yet it will take cash and gifts from the poorest supplicants at its shrines, and use their money to maintain properties like this for its officials, whilst persuading the supplicants they are somehow buying divine blessings. If a vow of true poverty had to be made and kept, there'd be far fewer applicants for the roles of Orthodox priests, in my view. Our statue here is, as you probably know, Priapus, in legend both father and son of my namesake, Hermes. He had, many years ago, a small cult of worshippers who liked to engage in orgies, and he was the deity to approach if you suffered from impotence. I noticed you have satyrion growing in your beds over there; that was a popular plant in their rites. It is a powerful aphrodisiac—were you aware of that?—and excellent for increasing the milk yield in cows, who love the taste so much they go almost mad for it. He's an odd-looking fellow, wouldn't you say? He was the god of freaks, too, the patron saint, if you like, of dwarves and giants, amongst others. In short, a very interesting character. So you should give him some respect, don't you think?"

Agiris chose a cigarette for himself, and held the packet out to the fat man, but the fat man declined. Agiris lit his cigarette and drew on it, watching the fat man with eyes narrowed against the smoke of both fire and cigarette, giving himself the appearance of slyness.

"You're not from here, I know," he said, slipping the cigarettes back into the satchel. "And you're not here to pay your respects to our venerated Lady, are you?"

"I'm a traveler," said the fat man, "and my feet have led me here. I have an interest in the old gods, and mythology, and in antiquities. It's my interest which engenders my wish to see old images respected."

"Have you been to visit our Lady?"

"I have indeed, and I admired her greatly as an example of the icon painter's craft. Speaking of which, are you not shaken by your experiences this morning? Were you well acquainted with the man who died—Sotiris, I believe they called him?"

Again, Agiris pulled up his lip; but then he released it, and inhaled deeply on his cigarette.

"I knew him," he said, breathing out smoke as he spoke. "Everyone knew him."

"But?"

Agiris shrugged.

"I'd be lying if I told you we were close. We were never friends, not from being boys. Sometimes, you take a dislike, and it sticks. I had little to do with him; he had little to do with me. We had one thing in common—a love of fishing—but even in that, we kept our distance. But seeing the boy in the water—well, whatever you thought about a family, you'd have to have a heart of stone, wouldn't you, not to have pulled the poor lad out?"

"Perhaps I will have a cigarette, after all," said the fat man. He took his own cigarettes from his pocket, and lit one with his gold lighter. "How was it that you came to find him?"

"Luck, on his part, pure luck. They'd been out all night, I knew that; the boat wasn't at its mooring this morning, and he's never out earlier than me. I didn't give that any thought—if they did as badly as I did last night (I came home with nothing: an octopus not worth the trouble and a few tiddlers for soup), he would have slept on board and be trying again this morning. He was—I don't want to speak ill of the dead, so let's just say he was careful with money. Tight, he was. He was well known for it, and he'd see no point in using fuel to get home just to use more to get back to where he'd been in the first place. If it rains, there's mud, I say; if he'd spent a few drachmas to replace those worn-out engine parts, the boy might have got the boat started and Sotiris to a doctor. The old fool might be home in his own bed, instead of being laid out in his coffin.

"I didn't know where he'd be, this morning. I gambled he'd have moved on from where he was last night, if he was having no luck. But he hadn't moved. Soon as I saw his boat, I turned around. I was turning the boat when I saw the boy. Clinging to the rocks, he was, barely alive. I took him for a seal; his head in the water looked just like one. I was being nosy, really, or I might just have motored away."

"So the boy had swum some distance from his grandfather's boat?"

"Oh aye, a good distance from there. Opposite side of the bay." Agiris ground out his cigarette beneath his foot.

"Why did the child not use the radio? Was there no VHF in Sotiris's boat?"

"If there was or if there wasn't, would the lad know how to use it?"

"But what about you? Did you not think of using your VHF to call for help?"

Agiris smiled and shook his head.

"My VHF packed up months ago. I don't go far. Never seen the need to replace it."

"Until today."

"Wouldn't have made any difference, would it? I was the fastest way to get the boy home, and old Sotiris was already dead."

"How do you know that?"

"At the time, I didn't. The boy didn't know himself. But he was in a bad way. I thought I should save him rather than the old man." He frowned. "You're not from the newspapers, are you?"

"I?" The fat man laughed. "No, I'm no journalist. Do you not like journalists? I wondered why you left the scene so fast, when you were the primary witness in the case. You might have had drinks bought for you all morning, if you had joined your neighbors in the *kafenion*."

"I try and avoid my neighbors, when I can; they gossip worse than women. If you're not a journalist, what's your interest?"

"My interest is only casual, at present, though I always take an interest in my fellow men. It seems a sad tale, and the boy will struggle to get over it, I'm afraid. Now, can I trouble you to get me some peaches? I don't want to take up too much of your time."

"Gladly. Come this way."

"May I just have another look at this old fellow?"

The fat man moved close to the statue, and laid a hand on Priapus's stone head.

"He's beautifully executed, so lifelike. Almost as if the man who made him knew him."

"You know," said Agiris, considering, "if you're a man who's an interest in antiquities, you'd maybe be interested in the tomb."

"Tomb? What tomb?"

"I could show you. Though it's against the rules, since it's on church property. But then, you're on church property now."

The fat man laughed.

"If you're calling me a trespasser," he said, "you'll find I have no conscience in the matter. I regard myself, generally, as free to travel where I will. But if I'm not mistaken, what I'm hearing is a request for a fee." He found his wallet, and took out a 5,000-drachma note. "Take this as a tip, and put as much as you see fit into the offertory box as payment for my fruit. Will that cover both?"

Agiris seemed disappointed.

"I'll tell you what," said the fat man. "You show me your tomb, and if I think the tour is worth more than I've paid, I'll increase your fee."

Agiris shoved the note into his pocket.

"This way, then," he said, ushering the fat man towards the house.

"What about your fire?" asked the fat man. "Do you think it wise to leave it?"

Agiris glanced at the smoldering pile of greenery.

"Without me to tend it, it'll be out in no time," he said. "I'll come back to it, by and by."

"So what is this tomb?" asked the fat man, as they passed a line of potted herbs. "What era is it from?"

"I've no idea," said Agiris. "That's a question for archaeologists to decide, and there have been no archaeologists through here, as far as I'm aware. The tomb's hidden away, and secret. The bishop wouldn't want archaeologists tramping over his property."

They reached the back door of the house, which, like the front door, was sealed with a padlock and chain. Agiris took a bunch of keys from his pocket—there seemed, to the fat man, to be an extraordinary number, of all types, sizes and vintages—and without hesitation found the right key for the lock, inserted and twisted it, so the padlock popped open. He removed the lock, and hung it in the hasp, then turned the handle and threw open the door.

"*Peraste*," he said. "After you."

Beyond the doorway, the room was dark, with no daylight entering through the fastened shutters. But the light from the open door revealed the outline of kitchen furniture—a table and chairs, a stove, a sink with a gas water heater above it, a row of wall-mounted cupboards. The house smelled of polish, and faintly of fresh flowers and smoke, though it seemed possible the fat man had brought these scents with him on his clothes; and whilst the house was cool, there was no smell of damp or mold. To keep it clean, the white cloth on the table was covered with clear plastic; on the stove back, and on the shelves beneath the tins for biscuits, flour and sugar, someone had placed delicately worked lace doilies.

"Is the bishop expected?" asked the fat man. "The house is very well kept."

"The bishop is always expected," said Agiris, "but he never comes. The house is kept in readiness by my sister, on Father Linos's instructions. Father Linos inspects it regularly; he insists everything is kept in order."

"Commendable," said the fat man. "I hope the bishop pays them well for their efforts."

"This way, friend," said Agiris. "Step this way."

He led the fat man to a door alongside the stove, which when opened revealed a number of steep steps heading downwards. Whatever place they led to was dark, and cold, and carried on its air the smell of mildew.

"After you," said Agiris.

The fat man hesitated.

"Is there no light?" he asked. "The stairs look rough, and I'd hate to lose my footing."

"There's a lamp down there, friend. We'll light it at the bottom."

"Then you must go first," said the fat man. "You know where to find the lamp, whereas I would merely flounder in the dark. Please, I insist."

Agiris gave a smile; his overlarge tongue glistened behind neglected teeth.

"You're the same as everyone," he said, tauntingly, as he started down the steps. "Folk don't like the feel of it, down here. I've seen more than one man run away from this place as if the devil were after him. It gives them the willies; they feel the hairs rise on their necks, and they don't like it. It's got some atmosphere, wouldn't you say?"

As he descended, his voice grew more distant, and his footsteps on the worn stone treads became faint. The fat man listened from the top of the stairs, and heard the rattle of metal and muttering, something dropped and the striking of a match. Below him, the darkness became lighter in an oil lamp's glow.

"You're safe now," called Agiris. "But watch yourself. These old steps can be treacherous."

Carefully, the fat man descended, into the cold of a vaulted cellar whose far end disappeared into darkness, making its length impossible to judge. The place smelled fusty, of damp that never dried, of candle smoke and lamp oil, and—to the fat man's nose—of the webbed, black hide of bats' wings. The ceiling—so low, it made Agiris, short as he was, seem tall—almost touched the fat man's head, and he looked up apprehensively for any telltale spots which might be the leathery, furry creatures he abhorred; but with no apparent opening for them to pass in and out, he dismissed the possibility of a colony as unlikely.

"What is this place?" he asked.

"It's what's left of the old house," said Agiris. "The house isn't what was originally on this land. The building here before—some say it was a church, some a farmhouse, some will even tell you it was a castle—came down in an earthquake, or so nearly down, they demolished what was left. You'll have noticed the steps; they're much older than the house. The bishop says they might go back a thousand years or more. It makes you think what feet might have trodden here before us. There's the mark of them in those steps."

The fat man looked back, and saw what he had felt through the soft soles of his shoes in his descent, that the stone steps dipped in the centers of their treads, hollowed by the feet of many generations.

"The house wasn't unique in being damaged," said the fat man, "if I may judge by the ruins I walked past to get here."

"It was a bad one that did the damage. A lot of the town was lost completely. We're susceptible, here, to earthquakes."

"As is most of Greece."

"We seem to get more rumblings than most. The old place here had a crack ripped from ground to rooftop, wide enough nearly to walk through. There were holes in the floors where the boards split so wide you could go down up to your waist. So they took the old place down, stone by stone, and rebuilt it, better than new. The church had money to rebuild when others didn't. But the cellars were undamaged, and they kept them as they'd been. They're not used now, except by me." He held up the oil lamp, and in its weak light the fat man saw a few items kept in storage—wooden packing cases of uncertain contents, a large band saw, nets for gathering olives. "They used to store oil and wine here, I suppose, but these cellars aren't much good for storage. The damp you can smell, and they're riddled with rodents. The rats are a damn nuisance; they put holes in everything, nest in the nets and gnaw through the boxes. I don't give in to them, mind! I put traps down; I make the poison for the bait myself. Look, here." Against the walls, hard to pick out in the bad light, were several saucers filled with grains of corn mixed with powder. "Lethal," he said. "A handful of that corn would kill a dozen rats."

"Really?" said the fat man, with a frown. "Tell me, how do you make a poison that's so toxic?"

Agiris put a finger to his nose, and smiled.

"That's for me to know, and you to wonder," he said. "It works better than anything you can buy, so well in fact I'm thinking of going into business. Make a rich man of me, my rat bait could. Come on this way, if you want to see the tomb."

He drew the fat man deep into the darkness of the cellar, towards a seemingly solid end wall. Puzzled, the fat man followed; but as they drew close to the wall, the differing depths of shadows thrown by the lamp showed that, where back wall and side wall met, there was a passageway. The passage was no more than a black, forbidding hole, its ceiling so oppressively low, the fat man would have to bend his back to enter.

Agiris held up the lamp, casting shadows which made his ugly face seem sinister.

"In that earthquake," he said, beckoning the fat man towards the passage, "part of this wall fell, and it turned out to be no wall at all, but stones lodged in there to block this entrance, and dressed with clay to make it seem solid. It's human nature to be curious, friend; they unblocked what had been blocked up by earlier generations, and in they went to see what they could find. And what they found were..." He laid a hand on the fat man's forearm, and squeezed his wrist. "Bodies. Many bodies, all reduced to crumbling bone, ten, twenty or more. Walled up for centuries, and no one knowing the poor souls were in there; and folk going about their business in the house, with the dead down here under their feet. It makes you shudder to think of it: a house built over a tomb. It made the house unlucky; the best thing they could have done was to take it down and rebuild it. Shall I take you inside, and show you where they found the bodies of those unfortunates? Though the bodies are long gone; there's nothing to see, now, except the shelves where they were kept."

For the briefest moment, the fat man considered the intimidating blackness of the passageway. Somewhere within, a draft disturbed the air, bringing nothing with it but the smell of rock and clay; but it was easy to imagine how it must have smelled, once: of putridity, decay, and the stink of rotting grave clothes.

The fat man shuddered, and turned away.

"Some other time, perhaps," he said. "I've visited many

catacombs, and find them without exception to be depressing to the spirits. So I'll decline, for now."

"As you wish."

As Agiris moved the lamp, the fat man noticed a tiny Maltese cross carved on the wall.

"Why did they seal them in?" he asked as they made their way back to the steps. "If these were Christian burials, what need was there to hide them?"

Agiris stopped and held the lamp up high between them, creating an unpleasant intimacy in its light.

"Father Linos says, to stop them walking," he said. "The people were troubled with vampires. They came in the night and drank the goats' milk and dug up the crops. So they sealed them in so they wouldn't come troubling the living."

"And what happened when these restless souls were removed from here, and sprinkled with holy water?"

"The people were troubled no more. They stay where they've been put, now they've had the proper offices."

The fat man looked him in the eye, and smiled.

"I'm sure they do," he said. "But in my experience, the dead don't walk unless someone digs them up, and makes them."

Outside, the air was blessedly warm, and aromatic with garden scents. The fat man breathed in deeply, and held up his face to the sun.

"We must not forget my peaches," he said. "I should be loath to leave here without them."

Agiris picked up a wicker basket which stood outside the kitchen door.

"I'll show you," he said. "There's one tree better than the others."

He led the way, along paths between beds of vegetables and flowers.

"That's your tree," he said, pointing to a mature tree against the high wall.

But as they approached, the tree was shivering and shaking; the branches rustled and bounced, as if birds or squirrels were fighting amongst its leaves.

Agiris frowned, and set off at an awkward run towards the garden gate. The fat man laid down his holdall, found a foothold in the stone wall and hauled himself up high enough to see over the coping stones into the lane outside.

A man of dark complexion stood in the lane; with a boat hook, he was stretching up into the peach tree, pulling down a branch heavy with ripe fruit to within his reach, picking peaches with his free hand. A shoebox by his feet was already filled; now he placed the fruit he was stealing in a cloth bag slung over his shoulder. He seemed unaware of the fat man, but Agiris, having reached the lane, came shouting along it, and the dark man quickly picked up the shoebox and set off at a brisk walk down the lane, away from the town.

Agiris reached the spot where the man had stood, and looked up at the fat man who still clung to the coping stones.

"Damned gypsies!" shouted Agiris after the dark man. His face was red with rage. "You thieving, filthy-souled robber! You cheating dog, you'd rather die than pay your way! I'll have you! I know where to find you!"

From his high vantage point, the fat man surveyed the lane, but the gypsy had vanished from view.

"He may be everything you call him," said the fat man, "but it's a rare man who has no good in him at all. Let him go for now, gardener, and I'll cover the cost of the fruit he has stolen. Come and help me choose the best of what is left, and let me deal with our friend there, in my own time."

The fat man found Enrico sleeping, stretched out on a bench in the shade. The waterfront was quiet: the travel agent was closed for the siesta, though the board advertising ferry tickets still stood outside; in the tavernas, a few tourists were eating lunch, and at the *kafenion,* a few more sipped beers and cold drinks. A fisherman making repairs to a pile of nets wiped sweat from his forehead with his shirtsleeve; a foreigner with a camera around his neck stood, hands on hips, gazing out to sea as if the ocean were a puzzle he must solve.

The fat man poked Enrico on the shoulder.

"You're slipping into Ilias's lazy ways," he said.

Enrico opened his eyes, and blinked; even seeing the fat man standing over him, he seemed disinclined to move.

"What time is it?" he asked. He yawned, and stretched.

"After one."

"You broke into my dreams," said Enrico, standing, smoothing his hair, tucking his shirt into his trousers. "I was with a blonde, a Scandinavian. Dreams like that don't come along too often."

"You should be grateful that I woke you," countered the

fat man. "Dreams like that are not for public places." He handed him the basket of peaches from Agiris's garden.

"Put these in the dinghy, if you would. Then come and find me, and I'll decide what to do next. Bring back the empty basket, as I must return it to its owner later on."

"Where shall I find you, *kyrie?* Where will you be?"

The fat man laid a hand on his stomach.

"There's a little souvlaki place, just along the way here, where the food smells particularly good. That's where I'll be; and if, like me, you're not in the mood for aubergines, it'll be my pleasure to buy you lunch."

# *Nine*

When they had eaten, the fat man and Enrico remained for a while at their table, drinking Dutch beer served in chilled glasses.

"We're ready to go," said Enrico, "as soon as you give the word. If we make good time, we can reach Kos by nightfall. We need to put in there to refuel."

The fat man was thoughtful.

"We may not leave today, after all," he said.

Enrico sighed.

"Don't say it," he said. "Don't say what I know you're going to say."

"Something about this business isn't right," said the fat man, as if Enrico hadn't spoken. "I was talking to an old man in the *kafenion,* earlier. We discussed this morning's tragedy. He knew the dead man well; Sotiris was his name, and he was the icon painter here. In his latter days, the old man thought Sotiris was losing his faculties. He'd developed a habit of sniffing lemons; *developed a passion for lemons,* was how he put it. Why would a man develop a sudden fondness for lemons, do you think?"

Enrico shrugged.

"I have absolutely no idea. Sounds to me as if crazy was the right diagnosis."

"I need you to make another phone call to Miss Athaniti," said the fat man. "She won't have reached home yet, of course, but leave a message. Tell her there's been some business with the icon painter, and it troubles me; tell her to take no action yet, not until she hears from me. Between us, I think there's more to his death than natural causes. They're saying he died of heart failure, and that may yet be the case; but to me, there's too much coincidence about all this."

"What coincidence?"

The fat man glanced around to make sure he wasn't overheard.

"Yesterday, I showed Miss Athaniti the discovery I had made about the Lady. Now, hours later, the man who might help most in the matter, the man who knew the Lady best of all, drops dead."

"Why should he know the Lady particularly well?"

"Because," said the fat man, "it is the icon painter's craft to copy. Most artists create and invent. Icon painters, though highly skilled, copy original forms. To deviate from an original is disrespectful. So Sotiris will have made many, many copies of the Lady, throughout his life. He would have known her intimately."

"You've become something of an expert on Orthodox art," said Enrico, "but it seems straightforward enough to me. Old people die: it's what they do. Likely as not, it's coincidence. Are we having another beer?"

"You may, if you wish. In my view, coincidence is rarer than people think. Often coincidences have a chain of events running up to them which make them inevitable, not random. The key, of course, is to uncover those events. Which reminds me: I found something today which might possibly be connected."

The fat man bent down to the front pocket of his holdall, and took out a matchbox. Sliding the box open, he picked up the mouse he had found at the bishop's garden and held it up by its tail.

"Poor creature," he said. "It's just a baby."

"Cat," said Enrico, draining the last of his beer. "I should put it away, if I were you. The patron here won't like you showing that to his customers."

The fat man turned the mouse in the air.

"I don't think it was a cat. No puncture wounds. No marks on it at all."

"You've had too much sun," said Enrico, "if you're investigating the murder of a mouse. They live, they die. There are a million more where that one came from. What's it to you?"

He signaled to the souvlaki shop's proprietor, and held up his empty beer glass.

"Well, let's see." The fat man lowered the mouse to his nose, and sniffed. "Here," he said, holding out the mouse to Enrico. "What do you smell?"

"Are you mad?" said Enrico, waving the mouse away. "Old men sniffing lemons, and now you sniffing dead mice—there must be something in the water hereabouts. I should get rid of that, before you catch its fleas."

"Smell," insisted the fat man, "and tell me what you smell."

With great reluctance, Enrico leaned towards the dangling mouse, and sniffed, wrinkling his nose in anticipation of putrefaction; but instead, his face took on an expression of surprise.

"It's very faint," he said, "almost too faint to detect. But I would say it smells of marzipan."

"It does, doesn't it?" Carefully, the fat man replaced the mouse in the matchbox. "Wrap this box well, and put it in the freezer, in case I need it later. And when you go back on board, I want you to find me a phone number. I think it's time I consulted a physician."

Enrico seemed alarmed.

"Are you ill, *kyrie?*" he asked. "I was only joking when I said about the sun."

"Not for my health," said the fat man, smiling. "I want to speak to someone who might shed some light on old Sotiris and his lemons. There's a doctor I know in Thessaly, a Dr. Dinos. He's well thought of, and decorated, so he should know. Rassidakis is his family name. Go through the directories in the office, and track him down. When you have the number for me, the good doctor and I shall have a little talk."

As the proprietor brought a fresh beer to their table, the fat man passed the matchbox to Enrico. At a table nearby, an elegant, middle-aged Englishwoman took a seat alone.

"Be good enough to change seats with me, *kyrie,* so I can catch her eye," said Enrico, his own eyes lively. "If we're to stay longer in this backwater, I'll be needing something to pass the time."

The fat man laughed.

"Here, take my seat, and good hunting," he said, standing up from the table. "I wouldn't want to be in your way. There's somewhere I must go, in any case. But don't disappear with her, Enrico. I want you to do those jobs for me, before I return."

At the counter, the fat man paid the bill. The tip he left was generous, and when he asked the shop's proprietor to take care of Agiris's basket for a short while, the proprietor was happy to oblige.

"I wonder," said the fat man, as he put away his wallet, "if you could tell me where I might find gypsies?"

The proprietor frowned.

"What would you be wanting with gypsies?" he asked. "Dirty thieves, every one. Pinch the food from your children's mouths, they would, and your children too, if they thought they'd fetch the right price. You want to stay well away from them."

"Happily, I have no children to be stolen," said the fat man, "only a matter of business to discuss with one of their party."

With reluctance, the proprietor told him where to look, and the fat man followed his directions, taking a path up to a road which led out of town, rising in a gentle incline into the hills. The road was not well made. Though used only infrequently by motorized traffic, the many flocks of sheep and goats herded along the route had eroded patches of its surface leaving the carriageway vulnerable to wear, and many winters' rain had washed away the hardcore underneath, opening treacherous pits and potholes. Still, the fat man walked briskly, until the gradient increased and his pace slowed. The scent of herbs and pine trees was in the air; clay dust coated the dry leaves of the thorny shrubs which grew amongst the rocks. A breeze caught the branches of an olive tree, moving the gray-green leaves from matte to silver, so the tree seemed to shimmer in the wind.

A mile outside the town, a track met the road. Signposted to the chapel of Ayios Panteleimon, the track was little more than a footpath overgrown with dry grasses and thistles, but the vegetation had recently been broken down, and the sweep of tire tracks followed the path's line to a hillock a short distance away. The hillock was covered in tall pines, and from amongst the trees rose smoke.

Without hesitation, the fat man followed the track, his feet raising puffs of soft, terra-cotta dust which stained his canvas shoes. As he drew close to the hillock, the ground dipped in a wide and shallow gully—a dried-up riverbed of sun-bleached rocks. The gully was not visible from the road, and in the riverbed, hidden from passersby, were three vehicles. An old truck in fading yellow, its paint flaking and dulled by years of burning sun, stood with its tailgate down and its bonnet propped up, the cab windows open because the glass was gone; the back was heaped high with domestic junk—blankets and buckets, a bicycle tire, a child's potty, a cardboard box holding tinned food and milk, a bale of hay with its string cut, a plastic water barrel tied on tight, and a number of baskets, some finished, some partly made with the willow lengths for completing them laid through the handles.

Nearby, a car (once scarlet, now faded to an unattractive orange) appeared to have two flat tires; but it was a second car which drew the fat man's attention. This car—rotten with rust, and wretchedly decrepit—had undergone an ingenious conversion, and was now a mobile shoe shop. The open boot was piled up with stock—sandals, trainers and slippers in cellophane-wrapped pairs—whilst a sample of each style was strapped on to the bonnet by a complex weave of inter-buck-led belts. More samples were strung on bootlaces threaded through the boot catch, and a microphone lay on the dash-board, attached by a coiled wire to a megaphone lashed on to the roof, so the salesman could call the housewives from their homes.

Amused by the owner's resourcefulness, the fat man picked his way across the rocky riverbed to take a close look at the car. Amongst the pine trees at the hilltop, a woman sang. By the car, the fat man reached out to examine a pair of sandals; but before he touched the shoes, the truck's open bonnet was slammed shut. A man stood by the truck, his hands shiny with grease and oil. In his right hand he held a wrench; his face was filled with anger and mistrust. The fat man knew him; it was the gypsy he had seen at the bishop's garden.

"What are you doing?" asked the gypsy, nastily.

The fat man smiled.

"*Yassas,*" he said. "I was merely admiring the cleverness of your enterprise. All your stock displayed, yet fully mobile.... Was this your idea?"

In suspicion, the gypsy narrowed his eyes.

"What do you want?" he asked. His accent was, in its

own way, as unusual as the fat man's; but where the fat man's enunciation was clear, the gypsy's was hard and guttural, with a sense of foreign influence. "If you're here to buy shoes, I'll be in town in a while."

The fat man smiled again and shook his head.

"No, no," he said. "My shoes, though not at their best, suit me very well, and I need no others. I am simply out for a walk, enjoying the scenery. Exploring the island, you might say."

"Explore elsewhere, then," said the gypsy. "It's not such a small place that we both need to occupy the same spot."

He took a step closer to the fat man, and slapped the wrench in his left palm.

"What an excellent place to set up camp," said the fat man, lightly. "From the road, no one would know you were here. It was the smoke from your fire which drew me."

"A man's entitled to light a fire. It's not an invitation."

"Fire is a dangerous element, more at this time of year than any other. You must take care that you don't get burned."

The gypsy looked at him with contempt, and once more slapped the wrench into his hand.

"Are you having trouble with your truck?" asked the fat man. "I know from past experience how troublesome those older models can be. I'd offer you assistance, but my knowledge of mechanics is very slight."

Amongst the trees, a dog barked. The gypsy did not speak, but lifted the wrench again, and took another step closer to the fat man, who returned his attention to the shoes strapped to the car bonnet.

"Where do you get your stock?" he asked. "Are these

all made in Greece? And how do you dispose of all the boxes? So many shoes must mean an awful lot of cardboard." He stopped as if a thought had just come to his mind, and pointed at the gypsy. "Of course," he said. "You and I have met before. Or should I say, our paths have recently crossed. You have a fondness for peaches, and you were making use of your boxes to collect them. At the bishop's garden, this morning."

From the top of the hill, a woman's voice called.

"Pavlos!"

"I'm coming!" shouted the gypsy; his eyes stayed on the fat man. "Leave," he said, "and you'll find no trouble."

"Yet somehow, trouble always finds me," said the fat man. "I had some of those peaches myself, you know; their quality is excellent. But since they were not mine, I paid the gardener for them, in a fair transaction of business. He grew them, I paid for them." He walked to the boot of the car, and picked up a pair of slippers in their bag. "If I took these slippers and paid you nothing for them, I know you would think yourself hard done to. You would think yourself robbed. And so, since you gave no payment for the peaches you took, you should be unsurprised to hear that the gardener felt himself robbed by you. I stood your debt to him. I paid for your fruit. So now you owe me."

"Why should he feel robbed?" asked the gypsy, defensively. "The fruit's not his; it belongs to his paymasters, to the church. Isn't it the church's job to feed the poor?"

The fat man dropped the slippers to the ground, and placed his foot beside them to compare sizes.

"These are too small for me," he said, "so my theft would be pointless. I don't think you're a stranger here, are you? When you went to take those peaches, you knew where you were going, and you know too whose property they are."

"I have eyes in my head, don't I?" said the gypsy. "A man can see a peach tree just in passing."

"With a box to carry fruit in under his arm? No, you're no stranger here, though you seem somewhat of a stranger to the truth. If you know this place, why not say so?"

"Why should I say so? Where I travel and where I don't has nothing to do with you."

Again, a woman called out the gypsy's name; the voice was closer, as if the caller was on her way to look for him. The gypsy glanced towards the trees, then looked back at the fat man.

"Go, friend," he said, in a tone which was not friendly. "If it's shoes you want, you'll find me in the town, after siesta."

The fat man seemed about to leave; but as if something had caught his eye, he moved forward past the gypsy, and leaned into the back of the truck, reaching for an old radio half-covered by unlaundered clothes.

"Would you mind?" asked the fat man. "Might I take a look? I haven't seen one of these in many years."

The gypsy was ready to object, but was distracted by the shouts of children's voices, and by the time he turned back to the fat man, somehow the radio was in the fat man's hands.

The fat man turned the radio over and round, examining the Bakelite frame and the age-yellowed plastic of its face; the gold mesh covering the speaker was spoiled by a tear, but the knobs were still intact, the on/off giving a smart click as the fat man turned it, the tuning dial moving the needle up and down a face numbered with transmitting frequencies. An electric cable dangling from its back ended in two naked wires where a plug had been removed.

"Where on this earth did you find this treasure?" asked the fat man. "A Telefunken, isn't it? What year—'51, '52? My father used to have one very similar; I remember it very well. He's quite a one for gadgets, but he's a hoarder, too. I wouldn't be surprised if he still has it, somewhere."

The gypsy glowered, and was about to snatch the radio away; but as he reached out, the fat man said, "I'll make you an offer for it."

The gypsy hesitated, and eyed the radio, appraising its value to a keen buyer.

"What did you pay for it?" asked the fat man. "Whatever you paid, I'll give you ten percent on top."

Unwilling to commit himself to a price, the gypsy remained silent.

"Surely you remember what you paid for it?" insisted the fat man. "You must remember buying such a rarity? Come, tell me what you paid. Ten percent is a fair profit for such an easy sale. Cash in hand."

"That ring," said the gypsy at last, staring at the ring on the fat man's little finger. "I'll trade you for that ring."

The fat man lifted his eyebrows in surprise, and, slipping the ring from his finger, held it out in the palm of his hand to give the gypsy a better view. Clearly antique, the plain band was set with an unusual coin, stamped with a rising sun on one side, and a young man in profile on the other. In the sunlight, the ring shone with the glow of old gold.

"It's nice," said the gypsy, "and I'd rather have gold than take cash. Gold holds its value; cash is here and gone. So I'll trade you, a straight swap: my radio for your ring."

The fat man laughed.

"A straight swap? This ring has a long history, and is of great personal value to me; it was a gift from my mother. You can hardly expect, surely, that I would trade such a piece for a mere curio."

The gypsy shrugged.

"Take it or leave it," he said. "You asked me to name my price, and I've done so. If you don't wish to trade, take yourself off."

From amongst the trees, the children's voices called again, one after another: *"Papa, Papa!"*

The gypsy turned again in the direction of their voices.

"I'm coming!" he shouted, and looking back at the fat man, once again slapped the wrench into his hand.

"If we have no trade, then go," he said.

The fat man turned over the radio and looked at its base, seeming to appraise its value more thoroughly.

"I'll tell you what," he said, at last, "we'll toss for it. One throw of a coin. If I win, I take the radio; if you win, you take my ring."

The gypsy smiled.

"For a gift from your mother, you're very careless with your property," he said. "It can't mean that much to you, if you're prepared to lose it on the toss of a coin."

"On the contrary," smiled the fat man, "I'm very careful of my property. I'm merely confident I can win when I want to. Here." He fished in the pocket of his shorts, and withdrew a 100-drachma coin. "Will you play the game?" He displayed the coin in the palm of his hand. The gypsy eyed it from every angle, as if he would like to see its underside, so the fat man held the coin out to him between a finger and thumb. "Here, check it," he said. "It's just a coin. If you're doubtful, shall we make it the best of three? I'll toss, you call."

But the gypsy shook his head, and reached into his own dirty trousers. He took out several coins, from which he chose a 20-drachma piece.

"We'll use my coin," he said. "Unless you've any objections?"

"None at all," said the fat man. "You toss, then, and I'll call."

The gypsy placed the coin on the back of his thumb, and flicked it expertly into the air. As it turned and fell, the fat man called out, "Heads!"

The coin dropped to the ground, and both men peered at it. The tail face was upwards.

"One to me," said the gypsy, bending to pick up the coin. Again, he set the coin on the back of his thumb; again he flicked it into the air, higher this time, so it spun and turned several times before hitting the ground; and as it spun, the fat man called out again, "Heads!"

But the coin again showed tails.

The gypsy gave a slow, malevolent smile.

"Best of three," he said. "I win."

The fat man's expression clouded.

"It would seem so," he said. For a long moment, he looked down at the ring on his palm, then held it out to the gypsy. "I charge you to take good care of it. It breaks my heart to see it go."

"You shouldn't be so careless then, should you?" said the gypsy. "You were mad to bet with it in the first place."

"Maybe I was," said the fat man, laying the radio down in the back of the truck, and shaking his head in apparent despair.

Down the hill, two children came running, a boy and a girl, both barefoot and bare-legged, with the skin up to their knees gray with dust. But whereas the gypsy was dark, the children, though brown from the sun, were fair-haired; where his eyes were black, both theirs were light, the girl's hazel, the boy's an exceptional blue.

*"Papa, Papa,"* they shouted. "Mama wants you to come."

"I'll say goodbye, then," said the gypsy, holding up the ring before slipping it into his pocket with the winning coin. "Better luck next time."

"Indeed," said the fat man. "But you still haven't paid me for the peaches. Don't worry, now; I'll collect the debt next time we meet."

The children grabbed the gypsy's hands, and pulled him to go along with them, though the gypsy resisted.

"Are these your children?" asked the fat man.

"Leave me!" said the gypsy to the children, bad-temperedly; but the children cheerfully ignored him, and dragged him away, and so the fat man's question went unanswered.

# Ten

When the fat man returned to the harbor side, siesta was coming to an end. The souvlaki shop's proprietor was missing, but the fat man found the gardener's basket on the counter, then asked directions of a young girl, who pointed him down an alley alongside the bank.

"First left at the end," she said. "Then right, then straight, then left again. You'll find the house next to a building site. You can't miss it."

The houses on the streets he followed were of modern construction, none more than forty years old; but though they shared a common period of origin, their state of repair and attractiveness was diverse. Some seemed cared for and prosperous, with newly varnished woodwork and well-cared-for gardens; others seemed more laundries than homes, with sheets hung on lines and underwear drying on racks, and yards scattered with the debris of young children—one-wheeled bicycles, limbless dolls, burst footballs. Through one upstairs window, a radio played at maximum volume, blasting out a popular tune; on the doorstep below, an old man, oblivious, turned to the sports pages of a newspaper. Next door, the house was closed up and silent, with discolored whitewash and a FOR SALE sign tied to the railings.

Around the corner, the fat man came across the butcher's shop. The butcher stood, arms folded, beside a blood-smeared table where his knives and saw were laid; a woman with a parcel of meat in her hand talked on as the butcher's bored eyes left her face and watched the fat man as he passed, acknowledging him with a slight incline of his head.

The fat man went on until he reached the landmark the girl had mentioned—an abandoned building site, no more than a single story of breezeblock walls overrun with weeds.

"Next door to there," the girl had told him. "Next door to the unfinished house, that's where they live."

As he approached the house he was looking for, it occurred to the fat man that the girl might have directed him more easily by telling him to follow his nose. The house itself was small, a single story without embellishments: no pots of flowers, or fresh paint, or decorative fencing. The front wall was low, but topped with chicken wire supported by iron stakes; chicken wire lined both sides of the path from the front wall to the house door and ran around the yard sides, marking out two pens of rough ground. In one pen were four turkeys, black-feathered and red-legged, the livid-blue flesh of their necks wobbling as they gobbled indignantly at the fat man's approach; pecking around them was a flock of skinny chickens, their feathers thinned from scratching at mites, and several fluttering sparrows picking at scattered corn. The bad smell—of the birds' droppings, and of their uneaten food: potato peelings, fish heads picked clean, the sauce from a stew that had seeped into the ground—came from this enclosure, and from the open poultry shed, whose floor and perches were thick with dried-on excrement and whose nest boxes were filled with filthy straw.

On the path's other side, the pen held a colony of rabbits, of all ages and many colors: some were the buff of wild rabbits, some were black, some gray, some white. For a few moments, the fat man stopped to watch the rabbits, stretched out and sleeping in the dust, nibbling at carrots strung from the fence, huddled together in the shade of their hut.

The church clock on the headland struck the half hour, and the fat man walked on up the path.

The house door was held open by a half-brick. The fat man raised his hand to knock, but before his knuckles touched the wood, a voice spoke.

*"Yassas."*

The voice was a woman's; but beyond the doorway, all seemed dark, and the fat man could not see the speaker.

*"Kali mera sas,"* he said, using the formal form of the greeting. "Do I have the right house? I'm returning some property to Agiris, the gardener."

"Come in," said the voice.

The fat man stepped across the threshold onto a mat woven from rags in the old-fashioned style, its fabric flattened by dirty feet. He found himself in a kitchen, a generous-sized room of contemporary proportions yet with none of the benefits of modern living. Instead, its owners had imported all the difficulties of old, rural homesteads: no electric stove, but a gas-burner hob connected to a weighty bottle of butane; for heating, an open hearth which would need chopped logs and the ash swept in winter; no cupboards or cabinets but wall-mounted shelves, where the necessities of everyday living were on view—mismatched plates, cheap glass tumblers, a ladle, a fish-slice, a slotted spoon hung on plastic hooks.

Beside the sink, unwashed dishes were piled up in unstable stacks; beneath the sink, a cotton curtain half-covered a tin bucket whose sides were rank with dried-on leftovers and chicken scraps. A broom leaned against an old table, whose shabby cloth was scattered with bread crumbs and spills of food where settled flies were eating; by the broom's bristles, the sweepings from the dirty floor—dust and straw, a feather or two, and black pellets of rodent droppings—awaited removal. On the dresser, a *kafebriko* stood in a pool of spilt coffee, next to a chipped cup with no saucer, and dregs in its bowl; beside the cup, a glass dish held a single peach too soft to eat, rotting amongst the stones of several others.

The kitchen was dark, the shutters closed; a length of electrician's tape covered a long crack in the window glass. Creased clothes lay across a wooden stool, waiting for the iron; but there was no scent of laundry, not of soap powder or starch, only the smell of yesterday's cooking, and the bad smell of the poultry, and beneath that, faintly, the nauseating smell of rotting meat.

Above the fireplace, a lighted wick floated in oil and water below a replica icon of the Lady; and before the icon, a woman sat in a wicker chair. The chair was designed for a rich man's garden, with high arms and great wings curving around the back; the woman sat on a ruby-red cushion to pad the seat, and rested her forearms on the high chair arms, like a monarch of ancient Crete. Her right leg was propped up on a milking stool with another cushion to support it; she wore no stockings, but the leg was bandaged up to the knee, the lint stained with the seepage of some wound.

The fat man placed the peach basket on the floor, and moved towards the woman, hand extended; but her hands remained where they were, on the chair arms.

"Who are you?" she asked, both loudly and abruptly, her eyes fixed on him. "Do I know you?"

Standing close to her, the smell of rottenness was stronger, coming, as it seemed, from the woman's leg. Dressed all in widow's black, her gray hair was tied so tightly in a knot, it stretched the features of her face. Her chair, he now saw, was positioned both to hide her and to provide her with a view of the yard and of the lane; everyone who came and went would be seen by her, whilst she herself was hidden by the house's gloom.

"No, *kyria*," he said, "you don't know me." He lowered his hand. "I am Hermes Diaktoros, of Athens. May I ask your name?"

"They call me Nassia," she said, "Nassia Delfis." She frowned, deepening the lines around her mouth and on her forehead. "If you don't know my name, why are you in my house? What do you say your last name is? Manikouros?"

"Diaktoros, *kyria*," he said, more loudly. "From Athens."

"Athens? I don't know anyone from Athens!"

"I'm returning some property of your son's."

"My son? My son's not here. You'll not find him here at this time."

"His property," repeated the fat man. "I am returning his basket."

"Basket? What basket?"

The fat man turned, and indicated the basket on the floor.

"I had some peaches from his garden, and borrowed a basket to carry them in."

She leaned over in her chair, squinting past him to see it, then looked back at him.

"Who are you?" Her face showed confusion. "Is Sambeca with you?"

"Sambeca?"

"My daughter. Is she there? Sambeca!"

"There's no one here, *kyria*. Your daughter isn't here."

"She's never here. There's always somewhere else she has to be, regardless of how ill I am. Where is she now?"

"I'm afraid I don't know, *kyria*."

"Did my boy let you in the bishop's garden? I've told him not to let folks in. The bishop wouldn't like it; the bishop likes his privacy. And my boy should have told you, there are bad things there. Bad things, and he knows it." Nassia took her hand from the chair arm, and shook a finger at the fat man. "If you stir them up, they'll come after you."

She made a triple cross over her heart, and muttered some words the fat man couldn't catch.

"What things?" he asked, curiously. "What kind of bad things?"

"Everyone knows it," she said. "He should have told you.

He's no business letting you go there unprepared." She stared at him; her left eye had the faded cloudiness of a cataract. "Maybe they have you already; how would I know? The dead walk that house, *kyrie*—revenants who find no rest. They want a human body; they'll slip inside you, and throw out your spirit. They oust your soul, *kyrie,* and live in your body as if it were their own. On the outside, you might look the same, but on the inside, you're not there. A dead man's eyes look through yours! You look the same, but inside, you're possessed. And then it's your soul that's damned to walk and seek a new body for its own. That's the nature of their filthy curse: possession. They've taken many, *kyrie,* over the years. They don't care who they take: little children, men and women. Not me, though. They wouldn't take me; I'm too old. They want a body that's got some life left in it, a good strong body. Like yours, *kyrie.* They'd like a body like yours. Don't go there again, *kyrie;* heed an old woman's warning, and stay away."

"Fortunately," said the fat man, cheerfully, "I have come away very much myself, and still intact. And I assumed it was your son who gave me peaches; am I to think now I was wrong, and that it wasn't your son, but some stranger pretending to be him? Since I didn't know the man previously, how could I tell?"

"My son knows how to protect himself," said Nassia, darkly. "He's always careful. He carries garlic in his pocket, and wears the charm I made him around his neck. They can't bypass a charm. But I don't make those charms anymore; I have no protection to offer you. Don't go there, *kyrie!* If you do, it might not be you who comes back!"

"You intrigue me," said the fat man, "not least because, everywhere I travel, similar stories surface. If every story were true, there'd be no mortals left; our whole country would be possessed by ghosts and vampires. But there's always something hidden behind these tales; and if I dig deeper, I usually find some family business at the root—a falling-out, or disagreement, very often a guilty conscience. I remember once in the Cyclades, a woman who had ripped up her mother's will, and cheated her own sister of some inheritance. It wasn't long before the vampires were tapping on the windows." He pointed to the electrician's tape on the window. "I see you have some trouble there yourself—not caused, I'm sure, by an undead hand? Or perhaps you do have family business, *kyria,* that keeps you awake at night?"

"Sambeca broke the window," said Nassia. "She's such a clumsy girl. Is she there? Sambeca!"

"Your daughter isn't here, *kyria.*"

"Well, where is she? I need her here."

"I'm afraid I don't know where she is. But if she's gone, I'm sure she told you where she went. Can you remember?"

She glared at him, as if he had been impertinent; but then she gave a nod, and said, "She's gone to the vigil. Old—what's his name? What do they call him?"

She looked again at the fat man, expecting from him the answer her memory couldn't provide.

"Do you mean the icon painter?" asked the fat man. "I believe they called him Sotiris."

"Sotiris." She makes a triple cross over her heart. "May his memory be eternal."

Her words had no sincerity; they were merely the right form for the occasion.

"You knew him, I expect," said the fat man.

"Oh, I knew him. He married that—what was her name?"

"I'm afraid I don't know, *kyria*. I am a stranger here."

"She died young. Or was that her sister? She's left me with nothing to eat, you know. I can't offer you anything, if she's left nothing."

"I want nothing," said the fat man, "thank you. I am simply returning the basket. I'm sorry to have disturbed you; I shall go now, and leave you in peace."

"There might be biscuits," she said, "in the tin."

"Truly, I want nothing."

"Not for you, for me," she said, with irritation. "The tin's over there, where she left it. She puts nothing away. When my husband was alive, I kept this house as it should be kept. That girl takes pride in nothing. Hours and hours, she'll clean that church, and this house not fit for pigs. It makes you hang your head in shame. They're over there."

She waved a hand to where the dishes were stacked.

The fat man crossed to the sink. That corner of the kitchen smelled of standing dishwater, and of the chicken bucket's waste. At the bucket's foot was a saucer of wheat grains mixed with powder: the same bait Agiris had laid at the bishop's house.

"Are you troubled by rodents, *kyria?*" he asked.

"By what?"

"By rodents. Mice, rats."

She gave a snort.

"We're overrun with mice. He wants to keep all that poultry; what does he expect? They come for the feed, then they come inside the house to be warm. They come in in winter, and by summer they've bred. I sit here and they play by my feet, happy as you like. It's shaming; they bring shame on me, but he doesn't care. His own mother's comfort matters less than his precious birds."

The fat man looked down at the unwashed crockery: dinner plates and cutlery, saucepans and baking dishes. Beneath a bowl holding the remains of a salad was a gold and red tin. As he lifted the salad bowl to take out the tin, he noticed a stoneware pot: the pot Sambeca had removed from Sotiris's boat.

Lifting out the tin, he carried it to the old woman, and with a flourish opened it to show her the sweet biscuits inside.

With a fingertip, she poked around the tin, moving the uppermost biscuits to see those underneath.

"Aren't there any wafers?" she asked. "I told her to get wafers. She never does as she's told." She chose a round biscuit with a center of red jam. "Are there any more of these? Find me another, will you?"

Graciously, the fat man obliged.

"Do you have enough?" he asked.

"I'll make do," she said. "I eat very little. Wouldn't you think she could get me the biscuits I like?"

Closing the tin, he crossed back to the sink, and, seeing no alternative in the chaos, replaced it under the unwashed salad bowl. As he did so, he quietly lifted the lid of the stoneware pot.

The pot was empty. He lowered his head to sniff, then sniffed again, and frowned.

Standing again before Nassia, he looked down at her leg.

"Your leg must trouble you," he said. "Is it painful?"

"Of course it's painful," she said, with bitterness. "There's a hole in it as big as your fist. She should be here to change the dressing, but she doesn't care. She let it get infected, and now it'll never be right. She's supposed to bathe it with salt water, but she's never got time. It's other people's dead today that make her too busy to bother with me."

"Does the doctor give you painkillers?"

"I won't take his tablets. They'd poison you soon as look at you. Doctors know nothing, nothing at all."

"Are you a believer in the old ways, then, Nassia?"

"There was nothing wrong with the old ways. The new ways aren't always better. Why should they be? Not everything good was invented yesterday."

"If you approve of the old ways, I can bring you something which may help you," he said, "a cure which is becoming very fashionable in modern hospitals. It is not, of course, to everyone's taste, but it is both cheap and effective, if you can stomach the idea. I mean maggots, which are common enough, and easy to find, if you would like to try them."

"Maggots!" Her face creased with disgust. "Dirty, nasty things! What would I want with maggots?"

"I really think you should consider it," said the fat man.

"Their use is very simple; place two or three in the wound, and cover them with gauze so they can breathe. They have an appetite for decay, and putridity, and—as I myself have seen—will happily eat the rottenness in your leg, and leave behind the healthy tissue. In other words, they'll clean your ulcer, destroy the badness and leave the good. But those you don't immediately use must be kept in a cool place, or you'll have nothing but bluebottles—one of nature's magic tricks. What do you say?"

"I say you're mad!" Angrily, she slapped her hand on the chair arm. "Maggots are creatures of the grave; they eat the dead, and shouldn't touch the living! You insult me, suggesting I should have the foul things in my home!"

"Are you sure you wouldn't like to give them a try?" persisted the fat man. "I think perhaps you should. It would take no time to find a supply, and a rotting wound such as yours—forgive me, Nassia, but the smell of it tells me all is not well—can spread to healthy flesh. If you don't take care, you'll lose the leg entirely."

"What do I care?" she said. "I've learned to live in this chair, and I need no legs, these days. Where is my daughter? Sambeca!"

The fat man gave a small bow.

"If you do not wish for my help, then I must leave you. Though we may meet again, Nassia."

At the door he stopped to say goodbye.

"*Yassas,*" he said.

But Nassia gave him no reply; she turned away her face, and bit into a biscuit.

\*      \*      \*

Outside, the fat man paused again to watch the rabbits (their burrows were numerous, and the rabbits were entertaining, appearing from nowhere and disappearing down holes), and as he prepared to move on, Agiris pushed open the gate, his arms filled with hay which he dropped over the fence into the pen.

"*Kali spera,*" said Agiris. "We meet again. Did my sister give you coffee?"

"Your sister isn't here," said the fat man, "and I called only to return your basket. I believe your sister's at the icon painter's vigil. I was thinking of going to pay my respects there too, if you would tell me where to find the house."

"Not far from here," said Agiris. "Just a little farther along the lane, and to the right. But have something with us, before you go. I expect Mother offered you nothing?"

Behind the darkness of the open doorway, the fat man sensed Nassia listening.

"On the contrary," he said, "I was able in a small way to make her more comfortable, as befits a woman of her seniority."

"Come back inside. There'll be a cold beer in the fridge."

The fat man remembered the kitchen, dirty and infested.

"You're very kind," he said. "Another time, perhaps."

But Agiris was not listening; his attention was on a large, brown buck, enthusiastically humping an indifferent doe.

Agiris laughed, clapped the fat man on the back and pointed at the rabbit.

"That's the way to be, friend!" he said. "Put it to 'em, whenever you've the chance! Like this fellow here! Get to it, Pluto! That's the randiest rabbit you'll ever see," he said, with pride. "At it day and night, he is."

The fat man's eyebrows lifted slightly.

"And all on a diet of dried grass," he said, politely. "Most impressive; but you yourself should take care not to fall too far under Priapus's influence. Too much time spent in his company might prove unhealthy. Which reminds me—on the subjects of health and rapid breeding, I wonder if I might ask you—I have a friend who is troubled with mice, and I see you have your special bait laid in the house here. Is it safe, then, for domestic use?"

"Safe enough, if you don't put it in your coffee. I'll give you some to try, and if it works like it should, come back and buy some from me. Just tell your friend to wash his hands when he's used it. It'll give him a nasty bellyache, otherwise. Wait a bit, and I'll fetch you some."

He went into the house. The buck rabbit lost interest in the doe, and gave its attention instead to the pile of hay. Behind the hut scuttled the dark shape of a rat.

Agiris came from the house, and handed the fat man a small tin still labeled with a brand of iron tablets.

"You tell your friend to mix a bit with something tasty," he said. "Half a teaspoon's plenty. Try it in a few biscuit crumbs, or on some peanuts. He'll soon find the little beggars with four legs in the air."

The fat man thanked him, and slipped the tin into the pocket of his jacket.

"I'll see you again, no doubt," he said.

"If you're going to the vigil, please tell my sister I'm ready for my dinner," he said.

"I'm sorry, but I don't think I know your sister," said the fat man.

"You'll know Sambeca easily," said Agiris. "She loves a death. She'll be the one amongst the wailers who's wailing loudest."

The fat man rounded the corner, out of sight of the house, before he unscrewed the lid of the little tin Agiris had given him. He peered in at the contents, which seemed to be a lumpy substance, creamy brown and roughly ground. Cautiously, he put the tin to his nose, and sniffed. The smell was faint, but unmistakable—the distinctive, deadly smell of bitter almonds.

## Eleven

As soon as the fat man turned the corner at the end of the lane, Agiris's directions became unnecessary. The wails and laments of women rose and fell; when one ran out of breath, another voice took her place, and beneath it all was the softer crying of genuine bereavement.

The fat man stopped and sighed, then seemed to make up his mind to press on, and followed the mourners' wailing to the icon painter's house.

To one side of the door, the unvarnished lid of a plain coffin was propped against the wall. Several chairs had been carried into the street for the men, and in two of these, either side of a small table, sat Father Linos and Mercuris. Between them on the table was a whisky bottle, half empty; before each of them was a tumbler of whisky, half full.

The fat man was about to greet the men, but caught behind him the sound of a stone hitting a tin can, and the scuttering of the stone as it landed amongst dried thistles. He looked over his shoulder, towards a neglected garden plot where the sound had its source, and found himself watched by a sullen-faced boy, who dropped his eyes when the fat man saw him, and moved towards the tin can to set up his target for another shot.

The fat man knew him; it was the boy he had seen carried off Agiris's boat. The boy looked unwell, drained by exhaustion; under his eyes the skin was black like bruising. He was a thin child, lightly built; the shorts he wore were long on him and loose at the waist, and his wash-faded T-shirt was too big for him, as if it were a hand-me-down he had not yet grown into.

"*Yassou,* Sammy," said the fat man.

The boy did not reply, but bent down to hunt for stones to use as ammunition.

"I'm sorry about your grandfather. May his memory be eternal."

With tear-filled eyes, Sammy looked at him. His face was creased into a scowl, not of discontent but with the effort of holding back the tears. He walked back to the point where he had marked a line in the dirt, chose the biggest from his small handful of stones and took aim at the can, throwing the stone with all his rage behind it. He missed his target; the stone flew too far, shaking the stalks of the dried-out grasses where it landed.

"Bad luck," said the fat man. "You looked an excellent shot to me, just now."

Still the boy didn't speak. Narrowing his eyes to take aim again, he threw another stone and the shot was good; there was a ping as the stone hit its target, and more rustling in the dead weeds; then, more rustling still, as something hiding in the grass slithered away.

Startled, Sammy looked at the fat man, who opened his eyes wide and beckoned to the boy.

"Snake," he said, quietly. "Come over here, to me. In those sandals you're wearing, you're an easy target if you make him angry."

The boy's fear of snakes overcame his disinclination to speak to the fat man. With his eyes fixed on the ground, he high-stepped to where the fat man stood.

The fat man gave a theatrical shudder.

"Snakes!" he said. "I'm no great lover of those temperamental creatures. But if you know how to handle them, they pose no danger. Do you know how to take hold of one so he can't bite you?"

Sammy intended to walk away to join his father, and had already taken a step past the fat man; but the fat man moved in front of him and towards the spot where they had seen the grasses move, and laying down his holdall, he carefully parted the stalks to hunt the snake.

"There he is," he said, in a low voice; but he spoke loud enough for Sammy to hear, and, his interest piqued, he turned back to the fat man.

The fat man beckoned to him again.

"Here," he said, "come closer, so you can see how I do this."

Vigorously, Sammy shook his head, and the fat man smiled.

"Wise boy," he said. "But it's only a matter of technique."

Quick as an adder-strike, he plunged his hand amongst the weeds, and brought out between his thumb and his two first fingers the head of a snake, whose olive-green body writhed as the fat man held it up for Sammy to see. The boy's face showed revulsion and fascination, both at the same time.

"Be still, handsome one," said the fat man to the snake. "Sammy would like to get a closer look at you, wouldn't you, Sammy?"

Again, the boy shook his head, but this time with less conviction. With the forefinger of his left hand, the fat man stroked the snake's head, watching the slender fork of the snake's tongue flash in and out.

"He wants to bite me, and make me let him go," said the fat man, "but he knows that I'm his master, and he won't be free until I'm done with him."

"He'll bite you anyway," said Sammy. "Soon as you let him go, he'll bite you."

"Not this one," said the fat man, with confidence. "This one can do us no harm. He's no threat to us; he's a rat snake, and actually brings us benefit, by keeping down the population of rats and mice, which by coincidence I was discussing with a lady just a few minutes ago. His kind were for many centuries held in great esteem; he is the symbol of the great healer Asclepius, and it is his species that winds itself around the staff which is the symbol of the medical profession, even today. He won't hurt you, or me. He only wants to leave us, and go free. That's common sense, after all. There is only one of him, and there are two of us. Would you like to stroke him?"

The boy shook his head more vigorously than ever.

"You've been taught that he's bad luck," said the fat man.

"Well, you've had the worst luck a boy could have already today, haven't you? Trust me, he will not harm you, though that's not the case with all snakes, as you know. Some are treacherous, and will turn on you, given a chance. Those ones are poisonous."

He bent to the ground, and released the snake, which glided away into the undergrowth, leaving no trace it was ever there.

Anxiously, Sammy watched the now-still vegetation, afraid to move.

"I suppose he has spoiled your game for you, even though he poses no danger," said the fat man. Behind them, at the house, the wailing reached a new pitch of intensity; one of the women screamed, whilst others dramatically wept. The priest and Mercuris grimaced, and each took a swig of whisky. The fat man laid a fatherly hand on Sammy's head. "You should be sleeping, young man," he said, "sleeping for a few hours of forgetting. But who could sleep with such drama in the house? Have you no relative you can go to for a few hours, no aunts or cousins?" Under the fat man's hand, Sammy shook his head. "I suppose they are all here, at the vigil. Well; it is to pay my respects to your grandfather that I am here myself. Come, walk with me; you can show me where to go."

The fat man picked up his holdall, and followed Sammy towards the house. As they approached, Mercuris reached for the whisky bottle, and the priest quickly covered his glass; but a word from Mercuris was sufficient, and Father Linos removed his hand to accept another drink.

"Though I'd prefer a lemonade," said Father Linos, "if you have one."

"Lemonade be damned," said Mercuris. "Lemonade's for women."

*"Yassas,"* said the fat man. The two men looked up at him from their chairs. *"Papa,* we have met already. And I believe you're Sammy's father." He held out his hand to Mercuris. "I am Hermes Diaktoros, of Athens."

Mercuris stood, and took the fat man's hand.

"Mercuris Stefanakis," he said. "I'm pleased to meet you."

"It would be more of a pleasure," said the fat man, "to meet under happier circumstances. I'm sorry about your father-in-law. May his memory be eternal."

"May I offer you a drink?"

"You're very kind. You may indeed, once I have paid my respects inside."

The room where the body lay was lit by candles, and by the flames of lamps burning beneath the icons on the wall. Sotiris's coffin lay on the table, its head and foot protruding beyond the table ends; along two sides of the room, women sat. They had for a brief while been quiet; but as the fat man entered the room, one or two recommenced wailing and moaning, though most simply stared at him, intrigued by a stranger in their midst.

From amongst them, an old woman rose from her chair. Her face was pale, and drawn; her eyes were bright with tears, her cheeks flushed with weeping.

"Welcome," she said. She passed her white lace handkerchief into her left hand, and held out her right. The fat man touched it briefly, and inclined his head.

"Thank you," he said. "I'm sorry about your relative. May his memory be eternal."

"Sotiris was my brother," she said, and pointed to a younger woman, whose black clothes were new, and whose eyes were hollow with weeping. "His daughter Tina, my niece."

The fat man offered the dead man's daughter his hand, and she touched it with limp fingers.

"I'm sorry for your loss," he said. "May his memory be eternal."

She bowed her head, but did not reply, and the fat man turned from her to the coffin on the table.

Beneath the shroud which covered him to the waist, Sotiris was smartly dressed in brand-new clothes: a suit, a shirt too big around the neck, a tie. His body smelled of the ouzo they had used to wash his corpse, and of the fresh flowers that the mourners had placed inside the coffin, both loose and tied in posies. A bandage tied around his head held up his jaw; on his sternum, a long white candle burned, and on his legs lay an icon.

The fat man took a coin from his pocket, and placed it with those already on Sotiris's chest. By convention, the fat man must now kiss the icon, and not wishing, in this setting, to break with protocol, he bent his head down to the painting.

The image was of St. Nicholas, his gray hair and balding scalp distinctive. The icon seemed from its style to be of considerable age, from the twelfth or thirteenth centuries;

its finish seemed to fit that era, with its imperfect gilding damaged and worn, its colors faded and its glaze flaking and cracked. Taking care to show no surprise, for as long as he dared the fat man studied what appeared to be an artifact of great value, then brushed his lips on the icon and moved to kiss the old man's forehead. As he leaned over the corpse's face, cautiously he sniffed.

He smelled nothing but aniseed and roses. Drawing back, he studied Sotiris's features. They seemed composed, as if death were a welcome sleep; only his lips showed irregularities, being freckled, in places, with small, white spots, which the fat man was quite certain were unburst blisters.

Outside, Mercuris had drawn a third chair up to the table, and half filled an extra glass from the whisky bottle. Sammy sat on the ground, his back against the house wall, unraveling the tar-stained filter of a discarded cigarette.

"Sit," Mercuris urged the fat man. "Sit, friend."

The fat man did so, placing his holdall between his feet. He picked up his glass, and raised it to the sky.

"To your father-in-law," he said. "May his memory be eternal."

Mercuris and the priest clinked their glasses to the fat man's, and all drank. The whisky was rough-tasting, but its strength and warmth were not affected by its cheapness. Father Linos looked flushed under the weight of his robes and hat. The first stubble of mourning darkened Mercuris's jaw; his eyes were bloodshot, the lids drooping from the alcohol, and when he lifted his glass, his hand was not steady.

"How did you know Sotiris?" asked the priest, replacing his glass on the table. Beneath the polite inquiry, an undertone of interrogation spelled out the real question: *What are you doing here?*

"The truth is, I didn't know him, personally," said the fat man, taking a second sip of whisky before putting down his own glass. "But I know of the long tradition of Kalkos's icon painters, and I had the unhappy experience of seeing him brought home this morning, and being carried from his boat. Will it be a big funeral, do you suppose? Was he well liked, as a man?"

Father Linos and Mercuris regarded each other, until Mercuris lowered his eyes and took another drink.

"He was a very devout man," said Father Linos, carefully. "A pillar of the church, and a man with a true vocation. He believed wholeheartedly in the usefulness of his work. He saw it as it should be seen, as a calling and a service to God. He was devoted to the Lady, absolutely devoted. And his devotion was a credit to him."

Half frowning, half smiling, Mercuris looked at the priest over the rim of his glass.

"You've painted a picture there," he said, "about as close to the life as one of his own paintings. Which is to say, it's a pretty picture, but nothing like the life."

"Mercuris!" said the priest. "Show some respect for the dead!"

"I did respect him," said Mercuris, "but he was no saint himself, was he? I won't speak ill of him, and you tell no lies."

The fat man looked quizzically at the priest, encouraging

him to go on. Father Linos hesitated. He took another draft of his whisky, and set the glass back on the table.

"The truth was," he said, "Sotiris had lost his faith in life, and in his fellow men. There was—an incident, shall we call it, which he saw as a betrayal. He couldn't feel the same about the world he lived in, afterwards."

"What incident?" asked the fat man. "What mere incident would change a man's view of his whole world? Please, tell me; I am intrigued."

Mercuris kicked his foot in the priest's direction, catching the priest's censer under his chair, rattling it onto its side and releasing the smoky smell of incense.

"Yes, come on, *Papa,*" he said. "You tell a good story, when you've a mind to."

The priest looked around himself, afraid to be caught gossiping.

"He had a wife," he said. "Not the best of women, and not the worst either, but she wasn't from here. She used to like to go and visit her family, who lived some way to the north. Sometimes she'd go for a week, sometimes for two, and old Sotiris was thrown back on his own resources. He didn't mind her absences, I don't think; he used to take himself off fishing, and play a few games of backgammon without having to watch the time. Well, came this time..."

"Eight years ago, it was," interrupted Mercuris. "Maybe closer to nine."

"...Came this time she'd been away a while," went on the priest, as if Mercuris hadn't spoken, "and Sotiris was expecting her back any day, and one morning down the lane here

173

come his wife's relatives, all dressed up for visiting and, to all appearances, come to stay. So Sotiris asks them into the house and asks where his wife is, and they say, she'll be here shortly, she's on her way; and they ask him to send for his daughter, and for Mercuris here. So Sotiris leaves the relatives in the house, and goes to fetch his daughter..."

"I came with her," Mercuris interrupted. "I remember it like yesterday."

"... Goes to fetch his daughter and Mercuris here, and back they all three come smiling to the house. But whilst they've been gone, the relatives have changed—they've changed their clothes, and now they're all in black, with their visiting clothes packed away in their traveling cases. And now he's got his daughter there, they tell him that his wife is dead, and waiting round the corner in her coffin."

"It was a shock to him," said Mercuris. "It was a shock to us all. Pass me that bottle, *Papa*. It was a bad way of handling it, was that."

"It was indeed," said the fat man. "They meant well, no doubt, wanting Sotiris to have the comfort of his daughter when they broke the news. But even so..."

"He took it as deception," said Father Linos. "It seemed to turn something in his mind. He lost all trust in people; I think he never trusted anyone again. From that day on, he was suspicious in his nature. He thought the worst of everyone, and could see the good in none. Except for Sammy, of course."

They looked across to where Sammy was tearing the paper from the cigarette into tiny shreds.

Glass in hand, Mercuris waved a hand towards the boy.

"He's a fine lad, my boy," he said. "He'll get over it, soon enough."

"He has had a terrific shock," said the fat man. "Witnessing his grandfather die that way must have been very traumatic."

Emphatically, Mercuris shook his head.

"He didn't see him die," he said. "He didn't know he was dead until he saw the coffin at the door."

"Oh?" said the fat man. "How was that?"

Becoming suddenly maudlin, Mercuris wiped a tear from the corner of his eye.

"My boy's the bravest, the best of boys," he said. "They all say he's shy, a mouse of a lad. But when the time came, when it mattered, he was brave as a lion. Isn't that so, *Papa?*" He drained his glass, and seemed disinclined to go on, looking to the priest to continue the story.

The priest lifted his hat, and scratched his head, then placed his hat on the table beside his glass. His long ponytail was pinned up in a knot; his hair was not luxuriant like a woman's, but thin and straggling, growing only from the perimeter of his scalp.

"Oh yes," he said. "He was a brave lad, all right."

From inside the house, the laments began again, underpinned by weeping. The boy looked at the house with a troubled face. Mercuris beckoned to his son, but the boy ignored him, giving his attention to his paper-shredding.

From his pocket, the fat man withdrew his cigarettes and, opening the box, offered it to Mercuris, who declined with a shake of his head. The fat man offered the cigarettes to the priest, who thanked him and took one. The fat man held the flame of his gold lighter out to the priest, who placed the cigarette in his mouth, and, as the blue flame touched the cigarette's end, inhaled deeply.

"Thank you," he said.

Mercuris and Father Linos now seemed inclined to reflective silence. The fat man reached out for the whisky bottle.

"May I?" he asked.

"Gladly," said Mercuris, slurring the word. "Fill us up, friend. Fill us up."

The fat man poured more whisky into all three glasses, adding only a splash to his own, where a good measure of whisky remained.

"Tell me, then, about the boy's bravery," he said. "It was obvious when I was talking to him what a bright lad he is."

"I'll tell you what, friend." Mercuris leaned forward, and placed a hand on the fat man's forearm, wagging a finger in the fat man's face. "If there's a braver boy on this island, you show him to me. Go on, show me. My boy's a hero."

"A hero indeed," echoed the priest.

"Listen." Mercuris squeezed the fat man's arm. "Picture the scene. There's the boy and his grandfather, out on the sea, fishing away as they like to do. He's always been one for fishing, has Sammy. He's a good little fisherman, is my boy."

"Oh yes," agreed Father Linos. "He's a good fisherman."

"And then the old man took sick."

"Took sick in what way?" interrupted the fat man.

"Sounds like it was his heart," said Mercuris. "Wouldn't you say so, *Papa*—his heart?"

"That's what the doctor said," said the priest.

" 'He said it burned, *Papa*,' is what Sammy said to me. The old man was doubled over, he said, staggering about, nearly went over the side. My boy laid him down in the boat, and he would have driven it home. He could have done it—he's not a bad little sailor, not bad at all—but there's a knack to starting that old engine, and he couldn't manage it. So without a thought for himself, in he went, swimming hard as he could to get help. Brave, you see, friend. A young boy like that, and that great, treacherous sea. He didn't think about himself. In he went, and started swimming." He drank more whisky; the priest exhaled, and flicked ash from the end of his cigarette. "But it wore him out, before long. His heart was willing, but he didn't have the strength. He made it across the bay, but no farther than that. All night he clung to the rocks." Suddenly Mercuris bent to the table, and buried his head in his hands; when he raised it again, his face was wet with tears. "My boy clinging to the rocks in that cold, dark sea, and where was I? I was home in bed, sleeping whilst my boy might have been drowning! May God forgive me!"

"God will forgive you," said Father Linos, with confidence. "You weren't to know."

"He must have been shouting for me," said Mercuris, "and I didn't hear! Slept through the whole thing! I tell you, friend..." He clutched again at the fat man's arm. "So easily we might have been burying two bodies, and one of them my boy! Someone protected him for me. The Lady was watching over him."

"You should make an offering," said Father Linos. "Go to the church, later on, and give thanks to the Lady."

"Speaking of the Lady," said the fat man, "what will happen now? No miracle has occurred, it seems, and the gift has not passed on. Kalkos has no icon painter."

Mercuris leaned back in his chair. A slow smile spread over his face.

"What do you think, friend, that we Kalkians are stupid?"

"Not at all," said the fat man, holding up both hands to refute the suggestion. "I am merely inquiring as to what will happen in the interim, whilst Sammy is trained in the art. If that is what is to happen."

"Oh, Sammy will be trained in the art, in due course," said Mercuris. "But Kalkos still has an icon painter."

"Really?" asked the fat man. "Who?"

Mercuris's smile widened.

"Me."

"You?"

"I had an interest, so Sotiris taught me. I don't have his years of practice, but he taught me what he knew. And what he didn't know, I taught myself. You'll understand..." He leaned forward, exhaling hot, alcoholic breath into the fat man's face. "...This is between us. As far as they're concerned..." he waved an arm to indicate the world in general, "...the miracle has happened."

"Mercuris," objected the priest. "Watch what you say! God hears all."

"Oh yes," said Mercuris. "He hears and sees a lot more than he lets on. Wouldn't you say, *Papa?*"

The priest was silent.

"If you're the new incumbent," said the fat man, "I wonder—though I realize now may not be the time, under the circumstances—if you might show me the workshop? I'd like to buy a genuine Kalkos icon, whilst I am here."

"Gladly," said Mercuris. "It would be a blessing to leave this wailing and misery for a while."

"Will you walk with me now? I'll only take a few minutes of your time."

"Yes, I'll come. I can trust Father Linos to mind the ladies whilst I'm gone."

The priest shot him a look of displeasure, but Mercuris was keen to go. Standing, he drained his glass.

"Speaking of the ladies," said the fat man, "I was charged to tell a lady named Sambeca that she's required at home."

Mercuris cocked an eyebrow.

"You brought a message from that house? You haven't been there, have you—to their home?"

"As a matter of fact, I have," said the fat man.

"And lived to tell the tale! You're lucky you didn't come out of there transformed, turned into a frog, or something worse." He made a cross over his heart. The priest opened his mouth to speak, but Mercuris held up a hand to stop him. "Don't you be telling me not to tell him what's what," he said. "We all know what she is; no need for him to stay ignorant."

"Who do you mean?"

179

"Nassia. The mother."

"What is she, then?" asked the fat man.

Mercuris leaned forward on the table.

"A witch, friend," he said. "Stay well away. She keeps her children bound to her with a curse. The whole family's cursed."

"Sinning more than cursed," said the priest, himself making a cross. "There's unholy things gone on in that house, if the truth be told."

"Tell him," urged Mercuris. "Tell him what's gone on."

"I'll not," said the priest, "and neither will you. It's not our place to repeat all the island's gossip."

"Gossip isn't gossip when it's fact," objected Mercuris.

"You keep your mouth shut," said the priest. "Leave those people be."

"She scared me with tales of vampires at the bishop's house," said the fat man. "Vampires and revenants. I didn't realize until now there was a difference."

"I sense," said Father Linos, seriously, "that you doubt the verity of her story. But if you'd seen what I've seen, you'd have no doubts. Apparitions too horrible to relate, and only the love of our Lord and our Lady to protect me from the evil that resides in that damned place. You'd do well to stay away."

"Stay away," repeated Mercuris. "Don't go near there, or they'll take you."

"Do you think so?" asked the fat man. "I should like to see them try. Now, time is pressing, and I must move on. Please, point out this woman Sambeca to me, so I can pass on the message."

"I'll tell her," said the priest.

"Don't drink all the whisky, *Papa,*" said Mercuris, clapping the priest on the back. "We've a long night to get through, and only one more bottle, when this one's gone."

"Shall we ask Sammy to come with us to the workshop?" asked the fat man.

Mercuris didn't reply, but through the corner of his mouth gave a shrill whistle, as if to a dog.

"For heaven's sake, Mercuris," said Father Linos. "You might show your father-in-law a little respect, at least."

Mercuris led the way, unsteady on his feet and slightly stumbling. Sammy stood up from his place against the wall, and silently followed Mercuris and the fat man at a distance.

Mercuris walked slowly, hampered by whisky. Around the first bend in the lane, they heard behind them a woman's voice as she walked fast to catch up with them. The fat man recalled the woman handing out candles in the church; he had seen her too at the harbor side, as Sotiris's body was carried off his boat.

"*Ela, kamari mou!*" It was to Sammy that Sambeca called out; reaching him, she hugged him to her and ruffled his hair, not noticing his embarrassment. "How are you, my baby? What a terrible time you've had, terrible! Never mind, my precious one, my lamb. Such a good boy, this one!" she called after Mercuris. "A better child than this one never lived."

But as she said these last words, a shadow crossed her face, and she let Sammy go.

"I must hurry," she said. She increased her pace, passing both Mercuris and the fat man. "He'll be angry, if I'm late with his food. He doesn't like to be kept waiting. Mercuris, you take care of that boy. You look after him!"

She turned a corner ahead of them, and was out of sight.

"Madness runs in that family," said Mercuris to the fat man, screwing a finger to his forehead. "The whole family's touched. You want to stay out of all their ways, friend. There are some who say you can catch their kind of madness like a disease."

# Twelve

The afternoon's shadows were growing long as Mercuris led the way through narrow backstreets, assuring the fat man that the convoluted route was a short cut. The people they passed offered their condolences, and Mercuris mumbled his acknowledgments. Already the shops were reopening for the evening's business; up on the headland, the campanile clock was striking five.

At the workshop door, Mercuris fumbled in his pocket for the keys. His key ring, when he found it, held a varied collection, and he hunted amongst them for a while to find the correct key, only to drop the whole bunch once he had. Picking up the key ring from the ground, he staggered, and put a hand on the wall to steady himself; finally, he found the right key once again, and, by making an effort to focus on the lock, was able at last to insert and turn the key.

"Come in, come in," he said, beckoning tipsily to the fat man. "And mind that step."

Sammy, sad-faced, hung back; his father was impatient to close the door.

"In or out, son," he said. "Which is it to be?"

Sammy came slowly across the threshold, and stood close to his father as the fat man looked around the room. The workshop had once been a warehouse, or storeroom; the roof was high, with open rafters on the bare underside of red clay tiles. The stone walls were unplastered, and the floorboards had no covering, or varnish. The windows were high arches, their shutters fastened back to let in the light, and it seemed to the fat man that at the right time of day—early in the morning, especially—the light would be excellent for an artist, though at this hour of early evening too many shadows had set in. Around the walls were icons, of many different saints in various styles, all hung by loops of leather thong on nails knocked into the mortar between the stones. Under the tallest window, an old executive's desk made a workbench, with a set of drawers to each side of the kneehole, and stains of dark-blue ink set in the wood alongside splashes of paint; on its top, on a stand, was an icon barely begun. At the desk's flanks were wooden tables, both cluttered with the painter's paraphernalia: jars of pigments, pots of brushes, rags and pencils, rulers and set squares, a box of eggs, whilst pine panels cut to size and ready for painting were stacked on the floor, one already prepared with marble-smooth gesso. There was a radio, and a newspaper, a coffee cup and a water glass; and to one side, a sink, whose single tap dripped rhythmically on the porcelain like a tolling bell.

Mercuris lay down on a chaise longue behind the door, plumping up the pillow to his liking and balling up a sheet he didn't want.

"Help yourself, friend," he said, turning his face to the

wall. "Have a look around whilst I grab forty winks. My boy can tell you anything you want to know. Everything's for sale; you make your choice, and let my boy know which one you'd like. There are tickets on the backs, but we can talk price when you've chosen."

He folded his arms on his chest, pulled up his knees, and in only a moment seemed to slip away, giving out the bubbling snore and whistles of a sleeper.

The fat man walked around the walls, pausing before the icons he found most attractive. The boy climbed miserably into his grandfather's chair. He picked out from the jar a paintbrush so fine only a few hairs were fixed in its end, and absently flicked the bristles backwards and forwards across the desktop.

The fat man admired the painter's work; traditional in its style, as was demanded, its gold leaf shone with burnishing, and the vibrant colors glowed. But the faces were irritating to him; so many were dour and dismal, perpetuating a view of life as suffering, and nothing more. He paused before several, appearing to be considering his choice, until he drew close to the chaise longue, where he took a long look at Mercuris to confirm that he truly was asleep.

Satisfied, he turned to Sammy.

"I expect it makes you very sad to be in this place without your grandfather," he said.

The boy did not answer, but poked the paintbrush back into the jar, and lowered his head. The fat man went across to him, and placed a hand on his thin shoulder.

"You're sitting in the seat which will one day be yours,"

he said, "but it must feel uncomfortable, just at this moment. I need advice, and your father's sleeping. Do you think you could help me with my choice? Which is your favorite?"

The boy hesitated, then climbed down from the chair and ran to point at an icon at the center of the wall.

"This one," he said. "It took *Pappou* weeks to finish it."

The icon showed a seated figure of Christ with all the apostles gathered round him; the brushwork was intricate and painstaking, the colors bright.

The fat man stood next to Sammy, considering.

"It's an excellent example," he said, "and beautifully executed. Can you tell me how much it would be?"

The boy lifted the icon's bottom edge from the wall to show the handwritten sticker on its back.

"Thirty thousand drachmas," he said, before adding words he had clearly often heard. "It's a fair price for the work of a skilled craftsman."

"Your grandfather was certainly that," said the fat man. "But you know, this is a modern-looking icon, and my taste is more for the antique. Something more like the Lady herself. Something very old, or at least old-looking. Is there nothing like that?"

"There are some special ones," he said. "You might like those."

"In what way, special?"

Sammy didn't answer, but returned to the old desk and dived into the dark beneath it, where several objects were covered by a bedsheet. Lifting the sheet, he revealed three icons, and clutching the frontmost of them, crawled out back into the light, and handed the retrieved painting to the fat man.

The icon was of St. Michael, in classical Byzantine style, and appeared, like the icon in Sotiris's coffin, to be of considerable age, battered and abraded in the expected places, with some damage to both the painted surface and the raised border which framed it. At a glance, it appeared to be an object worth many million drachmas.

"Where did your grandfather get this?" asked the fat man.

Proudly, Sammy smiled.

"My father painted it," he said. "I painted some of this bit in the corner." He pointed to the background near the saint's right foot.

"It's a fake, then?" asked the fat man.

"Not a fake, a copy," corrected the boy.

"Why isn't it on display with the others?"

"It's one of the special ones," said the boy. "*Papa* doesn't do many because they take so long. He worked on this one for over a year."

On the chaise longue, Mercuris opened his eyes.

"Sammy, what are you doing?" he asked, without turning from the wall.

"I'm showing the man the icons, *Papa*."

"Well, don't show him those. They're not for sale. Put them away."

"Perhaps you'd better put this back," suggested the fat man quietly, as he handed back the icon. "I think it would be better if I made my choice from the display. Christ and his apostles, the one you like best: could you wrap it up for me?"

The boy replaced the icon of St. Michael under the table, covered it with the bedsheet and took down Christ and his apostles from the wall. In a desk drawer, he found wrapping paper decorated with fighting Trojans; cutting a piece to size with dressmaking scissors, he wrapped the icon and handed it to the fat man, who unzipped his holdall and slipped the icon inside.

The fat man took out his wallet, and placed 30,000 drachmas on the desk.

"Tell your father I'm happy to pay the price your grandfather asked," he said. "The work deserves it. You'd better put the money somewhere safe. Do you know where it goes?"

Sammy nodded, and the fat man turned his back.

"I'm not looking," he said. "You put it away."

He heard the sliding of a drawer and the opening and closing of a tin, before the boy said, "Ready."

The fat man turned back to face him.

"Now," he said, "I'm sure your father will sleep awhile, and he's better sleeping here than drinking at the house. The mourners will be wailing all night long, so wouldn't it be a good idea for you to bed down here too, out of the way?"

Sammy shrugged, unsure.

"I'll tell you what I'd do," said the fat man. "I'd run home, and tell your mama where you'll be. Then borrow a pillow off your bed at home, and come and camp in here with your father. What do you say? It would be a good way for you to honor your grandfather, spending the night watching over his work. What do you think?"

The boy nodded.

"But I'll tell you what," the fat man went on, "before you do that, I'm thinking about going to get an ice cream. They do sell ice cream at the *kafenion,* don't they?"

Again, the boy nodded.

"Maybe you would come and be my adviser. If you'll tell me which ice cream is the best, I'll gladly buy you one, and I might throw in a lemonade as well—how would that be?"

Sammy's sorrowful mood showed no sign of lifting, but he nodded his agreement to the plan. He pulled the door closed on his sleeping father, and he and the fat man made their way to Apostolis's *kafenion,* where old men had already begun the evening's backgammon.

The fat man chose seats still warmed by the sinking sun. At the backgammon tables, dice rattled in the boxes, and shouts went up as counters were slammed down on the boards. A group of young soldiers sat in camouflage fatigues, arguing as they drank iced coffees. In the doorway, Apostolis held his tray under his arm and scratched the bite still irritating his arm.

"Before you sit," said the fat man to Sammy, "run inside, and fetch us two of what you think best from the freezer. And tell our host there to bring us something cold to drink. What do you think—orange, or lemonade, or Coca-Cola?"

"Coca-Cola," said the boy, immediately, and the fat man smiled. "My favorite too," he said. "Tell him to put them on my bill."

Sammy returned quickly, carrying tubs of strawberry and vanilla ice cream with shovel-spoons sealed in paper. The boy sat down next to the fat man, peeled the lid from his ice cream and the wrapper from his spoon, and dug into the pink and

189

white ice cream. Apostolis brought them glasses filled with ice cubes and a straw each, and popped the caps from two bottles of Coca-Cola without either a smile or a word of welcome.

"Thank you," said the fat man, but Apostolis tucked his tray under his arm, and walked away as if he hadn't heard.

The fat man poured Coke into his glass, and took a long drink through his straw. As the first spoonful of ice cream touched his tongue, he closed his eyes to savor it.

"I remember the very first time I tasted ice cream," he said. "I remember as if it were yesterday, even though many, many years have gone by since then. I was with a cousin of mine, and we were offered this new confection, and I remember that unique sensation, of sweetness, and cold. It was billed as an iced dessert, and we really had no idea what to expect. My cousin ate so much of it, he made himself sick." He opened his eyes, smiling at the memory. Sammy's eyes were on his own ice cream; he was eating all the vanilla before he touched the strawberry.

"That's an interesting technique you have there," said the fat man. "Do you eat the vanilla first because you prefer it, or because you prefer the strawberry and wish to save the treat?"

Sammy did not answer, but swallowed another mouthful of vanilla.

"Sometimes, I can't make up my mind," said the fat man. "Do I like vanilla best for its creaminess, or strawberry for its fruit? I can't decide, so I eat the two together to avoid the decision. Do you ever have trouble making decisions, Sammy?"

Again, the boy didn't answer, but reached for his Coke and sipped on it through the straw.

"Some choices are very hard to make," said the fat man, "though this one is unimportant. Sometimes we have to make decisions that are very hard indeed, and their consequences can stay with us a lifetime. Thankfully, those choices come to us only rarely; but when they do, we have to make our choice as best we may. Do you know what I mean?"

The boy continued eating as if he hadn't heard; the fat man took another spoon of ice cream.

"Like the choice you had to make last night. That wasn't easy, was it, son?"

For a moment, the boy's hand froze; then he dug again into the ice cream.

"Do you think you could tell me, Sammy, what happened last night?"

Now the boy looked at him, wide-eyed; the fat man sensed his wish to run vying with his desire for the sweet things on the table.

"Your grandfather became ill, didn't he?" asked the fat man, gently. "How did you know he was ill?"

The boy lowered his head.

"Had he just eaten? Was it after dinner he got ill?"

Sammy nodded.

"But you weren't ill, were you?" asked the fat man. "Did you eat the same as him, or something different?"

The boy's spoon was ready with the first taste of strawberry ice cream, but he paused with it halfway to his mouth.

"I had the milk pie," he said, in a small voice. "*Pappou* said I could, and he'd have the food in the pot."

"What was the food?"

"Avgolemono. Sambeca gave it to him. I don't like soup."

"And then what happened?"

"He ate it."

"All of it?"

"I don't know. He doesn't eat much. Mama worries."

"And then what happened?"

"He held his stomach, and said he had a pain."

"Can you show me where?"

"Here." The boy placed a hand below his breastbone.

"And then?"

"And then he said it burned. He told me to fetch him water."

"Which was where?"

"Inside the cabin."

"So you fetched him water?"

The boy nodded.

"And he drank some," he said, "and then he was holding his throat."

"What was he saying?"

The boy seemed pale; his treats were forgotten.

" *'It burns,'* he said. That's what he kept saying."

"And then?"

"I didn't know what to do. I thought I should get the doctor but I couldn't start the engine. So I jumped in, to swim for home."

"That was very brave, Sammy. You tried to save your grandfather, and that was the act of a hero."

But the boy's eyes filled with tears.

"I wasn't a hero," he said, "because I couldn't swim far enough. My legs got tired, and my arms. The water kept going in my mouth. I only got as far as the rocks opposite. I should have stayed with him and not let him die alone. But I didn't know he was going to die! I thought he'd be all right by himself, if I went for help."

He put his face into his hands to hide his distress. The fat man laid an arm across his shoulders.

"You were the bravest of the brave, Sammy, and your grandfather knew it. The truth is, you had no other choice but to try and get help. You tried your very best, and that's what counts."

"I tried and I failed, and that's what counts," said the boy.

He jumped up from the table and ran away down the alley, leaving the uneaten strawberry ice cream to melt in the evening sun.

The fat man abandoned his ice cream, too; the boy's distress killed his appetite. He sipped at his Coke through his straw, but found the drink too saccharine for his taste.

Dusk was falling, and Apostolis switched on the lights which hung from the overhead canopy. A mosquito whined, and landed on the fat man's wrist; he killed it with a slap, and brushed away its leggy body.

Along the waterfront, a car moved at slow speed and, seated at its wheel, the gypsy held a microphone to his mouth, his voice blaring through the roof-mounted loud-speaker.

"Come and take a look! I have shoes, all styles, all colors, all sizes, ladies shoes, shoes for children, shoes for the gentlemen. Come and take a look, and choose yourself a pair of my fine shoes!"

At the spot he judged he would draw the most customers, he parked the car and climbed out, still holding the microphone and continuing his call. Within only a few moments, he attracted several women, who gathered by the bonnet and browsed the shoes strapped on there as if the car were a conventional shoe shop. Before long, one asked for a low-heeled sandal in a particular size.

"In a thirty-six, *kyria,* yes, yes," said the gypsy. He walked quickly from the front of the car to the boot, and began to dig amongst the shoeboxes for the size he needed.

The fat man left his payment on the *kafenion* table, picked up his holdall and wandered in the direction of the gypsy's car. A woman trying on sandals was complaining to her friend about the fit.

"It's too tight across the top of my foot, *kalé.* I'll have to have a thirty-seven." She turned to the gypsy. "Have you got a thirty-seven?"

"Of course, of course," said the gypsy.

By the car boot, the fat man was waiting, examining a pair of trainers dangling from their laces.

*"Kali spera,"* he said to the gypsy. "We meet again."

"I'll give you a good price on those," said the gypsy. "What size?"

"No shoes for me," said the fat man. "Serve your customers, then you and I might have a little chat."

"What about?"

"About the money you still owe me for those peaches. Are you ready to pay?"

"As you can see, I'm busy now, so if you're not buying, leave me and let me make a living. Yes, *kyria,* a thirty-seven. Blue or red?"

"No matter, then," said the fat man. "We'll leave it for to-day. But we won't be leaving it much longer, my friend. You just come and find me, whenever you're ready to talk."

After dinner, the fat man took a glass of wine up to the prow, and leaned for a while on the railing, watching the sea. The evening's coolness had brought life back to the harbor side. Fragments of music—pieces of melodies picked out on a ringing *bouzouki,* lilting dance rhythms from a keyboard—drifted over the water to the *Aphrodite's* decks. The prospect of entertainment was tempting; and when the fat man finished his wine, he called Ilias from the galley and had him take him back to shore.

There, he strolled along the moorings towards the square where people were gathering. At the waterfront tavernas, trade was brisk. The smoke rising from charcoal grills carried scents of seared fish and pork, and the waiters carrying wine to cheerful tourists called out to him to take a seat, and eat; but the fat man dismissed their invitations with a tilt of his chin—in the silent language of the Greeks, *Ochi.* No.

The fat man stopped at a phone booth, and searched his pockets for change. Lifting the receiver, he deposited several coins, and dialed the number Enrico had found for him. For a long time, the phone he had dialed rang out, until at last an elderly man answered.

"Dr. Dinos?" asked the fat man. "Hermes Diaktoros, of Athens. Do you remember me?"

There was a short silence before the doctor answered.

"Now I've got you," he said. "Our city friend of the white shoes."

"The same," said the fat man. "How are you, *yiatre?*"

"Busy," said the doctor, happily. "No matter how old I get, they keep me busy."

"I am calling to pick your brains, if you will indulge me," said the fat man. "I wonder if you would answer me a question or two related to a medical matter."

"If I can be of help, it will be my pleasure," said Dr. Dinos. "Ask away."

"Thank you," said the fat man, "I appreciate it, especially since you may find my questions a little peculiar. They concern an old man, and a passion he developed for sniffing lemons."

When he'd finished his call, the fat man went in search of cigarettes. On the corner of a short lane running from the harbor side to the square, a despondent youth was minding a *periptero.* Elbows on the counter, his face leaning on his hands, he looked out of the wooden kiosk through a window half covered with merchandise: chewing gum in numberless flavors and batteries in all sizes, sunflower seeds and peanuts in their shells, potato crisps and biscuits, cheap razors and lighters, pornographic magazines and holiday postcards. By the kiosk's freezer, the fat man paused to consider the ice-cream menu taped to its lid; but a glance through the glass showed only a few children's lollies and a box of imported prawns for use as fishing bait. The drinks fridge, too, was low on stock; its upper shelves were almost empty, and those at the center were filled with boxes of chocolate bars. On the bottom shelf, someone had left their bags of shopping; a paper-wrapped parcel of meat was seeping blood.

Deciding on chocolate over ice cream, the fat man opened the fridge door, and the sour smell of feta rose from amongst the shopping bags. Dithering at first between Lacta with crushed almonds and Nestlé's milk, he chose eventually three sapphire-blue wrapped bars of Pavlides dark, approached the counter and laid the chocolate before the unhappy youth.

*"Kali spera,"* said the fat man, with a smile.

The youth stood upright, and removed his face from his hands. His jaw and chin were red with chronic acne, whose livid spots were centered with pale pustules; only the skin of his upper lip was clear of the condition, and there grew the sparse hairs of a fledgling moustache.

"Four-fifty," said the youth, and as he spoke, he blushed, deepening to purple the color of his afflicted skin.

"And I need matches, too, if you would be so kind," said the fat man. "Two boxes will suffice. And these too, if you have them."

He reached into his pocket and took out a pack of his cigarettes, and handed them to the youth, who seemed intrigued by the starlet's pretty face.

"We don't have those, *kyrie,*" he said. "I've never seen

them before. Perhaps you'd like to try a different brand. We have Marlboro, if you like American cigarettes; or some people like these French ones." He reached to the shelf behind him, and placed a pack of Gitanes on the counter, saying the name as if its strangeness was pleasant to him, though the soft sound of the "G" was beyond his tongue, and he pronounced the name "Tzitans."

The fat man's smile grew broader.

"Everywhere I go," he said, "they say the same. But often when people look, they find they have a pack or two of my brand tucked away. If you'll oblige me and just check, I would appreciate it."

With a melancholy sigh, the boy turned back to the kiosk's shelves, where every brand of cigarette, both foreign and domestic, seemed to be on hand. Carton by carton, pack by pack, he went through the stock, until at last he paused and, reaching up to the back of the highest shelf, lifted down two cellophane-wrapped boxes of cigarettes identical to that which the fat man held.

Turning one of the boxes, he squinted at its back.

"There's no price on them," he said. He laid the cigarettes on the counter beside the chocolate and placed two boxes of matches beside them.

"A reflection, no doubt, of their price's constant increase," said the fat man. "But I can tell you that for the last pack I bought—only three days ago—I paid 550 drachmas. Does that sound fair?"

The youth shrugged his indifference, and the fat man took out his wallet.

"Very good, then. I'll take both packs. In total, what do I owe?"

The young man's arithmetic was quick.

"Seventeen-fifty," he said.

From his wallet, the fat man handed the youth a 5,000-drachma note. The youth counted out his change; the fat man slipped the money into a pocket, and placed the cigarettes, the matches and the chocolate in his holdall.

At the center of the square, a band of three musicians was ready to play. A collection of old chairs had been arranged in a semicircle for the audience—mothers and daughters, grandmothers and grandfathers, the youngest of children.

At the small *kafenion* on the square's perimeter, old men fiddled with worry beads as they drank black coffee from tiny white cups. A group of foreigners in bright cottons chattered over beers and Campari; their bored children kicked each other beneath the table. As the fat man considered whether to sit down, a dust cart's two-man crew parked their half-sized, reeking truck only feet from the *kafenion's* door; oblivious of their own stink of rot and rubbish, they took the last free seats, dropped their filthy gauntlets on the table and called out for whisky-sodas.

Across the square, opposite the *kafenion,* a man in a white apron and cap sat alone at a table by a shop door. The pillared shop-doorway was imposing; the stone set over the pillars was engraved in old-style Greek with a single word—*Artopoleion*—which meant the place had been, at some time past, a bakery. The man's white apron and cap suggested it might be a bakery still; and hopeful this was the case, the fat man crossed the square.

Close up, the man's profession could be in no doubt. His gray hair was lightened and his face made cadaverously pale by a powdering of flour; his trousers, sandals and moustache were dusted with white. The black beneath his eyes suggested long-term lack of sleep; as he looked towards the band and its audience, his eyelids flickered, as if sleep were calling now. Before him on the table was a bottle of beer, part-poured into a glass; as the fat man approached, the baker poured out a little more beer, and raised the glass to his lips.

"*Kali spera sas,*" said the fat man. "Is your shop by any chance open?"

"Depends what you want to buy," said the baker, lowering his glass and looking up at the fat man from his chair. "There's no bread, not till tomorrow."

"Something sweet, perhaps?" suggested the fat man. "*Bougatsa?* Baklava?"

Wearily, the baker stood.

"This way then, friend," he said. "Come and take your pick."

The baker's legs were short and bowed, so the top of his head barely reached the fat man's shoulder. His gait was awkward, and to climb the single step into the bakery he took support from the doorjamb. As he crossed the threshold, the band in the square began to play: an island dance, brisk and uplifting.

Inside, the bakery's old origins were plain. The stone-built oven was set in the wall, its cast-iron door held open with a wedge of olive wood. Ash from the day's baking lay thick on the oven's brick floor; below the bakery's window, logs and sticks were stacked for the next day's fire. A scrubbed pine table held fire-blackened trays ready for the morning's loaves; resting against the table's edge, the pole of the iron paddle used to load the oven reached almost to the oak-beamed ceiling. Behind the door stood sacks of flour; in the far corner, the bowl of a commercial mixer held a batch of rising dough, whose musty-smelling yeast mingled with lingering woodsmoke.

Along one wall, a confectioner's glass-fronted cabinet displayed a range of baked goods: *koulouria,* round biscuits decorated with almonds, flavored with aromatic bergamot or drenched in icing sugar; pies filled with feta and spinach, or apples, or cheese and ham; and trays of sticky *kataifa* and baklava.

"No *bougatsa,*" said the baker, referring to the fat man's favorite custard pies. "She doesn't make them very often, these days."

"Are you not the pastry cook, then?" asked the fat man.

The baker gave a bitter laugh.

"No, I'm not the pastry cook," he said. "I'm the one who does the donkey work, the one who'll be up lighting the fire at two in the morning and hauling out the first loaves at four. I leave the easy work to the wife. What you see there's down to her."

The fat man chose *kataifa*—fine threads of pastry woven like a nest, filled with a paste of cinnamon-sweetened chopped nuts and baked to the gold of straw.

"The secret of good *kataifa* is in the syrup," said the baker. From under the cabinet, he took a pink cardboard box decorated with almond blossom and lined it with silver foil torn from a roll. "She puts plenty of honey in the syrup, and she makes it very thick, so it sinks through quickly to the bottom. That way, you get a crisp bite on the top, and a soft base to get your teeth into. She makes excellent *kataifa,* does my wife."

With a pair of aluminum tongs, he lifted four square pieces from the tray and laid them in the bottom of the box. Closing the lid, he cut a length of string and wrapped it round the box like a parcel; he tied the loose ends in a carrying handle, and passed the boxed *kataifa* to the fat man.

"Six hundred," said the baker.

The fat man paid for his purchase, and moved to the bakery doorway to look out on the square. The baker went outside, and sat down at his table.

"Sit," he said, indicating the chair opposite.

"Thank you," said the fat man. "I will."

The band had been joined by dancers—a troupe of young girls and self-conscious boys, all dressed in traditional costume. The girls wore long dresses of cream sateen, their heads covered by scarves of cream muslin, with white cotton aprons around their waists; and round their necks, gold chains were strung with gold coins and medallions which jingled like small change in a pocket as the dancers moved. The boys—in black knickerbockers, with white stockings and voluminous-sleeved shirts, and waistcoats embroidered in ruby and emerald threads—wore red fezzes with no tassels;

and the fezzes and the girls' jingling gold made the dancers seem exotic, more of Turkey or old Byzantium than of Greece.

The baker leaned across to the fat man.

"That's my granddaughter," he said, pointing. "There, second from the left."

The music's tempo had slowed, and, standing in front of the band, a slender, black-haired girl began to sing. Her nasal voice, though so young, carried the words of lost love and recrimination as if the story were her own. Placing their arms round each other's shoulders, the dancers, upright and elegant, moved in circles round the dance floor in a spectacle both timeless and touching. Mothers watched their daughters in the dance, and quietly clapped the rhythm; the old folk drifted on memories, back to their days of dancing and lost loves. Outside the *kafenion*, the foreigners laughed loud, and ordered up another round of drinks, whilst their heedless children ran amongst the crowd.

"Kids." The baker raised his beer glass, and drank half down. "They worry about nothing. To have nothing to worry about, and no regrets—that'd be something, wouldn't it, friend?"

The fat man watched the dancers, and was silent.

"When you reach a certain age," went on the baker, "these old songs break your heart. The young ones—the free girls and the youths—they laugh and chatter through them. But us old ones—they get us here..." He banged a fist on his chest. "See them all there, the old men half blind and lame, the old girls with their veins and their blood pressure, all misty-eyed with regret and might-have-beens. These young-sters don't know yet what life is. She's singing about love lost yesterday, and we're all thinking about those someones from decades ago. They're all fat or ugly or dead now, my yester-days. And yours the same too, friend, I'll bet."

The fat man turned his head from the dancers, and looked the baker in the eye.

"You didn't marry the one you wanted," he said.

The baker looked away.

"When I found her, I was already married," he said. He drained his glass, and tipped in what beer remained in the bottle.

"And so you let it go."

"What choice did I have?"

"Oh, we always have a choice," said the fat man. "But too often, we make the wrong one."

He himself was thoughtful.

"We're strange creatures, are we not?" he went on. "We make our choices with free will, and think we've done our best. And then, some summer evening like this, one song brings everything back: what went unsaid, what road wasn't taken, all our mistakes and stupidities recalled by a tune and regretted. But our regret is different, now—we regret that the road not taken can't be found. The only way is forward; and, as you say, there's nothing to go back to, anyway. We make our own tomorrows, baker, and this is ours. Keep the past in the past; consider it a moment, at a time like this, and let it go again. There's no way to make a past life what it wasn't."

The band played its final tune, and the dancers left the floor, joining family members in the crowd.

"I must go," said the fat man, holding out his hand to the baker. "Thank you for the seat."

"Don't go yet," said the baker. "You haven't seen the star attraction."

He gestured to where two more musicians, both dressed in white, were taking seats which the previous ones had left.

"What is the star attraction?" asked the fat man.

The baker named a singer of national fame.

"Our home-grown talent. He's a big star in the Athens clubs."

"I am myself from Athens," said the fat man, "and I recognize the name."

"We don't see him here too often, these days. But when he comes home, he always sings for us. Stay, friend, and listen."

From an alleyway, a small group of people emerged into the square. At their heart was a man dressed in the same white clothes as the musicians, though his trousers were stretched on plump thighs and his shirt was of a looser cut to hide a well-fed belly. A dour woman all in black clutched on to his arm; the other women with them were in heels and sequins, with the sleek-styled hair of Athenian salons. The group's men all wore suits, and looked around mistrustfully as if there might be trouble. Ahead of them ran two photographers, crouching to get their shots, their camera flashes dazzling in the night.

"That's him," said the baker, pointing to the overweight

man in white. "And that's his mother with him. He's a good son. He sends her money, every month. He makes sure she's comfortable."

The star took his place in front of his musicians, and the crowd applauded and whistled; his entourage seated themselves on reserved front-row chairs. The musicians played; as the star sang, many of his audience stood up to dance, echoing in less choreographed footwork the archaic style of the costumed dancers.

At the end of his set, the music slowed; the *bouzouki* rang out the mournful notes of a final, downbeat song. The audience found seats, and listened in silence as the singer delivered words of foolhardiness and remorse.

*My mother's eyes*
*I see them in my mind,*
*The pain that I put there:*
*I cut the ties that bind.*
*The bright lights called,*
*And I, the splendid youth,*
*Went traveling far from home.*
*It's time to tell the truth—*
*That I'm ashamed it didn't all work out:*
*No wealth, no dreams . . .*
*Just me,*
*My old suitcase in hand . . .*
*I'm coming home*
*To see my mother's eyes—*
*No splendid youth,*

*Just me,*
*The man she'll see,*
*And smile.*

As the last notes died away, the audience, applauding with delight, rose to its feet. Ushered forward with loud whispers, three small girls in pretty dresses presented bouquets to the band: one for the *bouzouki* player, one for the keyboard man, one for the singer himself. The singer took the flowers in the crook of his arm, and bent to kiss the child's head, thanking her by name. Then as one, the people moved towards him and, surrounding him, embraced him; they kissed his cheeks and shook his hands, shining with their pride in their home-coming son.

Making his way back to the quay where Ilias waited, the fat man seemed thoughtful, and when someone called out to him, he didn't hear.

"Friend! Wait!"

At a slow run, a man caught up with him, and touched him on the shoulder. The fat man turned, and recognized the butcher he had met with Kara the previous day.

"How are you, my friend?" said the fat man, holding out his hand. "Did you have any luck with your treasure hunting today?"

The butcher clasped the fat man's hand, and released it to reach into his pocket.

"No luck out there, no," he said. "I was tied to the shop for most of the day. But the talk we had at the beach made me think, and I paid my mother a visit before I opened up this evening. And it took some finding, let me tell you—but I think it's fair to say yes, I found some treasure." In the palm of his hand, he held a bronze coin, a hole drilled through its center. "She had it in a box of Pappou's things, amongst his old worry beads and watch chains. She said he used to wear it round his neck, the one bit of luck life had sent him. It's not a great deal to look at, is it? He told me it was silver, and it's not. But it's from that famous wreck, so it's worth a bit for that. Here, have a look."

The fat man took the coin, and held it up to the light from a nearby taverna. Its faces were worn, but on one side a wreath of laurels around the edges and the flourish of a monogram were easily made out, as was a date across the center: 1831.

"A treasure indeed," said the fat man, turning the coin over.

The reverse face was less clear, but the fat man saw a coat of arms—a double-headed eagle, and a crown—and on the bottom edge, two words, one containing letters he couldn't read. The second word, however, read as old Greek, the letters spelling *kopeks.*

"Well, well," said the fat man. "You were right. It is Russian."

"I told you," said the butcher, smiling broadly. "If my boy could find a few of these in gold, I'd be a happy man."

The fat man gave him back his coin.

"Good luck to you," he said, "and keep that heirloom safe. Its value in cash terms may be low; but as a piece of this island's history, it is invaluable."

# *Thirteen*

The fat man breakfasted early on the baker's excellent *kataifa* and a peach from Agiris's garden. When he had finished a second cup of coffee, he asked Enrico to ferry him across the bay and leave him at the foot of the church promontory, in the spot where Ilias had picked him up a day or two before.

"I have a mind to do a little walking," he said to Enrico, "and to keep myself to myself, just for the present. I have no idea how long I shall be, so go back to the boat and wait for me there. When I'm ready to return, I shall whistle."

At eight o'clock, the bells for Sotiris's funeral began to toll.

Just after eight, mourners started to gather at the icon painter's house. The incoming morning ferry came into view, and blew its usual mournful blast on its foghorn; and, as if that blast had provoked some avalanche or landslip, a low and angry rumble ran through the town.

As if shaken by some giant hand, the houses shuddered and the windows rattled in their frames; plates and glasses vibrated on the shelves, bounced to their very edges and fell to the floors. The shaking beds startled awake those still sleeping; the dogs chained in their kennels barked in alarm.

Then, the rumbling stopped. The people held their breath, squeezing the children's hands and speaking comfort, until they were quite confident the tremor had passed. They relaxed, and went back to their chores.

But the rumbling came again, much louder and deeper, and the shaking grew so violent, it knocked pictures from the walls and saucepans from the shelves. The people ran out-side, shouting to the neighbors, *Get out! Get out! Earthquake!* Some stayed inside, snatching babies from their cradles and diving under tables, whilst in the yards the madly barking dogs strained at their chains. Cracks appeared in walls, split-ting the plaster first and then the stone beneath; the window frames were parting from the walls, opening such gaps that daylight could be seen. Trees in the gardens rustled and dropped their fruit; the agitated sea rushed at the waterfront, sending up high waves and making the moored boats buck. In the grocer's shop, the rocking shelves spilt tins and jars which burst and splattered their contents—honey, mayon-naise, pickles—on the floors, whilst the fluorescent lights swinging overhead on their chains flickered like demonic lightning. The glass across the cheese fridge split like ice, cracking with a force which sent the frightened grocer run-ning, his arms covering his head against falling plaster. In the *periptero,* cigarettes cascaded from the shelves; coffee cups crashed from the *kafenion* tables; women shrieked, men shouted, children cried, whilst at the church the bell ringer dropped the rope and let the bell swing its own mad rhythms across the bay. The demented dogs barked on, in fear and warning, until the ground's terrible trembling became still, and the rumbling which had begun it died away.

In the aftermath, all was, for a short while, very quiet whilst this small world waited for worse to come. But the ground under their feet remained still.

Some people smiled and laughed—*Mori! The biggest one for years!*—but others, serious-faced, were still afraid. The grocer, though keen to assess the damage, was reluctant to reenter his shop; Apostolis sighed, and bent to pick up the shards of broken crockery around his tables.

At the icon painter's house, the earthquake's rumbling had turned the wails and moans of grief into shrieks and shouts of feminine alarm. Preparing to lead the service, Father Linos had instead led the exodus outside, and from the street listened with the women to the sounds of falling china and a loose tile which slid from the roof, and smashed on the courtyard flowerpots.

When the ground was still, the women gathered round the priest.

"That was a bad one," said one. "As bad as '62."

"The old houses will never have withstood that," said another. "*Papa*, you should go and see whether the bishop's house is still standing."

"It wasn't as bad as that," he said. "Surely?"

"Half the roof's off, and he says it wasn't bad," said a third, pointing to the broken roof tile. "That might have killed one of us, easily."

"We could have been burying two."

"Maybe we will be. A quake like that, there'll be casualties."

A thought seemed to strike the priest, who blanched.

"You ladies are quite right," he said, laying down his censer. "I must go, and make sure everything's all right up there. I shall be back, within the hour."

He lifted the skirt of his robes to walk faster, and left them.

"Run, *kalé*," one of the women called after him. "And be sure to come and tell us what you find!"


At the bishop's house, a great crack had appeared across its front; around the roots of the peach trees, fruit lay bruised and broken, the smell of it carried on the morning's breath of a breeze. The priest hesitated, made a cross over his chest and hurried to the kitchen door, which stood open with its padlock and chain dropped to the ground. Inside the kitchen, flakes of fallen plaster lay on the table, stove and shelves, whilst the caustic dust of quicklime dried the air, catching in his throat and making him cough. The household icon had fallen from the wall, and stood balanced on its foot beside the dresser, its lamp of water and oil spilt beside it. Down the wall, the crack which had seemed bad on the outside of the house seemed worse in here.

In his hurry, Father Linos did not register the fact of the cellar door being ajar. Carefully, he made his way down the steps into the cellar where the air was choking with gritty dust. Fumbling for matches, he lit the lamp, but the light it cast came back at him, like headlamps in fog. His plan was to be quick, straight in and straight out, but he was afraid, and his heart beat fast. Part of the cellar had collapsed, and as he picked his careful way towards the catacombs he glanced up in apprehension, looking for the place where the roof had come down. If there were aftershocks, more of the roof might fall; if he were underneath it, who would there be to dig him out?

But the dark portal in the cellar wall was gone, covered over by rubble and fallen stone. The obstruction was solid and immovable; the tunnel that was the catacombs was no more.

In dismay, his hands went to his face; he covered his cheeks with them, and stared at the obstacle that blocked his way.

"I wouldn't linger down here, if I were you." The voice came from behind him. In shock, Father Linos turned and in the gloom saw the fat man, made ghostly by the chalky dust which covered him. "It isn't safe."

"What are you doing here?"

The priest, bewildered, looked between the fat man and the buried tunnel entrance.

"You might expect me to ask you the same question," said the fat man, "but I have no need, since I already know the answer. Did I startle you? Did you think I was some revenant, or vampire, come to steal your body? No: I see the thought never crossed your mind. It isn't revenants and vampires that you fear, is it, *Papa?* It isn't the loss of your soul you're afraid of, but something else. But don't worry. I was in time to save her. She's over here, by the wall."

A long moment passed, before the priest gathered himself, and asked, "Who?"

"Who, indeed? Which one of them are you interested in?" Behind the fat man, a little dirt dropped from the roof. "Shall we go upstairs?" he asked. "I think it would be prudent. Perhaps you'd like to carry her."

From behind, he picked up an object wrapped in a linen tablecloth filthy with fallen dust. The object was the shape and size of a painting; the fat man handed it to the priest, who, without lifting the covering, clasped the object to his chest and made his way to the steps. The fat man picked up a second object—a shoebox, whose lid was also thickly covered with dust—and followed Father Linos up the stairs.

Outside, on the terrace, the priest laid the object he was carrying on the cerulean-blue table, where the fat man also. placed the shoebox.

"You should check she is undamaged," said the fat man. "Please. Don't mind me."

The priest was doubtful, but his concern for the rescued object overcame his wish to hide his secret from the fat man. He blew hard on the linen to remove what dust he could; then, with reverence and care, he peeled back the cloth, spreading the opened folds across the table. Inside the cloth lay an icon: an ancient image of a sorrowful Virgin, identical at first glance to the revered Lady hanging in the church.

The fat man leaned over the table to scrutinize the painting.

"Here she is, at last," he said. "The Lady of Sorrows. Not stolen at all, but hidden away in the bishop's cellar. You know, the copy was really very, very good. But when you see the real thing, the difference is obvious, don't you think?"

The priest looked at him with suspicion.

"Who are you?" he asked. "What's your interest in the Lady?"

"Well," said the fat man, "the truth is, if there hadn't been repercussions, I would have taken no more than a passing interest in the Lady's disappearance. I was prepared to hand the matter over to a good friend of mine, who takes the welfare of works of art far more seriously than I do. To me, the Lady—beautiful though she is—is just an image painted on wood, and of interest as a curio, because despite her fragility she has managed to survive this world so long. But to others of course—to you yourself, and to others of your faith—she is much more than the sum of her parts, isn't she? She's a gift to the faithful from God himself; not wood and paint and gold leaf at all, but an object through which He works His miracles on earth. And that is what you should have considered, before you removed her. Why did you hide her? And how long has she been down there? Come, sit, and tell me everything."

"You're from the police."

The fat man smiled, and pulled out a chair from the table. As he sat down, he indicated the priest should do the same.

"No, no, I am not a policeman. There is no police force in Greece which would hire me. My employers are higher authorities, who would not under normal circumstances trouble themselves with anything so petty as art theft. Our concern is not with the enforcement of written laws, but with the administration of justice, which is not at all the same. You may talk to me quite freely on this matter. For you, there are unlikely to be repercussions, especially since I suspect your motive was honorable."

From his pocket, the fat man took out his cigarettes, and offered the box to Father Linos before taking one himself. With his gold lighter, he lit them, and Father Linos drew deeply on his cigarette, holding the smoke in his lungs for a long moment before exhaling.

"It was Sotiris's idea," he said. "He reached a stage in his life where he trusted no one. The business with his wife's death changed him. He felt so betrayed by the deception of his wife's relatives—their disguising of bad news as good—it turned his mind a little, I think. Mercuris had made a copy of the Lady so exact, it was impossible for the layman to tell the difference. Mercuris plays with icons as a hobby, or has done in the past. He may have to take the work more seriously, now. But Sotiris pressed me to put Mercuris's copy in the church. I resisted, at first; it seemed to me a deception of the worst kind, to allow the faithful to venerate an icon which—even if painted with great faith, with obedience to the tradition and belief in holiness of the images—could never replicate the miracle-working power conveyed through this most sacred original." He made the triple cross. "It seemed an offense as bad as, or even worse than, the offense Sotiris saw in his in-laws. Deceiving is deceiving, regardless of motive. Our Lady here is a miracle worker, in a way God grants only rarely here on earth. She is irreplaceable." He drew again on his cigarette, then dropped it to the ground and extinguished it with his foot. "I forget myself; I should not be smoking in her presence."

He gave the fat man a look which suggested he, too, should put out his cigarette; but the fat man only smiled, and put his own back to his lips.

"Irreplaceable," he echoed, exhaling smoke. "And yet you replaced her."

"Sotiris wore me down. He was convinced that we would lose her. We are led to believe she had come to us through a miracle, but was that the truth? I have heard so many stories over the years, but the one that never goes away is that she had probably, in fact, been stolen once before, and that was how she came to us. Why should she not be stolen again? Then there was the theft at Patmos; you mentioned to me yourself the incident at Elona, and we spoke of Serres. And as you pointed out, she was impossible for us to protect from a determined thief. Sotiris badgered me, and I began to feel her vulnerability; and I believed if her power was truly needed, she would hear the prayers of supplicants, wherever she was—in the church, or this short distance away, protected underground. She was unlikely to be found here; the people have a horror of this place, of its spooks and bogeymen."

"You don't fear them, then?"

"It is they who must fear me. I am ordained a priest of the true church, and I have the Lady's protection."

"Is that so? Or was it, more simply, you who instilled thoughts of bogeymen in their minds in the first place?"

"Let us say rather that I did nothing to assuage the fears already in people's minds."

The fat man ground out his cigarette.

"Once you had your forgery, I assume it was very simple to make the swap?"

"Forgery's a strong word."

"I think it is the correct word. You deceived the faithful into thinking they were praying to an ancient miracle worker, when in fact she had no track record, and was fresh from the artist's brush."

The priest shrugged.

"Were they deceived? All faithful copies of our icons are legitimate vehicles for miracles and veneration; that is the tradition icon painting exists to preserve. What is unfortunate is that Mercuris cannot work with Sotiris's eye of faith or for the church; but his talent for the art is undeniable."

"Then the Lady's gift of artistry has changed bloodlines."

The priest sighed.

"When he's had a drink, Mercuris talks too much. So now you know there is no miraculous gift, no passing of the talent at the time of death."

"That fairy story? I needed no one to tell me that."

"Between them, Mercuris and Sotiris were a good team. Mercuris had an interest in the very old techniques. Sotiris had his years of expertise. Put the two together..."

"I have seen other examples of what was produced. Like the icon in Sotiris's own coffin."

"Mercuris copied it from books. The original was lost some years ago — another victim of thieves. His idea was, if his family was ever needing cash, it might resurface. A trip to Florence, or Istanbul, even to London, to offer it to a collector. Why shouldn't he, he said. Beauty is in the eye of the beholder..."

"You condoned it, then?"

"I told him he was wicked. And I don't think he has the nerve to try and pass his work off as the real thing. It's all talk; he simply likes the challenge. He thinks the icons beautiful, that's all. He's a man who's rarely left this island's shores. He'd never dare take on the experts and dealers of the European art world."

"Are you certain? My feeling is that Mercuris may have plans. If he does, please warn him that experts like my Athenian friend will see through his deception in a moment."

"I suppose he wouldn't expect an icon dishonorably acquired to meet with experts."

"You would condone it, then, if he sold his forgeries?"

The priest sighed.

"I have lived here many years," he said, "and watched the people struggle for their livings, passing trades which make no money from father to son. So I admit to being torn. Young Sammy might have an education, if there were money; he might have wider horizons than we do, a chance at life beyond this island's shores."

The fat man nodded.

"Your point is fair, even if your moral stance is questionable, in a priest. I agree that passing years remove the blacks and whites of rights and wrongs, and clothe all in shades of gray. And I'm sure you believe that, with the Lady, no harm's been done. You see her protection as your priority, and that's why, when the earthquake struck, you came running."

"The thought struck me, as I was on my way here, that we had moved her into greater danger than she had been in at the church. This part of town has always been more vulnerable to tremors."

"It would have been ironic, I agree. Happily for you, I was already here."

A thought seemed to strike Father Linos.

"How did you know she was here?" he asked. "And how did you get in?"

"The great care lavished on this house, and on its garden, made no sense to me," said the fat man. "The bishop, by all accounts, is never here; yet the house is kept immaculate, and the garden too. If the care was not for the bishop's benefit, someone—or something—of importance was being kept here. As for getting in, there are not many locks that will keep me out. You might assume my skill is a sign of a misspent youth, or too much time spent in bad company, but the truth is, locks and their workings interest me. Take a few locks to pieces, and you'll find there's no mystery to opening them."

"But how did you know when—how did you come in time to save her?"

"Call it instinct," said the fat man, "a nose for trouble, as you often find in animals. Years of experience have taught me that with earthquakes, there are many signs to look for, if you know where to look: a cat moving a litter of kittens, for example, or an overly anxious dog. There have been several small tremors over the past few days. But the fact is, I didn't come to save your Lady. I brought her out with me, because it seemed a shame to leave her. She is a good age, and venerable for that. But I came here for another reason, a somewhat better one. Sotiris's sudden death has puzzled me, and the answer to that puzzle is in this box."

He had the shoebox before him, and pushed it forward on the table. Father Linos, intrigued, leaned forward to touch it, but the fat man moved it out of his reach.

"This is not for you," he said. "The contents of this box are someone else's business. Our job, now, is to restore the Lady to a more appropriate place. My friend will be very pleased to hear that she is safe and sound; be grateful that I stopped her calling the police and alerting the museums, and be grateful, too, that the reputation of Kalkos's icon painters remains untarnished. Your position would have been difficult to explain if it had got back to the church authorities. I am prepared to make the swap back on your behalf, since it must be done discreetly, and I will not become the subject of gossip if I am seen wandering the midnight streets, or disgraced if, worse, I am discovered in the act. My price for this favor is the copy, for which I have a use—a worthy use, where it will be appreciated. Tell Mercuris, if it becomes necessary to mention the business to him, that you have given me the forgery as a gift for my silence."

Father Linos looked doubtful.

"You are suggesting," he said, "that I hand her now to you, a stranger?"

"You don't trust me."

"Where the Lady's welfare is concerned, I trust no one but myself."

"That is only natural," said the fat man. "But there are two things to consider here. Firstly, I did not have to wait for you to come. I had the Lady in my hands, and could easily have been gone with her before you got here, if it was my intention to steal her. Secondly, you have a practical difficulty. How are you to remove her from this place, in broad daylight, with a funeral to conduct? You are required back at Sotiris's house, are you not? How are you going to explain your arrival with the Lady under your arm? You can trust me, *Papa,* to do the job discreetly. Tomorrow I shall be gone, with just the copy for my trouble. I have ample time to take care of it before I go. So, will you trust me? What do you say?"

The priest looked into the fat man's eyes. The fat man seemed in earnest, his face honest.

"All right," said Father Linos. "I will entrust her to you. But will you take care to make sure everything looks as normal at the church?"

"The shrine will look as if it has never been touched, I guarantee it," said the fat man. "Now, you must go. Sotiris is waiting to be buried, and the mourners will be wondering where you are."

# Fourteen

After Father Linos was gone, the fat man took a silk paisley-patterned handkerchief from his pocket, and used it to brush away as much dust and dirt as he was able from the shoebox. He did his best, but the box was grimy from its time in the damp catacombs; its lid was fastened on with a dirty, once-white ribbon whose bow was still intact, the original careful arrangement of the bow's loops still in place.

Placing his holdall on the table, he unzipped it and opened it as wide as he was able, and spent some time tidying and rearranging its varied contents. He rewrapped the Lady of Sorrows in her cloth, and placed her faceup in the bag; on top of her he laid the shoebox, ensuring it was level; and, when he was satisfied that both the icon and the box were safely settled, he zipped the holdall closed.

He walked down the steps as far as the sea, passing many minor dramas whipped into crises. The older houses had suffered worst from the earthquake's impact: split masonry, buckled window frames with cracked glass, a hole opened up where a cesspit had fallen in. Beyond the steps, where the houses were of more modern construction, the damage was less severe. Four men stared at a TV aerial which had fallen from a roof, one of them leaning on a stepladder which could only reach the ground-floor ceilings; several women were gathered around a buckled water pipe, watching water trickle away down the street. An old man mumbled sadly as he lifted the planks of a wooden shed from the corpse of a nanny goat, its distressed kid bleating beside him; a housewife swept up the terra-cotta shards from a line of smashed plant pots which had fallen from a courtyard wall, scattering dark earth and broken plants into the road. A small child clung whining to its mother's leg, as she and her husband looked in dismay at the tangle of a venerable grapevine; a collapsed trellis had felled the vine, which now covered the house door like a jungle curtain.

The cemetery lay at the edge of town, almost in the shadow of the promontory. The fat man found a bench out of the way and in the shade, and sat down. Above him, the single church bell began to toll again, and was echoed by the bells of smaller chapels around the town, and before long the procession of Sotiris's funeral came into view. The mourners were quiet, and subdued by both the occasion and the earthquake's impact. Father Linos led the way; Mercuris held Sammy's hand, and supported his wife.

The fat man scanned the mourners, looking for the person he sought; and having seen the right face in the crowd, lit himself a cigarette, and settled down to wait.

She did as he expected, breaking away from the mourners as they returned from the cemetery, and making instead for the church. On the steps, she made slow upwards progress; hands on hips, she paused after every few paces to catch her breath. The fat man moved more quickly, and before she reached the top, he was beside her.

Down on the bay, the first of the tourist boats approached the quay.

"Sambeca," he said. "May I speak with you a moment?"

She looked at him, surprised to be addressed by a man she did not know.

"With me? What about? I am in a hurry, *kyrie;* the visitors will be here before long."

"I know your brother," said the fat man, "and I have met your mother, too. I wish to talk to you about the Lady of Sorrows."

"About the Lady?" Piously, she crossed herself, and started up the last few steps. "If you have questions about her, you should speak to Father Linos. He knows everything there is to know."

She crossed the courtyard ahead of him, and reached up for the key hidden in the wall.

"That's an ingenious hiding place," he said. "Do you not worry you have shown me where it is? There are thieves about, Sambeca. Perhaps you should take more care."

She didn't answer him, but unlocked the door and, with a squeal of its hinges, pushed it open, and signaled to him to go before her. As a man of the Orthodox faith would do, he crossed to where the offertory candles lay on their plate, and picked up one of the slender tapers.

But in the sandbox, no other candle burned from which

he might light his own; no lamp was lit before the Lady's shrine. The eternal flame was out, and without the warm light from lamps and candles, the church's magic was gone, and it could be seen for what it was: an old and cavernous building filled with gloom and shadows.

Sambeca was ripping paper from a pack of candles. He held his out to her.

"Do you have a light?" he asked. "There's nothing lit. The eternal flame is out."

She looked at him blank-faced, then seemed to come awake.

"Certainly, *kyrie,* certainly," she said. "Here, I keep the matches in this drawer, here."

She took out a box of matches, and struck a match. The fat man put his candle's wick to the flame; as the string burned away, it left a wisp of smoke hanging in the air. As the flame steadied, he held it up before his face. The light made his eyes like black glass, reflecting the flame as if a fire burned behind them.

Startled, she turned away, and replaced the matchbox in the drawer.

"I must get on," she said, to herself, or him. "Any minute, they'll be here, and I need a duster."

She was going to leave him to attend to her little chores, but the fat man touched her arm, and stopped her.

"Sambeca," he said, quietly. "Why is the lamp not lit?"

"I'm running late, *kyrie,*" she said. "I was attending Sotiris's funeral, and it's thrown me out. I'll get to the lamp in a moment, if you'll excuse me."

The fat man placed his candle in the sandbox, where its flame grew, and cast long shadows on the walls.

"You surprise me," he said. "I would have thought a woman as devout as you would have made that your very first task. Do you not do so, usually? Yet the Lady's lamp is out. Will she not be annoyed at your disrespect?"

"You're right, *kyrie*, of course," she said. "Of course you're right. I'll do it now."

She reached out for the matches, but he stepped forward, placing his hand on hers to stop her.

"Please, do not do it on my account," he said. "I am not of the Orthodox faith, and it gives no offense to me. I merely came to light a candle for old Sotiris, who died so needlessly."

He watched her, and she looked at him, but didn't speak.

The fat man filled in the words he had expected from her.

"May his memory be eternal," he said.

She repeated the phrase after him, but did not make a cross.

"Your heart just isn't in it, is it?" asked the fat man.

"In what, *kyrie?*"

"In any of it. What, after all, is the point of worshipping a false idol?"

Her expression showed shock; it was impossible to say if it was real, or acted.

"What do you mean?"

"You feel betrayed, Sambeca; of course you do; and like all injured humans, your instinct was for revenge. But I have something for you which I hope will placate you, to an extent at least. It is what you have longed for, these years gone by. Sadly—there are no words which can soften the blow—what I bring you is not in the form you have longed for."

The color drained from her face.

"Who are you?" she asked.

"Who I am is not important," he said. "But I bring you a gift which you must take, but for which you will not thank me."

He placed his holdall on the tiled floor, and unzipped it to take out the shoebox tied round with dirty, white ribbon.

"You should sit," he said, and he indicated the chair used by the offertory box's guardians. Sambeca hesitated. "Please."

She sat down, and took on the prim pose of pious women: knees pressed together, feet flat on the floor, hands in her lap.

"I have not opened the box," he said, "not since it was fastened up, and hidden. But I believe I know what's in there. It is your right to open it, not mine."

"Hidden? Where was it hidden? Who hid it?"

"It does not matter where I found it. What matters is that it has been brought back to the light of day."

Pale-faced and wary, she held out her hands to take the shoebox, which he handed to her with great care.

"What is it, *kalé?*" she asked, quietly. "I am afraid."

"Your fear is understandable," he said, "but there is no point in putting off the moment, which has, in my view, been delayed far too long already."

With shaking fingers, she pulled at the ribbon ends to untie the bow, and the ribbon fell from the box into her lap.

"Open it," he urged. "Have courage, and open it."

She placed the flats of her hands on the ends of the box lid; then, she hesitated. The box's odor—of damp earth and cobwebs, of age and withered roses—was discouraging, but she pressed her lips in determination, and lifted the lid.

She looked inside, and gave a cry.

He held out his hand to take the lid and, extending her arm slowly, she gave it to him. The open box was lined with torn sheeting, thickly folded and stained with dark fluids. The dried, dead heads of several rosebuds lay amongst the bones of a very young infant, mostly still in place to form the body's living shape, the tiny, toothless skull face up and staring.

She looked up at him with tear-filled eyes.

"Is it her?" she asked, in a voice barely audible. "Is this my little girl?"

"I'm afraid it is, Sambeca," he said, sadly. "All the years of prayers you offered begging for her return have yielded fruit, and brought her back. But not—I am so sorry, believe me—as the well-grown child you had so hoped for."

With the tenderest touch of her fingertips, she stroked the naked skull, and touched the skeleton's minute bones with such deep sorrow that the brightness of tears appeared in the fat man's eyes.

"This is not an answered prayer," she said quietly. "This is the Devil's work, to return my child to me in this way. Where did you find her?"

"In the same place I found the Lady of Sorrows, who guarded her. The Lady herself was keeping watch over your child. You know, Sambeca, I spent some time considering whether I should bring the child to you, or whether it was better to allow you to continue in your hope. But I realized that, for you to have taken the action you did, your hope was already gone."

"My hope was taken from me," she said, bitterly. "My hope was stolen."

"I know you think that," said the fat man. "But your daughter has been dead many years; and even miracle work-ers here below—even the Lady of Sorrows—cannot restore life to the dead. Do you want to tell me your story? Give me your version of events, and I will listen with my full atten-tion. And you have my word, I shall give fair judgment when I know the facts as you believe them to be."

"I'll tell you nothing," she said. "Mama will be angry if she knows I have said anything to anyone."

"I have no fear of your mother," said the fat man, "and you need have none either. There are much higher author-ities than your mother, Sambeca, and I will grant you their protection, if I think you warrant it."

"You can't protect me from her," she said, bending low over the skeleton in the shoebox.

"Her authority is only in your mind, and your fear of her disproportionate to the power she actually wields. She is an old woman, sick and dependent on you for her care, her survival even. You are afraid to feel anything for her but obei-sance; but I suspect she should have been the target of your rage. Which is not to say," he added quickly, "that you should take it out on her. Violence is only very rarely an appropriate answer."

"He deserved it," she said, once again stroking the skull. "He made fools of us all. He stole my only hope."

"Tell me your story, from the beginning."

She touched the tiny finger bones, being careful not to disturb them where they lay. Then she looked up at him, and began to speak.

"I was pregnant," she said, "pregnant and unmarried. I had disgraced her, she said, and the problem had to be fixed. She made all kinds of brews—foul stuff, from every plant in that garden. She might have killed me; she didn't care. She cared about the family name. I was sick, and ill for weeks, but my little girl hung on inside me; she just kept growing, and hanging on. Right to the very end, there wasn't much to see; Mama kept feeding me potions which made me ill, and stopped me gaining weight. When there was a danger I would show, she kept me shut indoors, and told everyone I had caught an infection so they wouldn't come visiting and catch it themselves.

"But she didn't have to shut me away for long. My little girl..." She bent over the box, and whispered endearments— *my little love, my little partridge, my baby girl.* "She came early, and she was very small. Mama wrapped her in a blanket, and gave her to me to hold. I held her for a while. I tried to feed her, but she only wanted sleep, so I just nursed her as she slept. Then Mama came in, and said I should sleep myself, that I should get some rest, that she'd look after my little one whilst I slept. And so I handed her over."

She fell silent. To comfort her, the fat man touched her shoulder, but her body stiffened and he took his hand away.

"What happened then, Sambeca?"

"From then to now, I haven't seen her. She gave my daughter away—her own granddaughter! She gave her to some gypsies who had been in town: gave them my daughter and paid them to be gone. She told me what she'd done, and I went after them. I tried to follow them, but I was weak from illness, and from giving birth. I didn't get far, and when I crawled home, she locked me in the house for the next week, until they were far away and I had no way to trace them.

"But I wasn't disheartened. I knew what to do. We had here in this very town the answerer of all prayers! I became a servant to our Lady. I took care of her home, and made her home my work. I put myself in her service, and every day I prayed to her, morning and night, for my daughter's return. I knew that she would answer me, in time. And these past few days, I thought that she had answered me. When I saw those gypsies back in town—who could forget him? I'd watched him from the window in the last days of my pregnancy, selling shoes from that old car of his. It's the same car still—can you believe it?—or one very like it, anyway. There aren't many cars that look like that one. I thought my prayers had been answered, that my little girl was back and I could at least see her, see what she had grown into, maybe even speak to her, face-to-face. Ten years old, she would have been. I went to find him, and he told me she was dead!"

She covered her face, and wept; but outside, voices were approaching, as the day's first visitors arrived. Carefully, he replaced the shoebox lid and took the box from her; raising her to her feet by placing a hand under her arm, he led her out into the courtyard, past the arriving tourists and round to the back of the church. There, he sat her down on a seat with a view of the sea, and gave her back the box, which she held between both hands like the precious object it was.

"What did you do then, Sambeca?" he asked. "When the gypsy told you your daughter was dead, what did you do?"

"I came to the church to pray, to say prayers for her soul. But there were others here, cleaning, so I couldn't pray. Instead, I helped them. Then you came in with that woman. I heard what you said, about the Lady having been stolen, and suddenly everything made sense. I knew she would have answered my prayers, if she had heard them; but she wasn't here to hear. I'd spent my years pleading with the Lady, but the Lady wasn't here. No copy can have her power. That's why she hadn't answered!

"And I grew angry. I grew angrier than I had ever been before. I knew what had happened to the Lady, even if you didn't. I knew who'd taken her, and put a copy in her place. Who is the only one who could copy her so we would all be fooled? Sotiris! Who else? He'd made a copy of her, and sold our beautiful Lady to someone else, set her adrift in the world and left us with no hope of answered prayers. He was to blame! He did this to us!"

She looked down at the box, and placed both hands on the lid.

"So what did you do?"

"I wanted revenge! I wanted to hurt him the same way he'd hurt me, and I wanted him to suffer. But I couldn't strike his heart, the way I've been struck, so I thought I'd strike him how I best could."

"And how was that?"

"I poisoned him."

"With what?"

"With what came to hand."

"Which was?"

"I'd been cleaning the lamps. I had the brass polish in my hand. I went and took the soup from Father Linos's—he never eats, not in this heat—and I poured in what was left in the bottle. Then I offered Sotiris the soup, and he took it. It was God's will; if God hadn't willed it, he wouldn't have let Sotiris take the soup, or eat it. I didn't think he'd eat it, anyway. It smelled bad, of the ammonia that's in the polish. I suppose I thought, if nothing else, he'd have a bad taste in his mouth."

"You really didn't think he'd eat it?"

She hesitated.

"No," she said. "No, I didn't. I wanted him to; I wanted him to suffer. But the polish smelled so strong. No one would have eaten it."

"And yet he did. When you knew that he was dead, what did you think?"

"I knew it wasn't my fault. No one would have eaten that soup. It smelled like Brasso."

"What kind of soup was it?"

"It was avgolemono," she said. "I always make avgolemono on a Wednesday."

The fat man smiled.

"How perfect," he said. "Absolutely the perfect weapon.

Soup flavored with lemons. There was a reason why he ate it, Sambeca, and you are responsible for his death. He died from your poisoning, though I am inclined to think your rage had made you mad, and you were not, at that time, responsible for your actions. Would you have acted differently if you had known the facts?"

"What facts?"

"The most important is that you targeted the wrong man. It was not Sotiris who painted the copy, but Mercuris, who seems to be considering a career in wholesale forgery. If you had set your bait for him, you are quite right, he would not have taken it, and your rage-filled gesture would have done no damage."

"Then it was meant to be. 'Vengeance is mine, saith the Lord.' "

"More often, he leaves it to men to sort out their own squabbles. You have suffered a great deal, Sambeca. But did you really have murder in your heart? Perhaps you did. Let me ask you this: when you became pregnant, was there no question of you marrying the father? Why was it not arranged that you should do so?"

"I have to go," she said, suddenly.

"Sambeca, answer me. Was there no question of your marrying?"

"None at all."

"Why? Was he a married man? Were there family issues, some rift or disagreement?"

"It was a family issue," she said, "though not the way you think. I must go."

But he grasped her arm to stop her.

"I have had many of my answers," he said, "so don't deny me the last pieces of this sad jigsaw. Who was the father, and why was it impossible you should marry?"

"I will not say," she said quietly. "My mother says, rarely in mankind's history has one little child brought so much shame upon one family. I won't add to that shame."

"The little one did no wrong," he said. "What do you think we should do with her, now you've found her?"

Sadly, she looked down at the box.

"What can I do with her? If the people find out, there'll be the scandal Mama always feared; but I want her to have a proper burial, the right services and blessings."

"I must speak honestly, Sambeca, and say I see in you no remorse for the course you took, even though I have told you that it was not the man you killed who painted the forgery. And murder is murder, a crime I can never condone. So I propose a solution that will satisfy my wish for justice, and yours for the best for your child. You are quite right that, if you have her buried here, you will bear the weight of disapproval and disgrace. The people here are no different from any others, and will pass their own judgment on you, right or wrong. I am going to offer you an alternative to family scandal. I shall take the child's remains with me, and have them interred in some place far away. I know a place to the north, where it is peaceful, where there are flowers in spring, and a view of the sea, and of the ships passing. There are other young souls like her there; she won't ever be alone. And you may be sure that, if you send a blessing to her with the northbound boats, in that place it will be sure to reach her.

"And what will be your punishment is the knowledge that you had her back with you, and lost her once again. That seems to me to be a fair exchange for taking Sotiris's life. I am sorry for you, but Sammy has lost his grandfather, Tina her father; and curmudgeonly and miserable and sick as he may have been, Sotiris's time had not yet come. So say your goodbyes to this little one you loved so deeply and knew so briefly, and hand her back to me. She will be well cared for, I promise you. The Lady will now be restored to her proper home, so change your prayers to pray for your daughter's immortal soul, and they will be heard."

She lifted the lid and gave a last long look at the tiny bones, bending to kiss the skull. He took both box and lid from her, and carefully zipped it back inside his bag.

He gave a small bow, and left her weeping with a view of the sea, and of the passing ships.

# Fifteen

The fat man returned to the shaded bench where he had waited for Sambeca, but the day had moved on, and the bench now stood in full sun. Another tour boat was arriving, tying up alongside those moored rail-to-rail at the quay; its passengers waited for the gangplank to be lowered so they could join in choosing postcards from the stands and ordering ice cream and coffee from unsmiling waiters. The majority of visitors already landed labored sweating up the church steps, on their pilgrimage to what they believed was the famous Lady.

The fat man's mood was pensive. Despite the sun, he took a seat on the bench, and, closing his eyes against the crowd and the bustle of the place, folded his arms over his stomach, thinking he might sleep; but his eyes had been closed only a minute when a hand touched his shoulder, and a voice spoke to rouse him.

"*Kyrie*," said the voice. "*Kyrie,* I need to speak with you."

The fat man opened his eyes. The gypsy stood before him, his dark face serious, his manner agitated.

"Ah," said the fat man, pulling himself up and indicating the seat beside him. "I've been expecting you. Please, sit."

"Expecting me, *kyrie?*" asked the gypsy, sitting down. "Why in the hell would you be expecting me?"

"You have come to return my property, have you not?"

The gypsy frowned; then he held out his closed hand, and the fat man, smiling, held his open palm beneath it. The gypsy opened his fingers, and the fat man's ring fell into his own palm, glinting in the sun. The gypsy quickly drew back his hand, and wiped it on his trousers as if he feared contamination.

"How did you know?" he asked.

"You didn't like my ring," said the fat man, still smiling. "People never do. It never leaves me for long." He slipped it on to his little finger, and held it up to admire it. "Perhaps it suits my hand better than yours. What do you think?"

"I think it's a thing of evil," said the gypsy. "A cursed thing."

"Cursed?" asked the fat man. "Now, why on earth would you say that?"

"It brings bad dreams," said the gypsy, his face showing distaste. "Ever since I had that damned thing, it brought me bad dreams."

"I'm sorry to hear that. What kind of dreams?"

"Bad things," said the gypsy. "That's all."

"You know," said the fat man, "people have said to me in the past that the ring acts like a conscience. Did it remind you of things past?"

"Past or future, what does it matter? I have no need of that ring's bad luck."

"Well, I can't say I'm sorry to have it back," said the fat

man. "And since you are here, I remember you still owe me for some peaches."

The gypsy delved in his pocket, and brought out a fistful of money.

"How much?" he asked. "I'll pay you, and then our business is at an end."

"Rather than cash," said the fat man, "I want you to pay me with answers. There are some questions I want to ask you. Put the money away."

Reluctantly, the gypsy replaced the money in his pocket.

"Please," he said, "be quick. I have customers who want shoes, and we leave this island tonight."

"My questions rely on your memory," said the fat man. "I want to ask you about a night some years ago. A night when you were last on Kalkos, when a woman here gave you an infant."

The gypsy put on an expression of bafflement.

"An infant, *kyrie?* I have no idea what you mean."

"Yes, you do," said the fat man. "And if you don't tell me the truth, I shall send you bad dreams for the rest of your life. Were you given an infant, yes or no?"

Reluctantly, the gypsy inclined his head.

"I want to know what happened to her."

The gypsy looked regretful.

"The baby wasn't well, not from the first. She was weak. I carried her myself at first, then gave her to my wife to nurse. By the time we got to the mainland, she wasn't breathing. My mother said it was *astera,* that she'd caught cold from the starlight. We shouldn't have taken her out by night, not with her so young. But we had no choice; the infant had to be hidden. There was some family difficulty. The child was a bastard, I knew that; that much was plain."

The fat man gave him a long look.

"Why did the woman give the child to you?"

He shrugged.

"The same reason they all do, the same reason they give us their unwanted dogs and cats. Anything they don't want, they give us. That old radio you liked came to me that way, as we passed some house. They'd give us their own grand-mothers, if they only dared. I've been offered other children, before now. Orphans, bastards. Children no one wants. They offer them to gypsies because we'll take them, and move on, and remove the stain from the family laundry. A baby and a few coins, and your embarrassment is gone."

"Are you in the baby-selling business, then?"

He laughed.

"I? No, *kyrie*. If I were in that business, would I be poor as you see me now? There's money to be made in that trade, in the cities especially; rich, barren women, rich men who want an heir and can't father one. Oh, there's money there, for the unscrupulous. And why not? Both families lose an embarrass-ment, the one of an unwanted child, the other the stigma of barrenness. But that has never been my motive." He spat on the ground to underline the truth of his words. "I swear it."

"So there was no other reason she gave the baby to you, other than that you were passing the door, so to speak?"

"I think she couldn't believe her luck, that we were in town at the time. A baby is a difficult thing to hide. The noise they make crying would make your ears bleed."

The fat man frowned.

"She was no relative of yours, then?"

"My relatives travel with me. All the relatives I know of, at least." He narrowed his eyes, and looked at the fat man. "What exactly do you mean, when you ask if she was a relative? You mean the infant, don't you?" He gave a wide and unkind smile, showing several missing teeth. "You think she was my bastard, that I fathered her!"

The fat man gave a nod of concurrence.

"The thought had crossed my mind," he said.

The gypsy gave a bitter laugh.

"No, *kyrie,* she was no daughter of mine. I was a married man then, as I am now, and I have kept the vows I made. I love my wife, and I would do nothing to disrespect her."

"So what did you do with the baby when she died?"

"I brought her back. I came alone; for us all to return would have drawn attention. I put the little one in a box, and pretended I was bringing a pair of shoes. I handed her to the grandmother with my apologies, and my tears—I admit it cut me to lose her; I felt my part in her death—and I left. She had paid me a good sum not to come back. I had promised her ten years."

"And now ten years are up?"

"By now, for sure. I kept my word on that."

"When you brought back the remains, you didn't see the mother?"

"She said the mother was unwell. I never saw the mother, until..."

"Until when?"

"Until a couple of days ago. She saw me in the church. She knew my face, I suppose, and followed me."

"What happened then?"

"She asked me in a roundabout way about her daughter. She wanted to be sure I was the man. Maybe she'd bothered every man of our tribe who came here; maybe she'd put her obtuse questions to a hundred others before me. Her questions were so indirect, I didn't understand her meaning at first. I thought she was some madwoman; I still think she is touched. When I told her I was the man who'd taken her baby, she grasped my hand and begged me to take her to see the girl. So it was down to me to tell her that the baby was dead."

"And when you told her that?"

"She said nothing. She left me."

"Why were you in the church?"

"Same as everybody. Paying my respects."

"Or asking for a miracle?"

"A miracle?"

"Why did you really take the baby? Weren't there mouths enough of your own to feed?"

"I have to go now. I have customers." He moved to stand, but the fat man stopped him.

"Give me a moment more," he said. "Perhaps I can help you. You may not be the world's most honorable man, but I think in this matter, where this child was concerned, you were prepared to take her in and love her as your own. Not every man would do that. But you had your reasons, didn't you?"

"Meaning?"

"Your impotence."

The gypsy flushed red, and angrily stood.

"How dare you!" he shouted. "*Pousti!* You insult me as a man!"

"I do not mean to insult you," said the fat man, calmly. "I mean to offer you help, practical help, and the possibility of fathering a daughter of your own. Please, sit down and listen to me. Your shouting will draw attention, which is the opposite of what you want. Sit down, please, or I may start shouting too, and then the world and his brother will know of your predicament." Reluctantly, the gypsy sat back down. "The children with you—whose are they?"

"They are other strays, poor wretches who had no home. My wife and I love them as our own."

"I'm pleased to hear it. But I must assume that, despite your devoted prayers and offerings here and elsewhere you've traveled, the saints have not responded?"

"There seems to be no help." Despondently, he lowered his head.

"Let me offer you this." The fat man reached down to his holdall, and took from it a bag of dried herbs. "Make tea with this, and drink it twice a day. The taste is foul, but take heart in the foulness. It will help. And promise me one thing: when your wife conceives, write and let me know. In my line of work, I need to hear good news from time to time. Here is my card. My help is your reward for your generous actions. You took the child with good intentions, and when she died you brought her home when you might have buried her in any ditch or forest. What happened next was not your fault."

"What did happen next?"

The fat man sighed.

"What happens too often. Lies, deceit and cruelty. When your own children come along, be kind to them, always. Before you go, I have one more question. Did you know who had fathered the child?"

The gypsy was silent for a moment.

"I knew," he said.

"And will you tell me?"

"What is it to you?"

"I take a poor view of a man who uses a woman, and fails to marry her. In my view, he should have stepped out of the shadows, and made her an honest woman. It is the baby's father who's at the root of this tragedy, and he should be confronted, and pay some price."

The gypsy shrugged.

"Your aim is noble, and to be applauded," he said, "but it was never going to be, in this case. A marriage was not possible between those two."

"She told you the name?"

"I know who it was."

"Then tell me, and let me tie up the loose ends in this case before I leave."

And the gypsy told.

## Sixteen

In the aftermath of the earthquake, the livestock in the pens at Agiris's house seemed subdued. The poultry were gathered together at the center of the run, crouched and blinking, abnormally still; the rabbits had scattered to the perimeters of their pen and made small groups, three or four together, huddled as if weathering a storm; their smell was somewhat reduced, sterilized by cement and plaster dust.

The doorway of the house was open, and on the path between the penned animals Nassia sat, disgusted and disgruntled, on a kitchen chair, her ulcerated leg supported on the cushion-topped milking stool. Her widow's black was gray with powdery dust; her frown was deep, and murderous.

The fat man stood before her.

"How are you, *kyria?*" he asked. "I'm pleased to see you survived the drama unscathed."

"Unscathed? I need a bed to lie in after the shock I've had, and here they have me sitting out in the yard! You see how my children care for me, *kyrie.* They give better care to the livestock than they do to me. They'll have me dead yet; they'll be glad to see the day!"

"Surely it isn't safe to be in the house at this time?" asked the fat man. "There is always a risk of aftershocks, as you must know. In fact your property seems to have survived very well. There is considerable damage elsewhere, I'm afraid."

"I feared for my very life, *kyrie,*" she said. "I feared for my very life." She crossed herself several times, and let her head fall back and closed her eyes, as if reliving the ordeal she had undergone.

The fat man looked towards the house.

"Are your family not here to take care of you now?" he asked.

"My son only," she said, her eyes still closed. "I think he is trying to make chamomile tea, to calm my nerves. Men don't know how to make tea! Sambeca isn't here; I have no idea where she is. Wouldn't you have thought she would be here? Wouldn't you think she'd come running to make sure I'm all right?"

"She has other things on her mind, just now," said the fat man. "By which I mean her own welfare, and that of another. She and I were talking, for a while."

"You were talking to my daughter? Why should you be talking to her?"

In the doorway, Agiris appeared, carrying a cup and saucer. On seeing the fat man, his expression remained indifferent. He walked cautiously down the footpath towards his mother, watching the cup for spills.

"Hello again," he said to the fat man.

"How are you, Agiris?" asked the fat man. "I was just

saying to your mother how glad I am your household has suffered no serious damage."

"A little plaster off the ceiling, is all. Nothing that can't be swept up when Sambeca gets back. Here you are, Mama; your tea."

He handed the cup and saucer to his mother, who glared at both him and the cup; she didn't thank Agiris, but he seemed not to expect it.

"I'm making coffee," he said to the fat man. "Do you want one?"

"Thank you," said the fat man. "I would appreciate it. No sugar."

"Pull up a chair," said Agiris. He pointed to a kitchen chair at the door; its cane seat was frayed, and one of its cross-supports was missing. "Here you are, Mama," he said, cheerfully. "This gentleman will keep you company whilst I make coffee."

As Agiris went inside, the fat man fetched the old chair from the door, and placed it opposite Nassia's, so he was facing her. Sitting close, the smell from her wound was pungent, quite distinct from the ammoniac smell of the livestock.

Nassia tasted her tea.

"Too sweet," she said. "He cares nothing for me, or my comfort."

"Is that truly so?" asked the fat man.

"Oh, I'm a burden to them. Make no mistake, *kyrie;* my own children consider me a burden."

"And are you a burden to them?" asked the fat man. "Is their view in any way justified?" In annoyance, she glared at him; her lips worked, as if she would damn his impertinence. "By which I mean, do you stay cheerful through your incapacity, and make it a pleasure for your children to nurse you?"

As if she had not heard him, she tasted her tea again.

"And it's too hot," she said. "I don't know where Sambeca is. She always adds a little cold water to the hot."

"If you asked your son, I'm sure he would do likewise," said the fat man.

She gave no reply, but laid her head on the back of her chair and stared up at the empty sky.

"The damage at the bishop's house is considerable," said the fat man. "That's what I came to tell your son. No doubt he will want to go and see what must be done. Happily they were able to proceed with Sotiris's funeral, despite the drama."

Nassia made a cross over her breast.

"May his memory be eternal," she said. "They'll do right by him, and grieve him properly. That family takes its responsibilities seriously. They know how to honor the dead."

"Most families do." The fat man folded his arms across his chest, and watched Nassia brush some of the dust off her clothes. "Most families, but not all. Sotiris was an old man whose time, it seems, had come. If you believe the doctor."

"Why shouldn't you believe the doctor? Sotiris was ailing, as I am myself. When the plaster started falling, I thought I was going to join him. I expected to be buried alive in my own home."

"Speaking of being buried," said the fat man, "and of the

bishop's house, the catacombs up there are in a state of collapse."

Nassia looked at him; her face grew pale.

"What do you mean, *kyrie?*" she asked, in a voice which began as a croak. She coughed to clear her throat, and her voice strengthened. "This dust everywhere is choking; it'll do damage to our lungs. In what way, in a state of collapse?"

"I've suggested to Father Linos they must be sealed immediately," said the fat man, dramatically. "Immediately. The whole roof is ready to collapse. There's no question of anyone going in there. Which should be good news, to you. There'll be no more trouble from vampires and revenants there."

Nassia's face showed nothing.

"Where is Sambeca?" she asked.

"You know," said the fat man, "to anyone going by, we look like ordinary folks just passing the time."

"What else should we be," she snapped, "except ordinary folks?"

"Normally, I would suggest holding this conversation inside, out of the sight of your neighbors; but your neighbors are anyway occupied with their own business after the earthquake. And since we can never be quite certain when the next shock may hit—today, or next week, or next year—we're better out here, out of harm's way, maintaining the pretense of a normal family entertaining a visitor. You've had many years of practice at normality, after all."

Nassia leaned forward to make her leg more comfortable, lifting her lower limb with both hands, and wincing at the pain.

"Whatever you have to say," she said, adjusting her leg,

"say it now, and be on your way. I smell trouble on you, *kyrie*. This family needs no more trouble."

"Well, then it's unfortunate you may find yourself once more in its way," said the fat man. "You know, I have often found that trouble stems from secrets. Secrets that are hidden in the dark have a nasty habit of sprouting shoots, which in turn are often determined to see daylight. And secrets fester; fester as your leg is festering. No matter what you put on a festering secret, it won't heal. Though your leg is in a bad way, there's a chance with the right treatment that the wound might close, the skin might grow back and no one would ever know the wound had been there. But secrets aren't like that, Nassia. With secrets, the favorite salve is lies, and the favorite bandage is deception. Secrets respond very badly to those treatments. They fester worse, until they burst, like boils. Here. I have brought something to show you."

He bent to his holdall, and unzipped it, whilst Nassia watched him with suspicion.

"I have here something you will recognize," he said.

He took out the shoebox, screening it with his arm until it was free of the holdall. He stood, and held it out to her. Her face showed no emotion, except for her lower lip, which trembled.

He let the silence between them lengthen.

"Well?" he asked, at last. "Do you have nothing to say?"

"What should I have to say about some old shoebox?"

"Some old shoebox, yes, and some old ribbon that you tied around it. Am I right?"

She craned her head, trying to see around him.

"Where is my daughter?" she demanded. "I need her to change my dressing."

"Someone tied the lid on this box to seal its contents, and hid it in the catacombs in a place where only the most curious of individuals—and yes, you may count me amongst their number—would venture to look. It took me a little while to find it, because whoever hid it did so very well. But since you claim it is nothing to do with you, I shall take it away again."

"Take it, and go," she said. "Be good enough to send my daughter to me. She takes no care of me at all; a mother's a right to better treatment than I get, God alone knows."

Carefully, he replaced the shoebox in his holdall, zipped it up and gave a small bow of his head as he turned to leave her. But as he walked down the path towards the kitchen, he turned back to her, smiling grimly.

"*Kyria*," he said, "I am sorry to have to tell you that your excellent act of indifference was flawed in one regard."

"What do you mean?"

"There is one trait amongst us Greeks which overrides all others—the trait of curiosity. You, when shown this box, showed me none. What woman in your position would not have asked me to open the box, and reveal its contents? You should know that before I brought it here, I showed the box's contents to Sambeca. You ask where she is; she is contemplating what lies within this box, and the fact that I am taking it far away, for burial in some place that neither you or she will ever know. You have shown no compassion, but that doesn't mean I shall myself show none. The contents of this box will be treated with dignity, and respect, but for Sambeca's sake, not yours."

He walked away, towards the kitchen door. Behind him, he heard her call him back, and he ignored her.

"May I join you?"

Agiris was standing by the stove, watching the coffee in the *kafebriko* as it rose to the boil.

"Coffee's ready," he said. "I'll bring it out to you."

"Perhaps we could drink it in here," said the fat man. "I believe your mother and I have said all we have to say to each other, at this point."

Agiris turned away, looking through the window into the poultry pen, where the birds were recovering from their shock, pecking and preening. He looked out for several moments, before looking back at the fat man.

"I hope you haven't come to cause trouble, friend," he said. "We're not a family that looks for trouble."

"What makes you think I've come to cause trouble? Do I look like a troublemaker to you?"

"Trouble comes in many shapes and many sizes."

"Indeed it does: tall and short, fat and thin, male and female."

Agiris poured the coffee into cups which were barely clean; coffee discolored their insides, and the saucers were no match for the cups in pattern or size. He made space on the cluttered table by pushing the objects there aside—used plates, a bowl filled with peaches, a pitcher half filled with water. Everything was dusty with plaster; white lumps of it lay on the table and dresser. The fat man looked up at the ceiling, where the uneven plaster showed paler spots where the upper surface had come away, and around the light fitting a hole had opened, with the plaster fallen from it lying on the floor.

"Sit, if you've a mind to," said Agiris, indicating a chair at the table. He handed a cup to the fat man, and sat himself down. "You'll not mind the mess, I hope. Folks must take us as they find us."

The fat man also sat down.

"I suppose you don't get many visitors, Agiris?"

"Now and then," he said, "just now and then. We're not very sociable, as a family."

He bent to blow on his coffee. Out of the corner of his eye, the fat man saw some vermin run along the skirting board and under the sink, not pausing even to sniff the saucer of poisoned grain laid out as bait.

"Still troubled by mice?" asked the fat man. "They don't seem to be attracted to your bait."

"It's not that," said Agiris, scratching vigorously at an itch inside his ear. "It's that the damn things aren't hungry. They find all they want outside, around the livestock, then come in here to get cool, or find warmth. I'd be better off leaving down poisoned water."

"Is your poison water-soluble, then?"

"No," said Agiris, "it's not. Shall I tell you the secret, friend? It's free, and it's simple. I take the poison from peach kernels, dried and ground. There's enough cyanide in one or two of those little nuts to kill several rats, or mice. If the buggers were only hungry enough to eat them."

The fat man nodded.

"Ingenious," he said. "But you would have to eat a lot of peaches to go into production."

"A lot of peaches," Agiris agreed. "Same as a man would have to eat a lot of kernels to do himself any damage."

"It's an interesting thing about poisons," said the fat man, lifting his coffee cup to his mouth. Before he drank, he gave a discreet sniff; noticing nothing suspect, he took a sip. "They come in so many forms. Quite noxious poisons can kill a man, and yet go undetected, if no one is looking for them. Take Sotiris's case, for example. The doctor has happily signed his death off as natural causes, because he suspects no other agent. Who would poison old Sotiris, after all?"

"Who would?" asked Agiris. "There was nothing out of the ordinary about Sotiris's death. The miracle is it didn't happen sooner. The old bugger was glad to go, I have no doubt of it. A more miserable old bastard you couldn't wish to meet."

"Well, there again, misery takes many forms, doesn't it? There's the melancholy misery of old age, and the undiluted misery of a mother who's lost a child. And then there's the long, drawn-out misery of people forced together by circumstances, who can't be free of each other because of some mistake one of them made."

Agiris shook his head, and gave his satyr's smile.

"You're a deep one, friend. Do you never talk in anything but riddles?"

"You know, I hate to add to anyone's misery if it is undeserved. Would you describe yourself as a contented man, Agiris?"

Agiris shrugged.

"As the next man. What's it to you?"

"I'll tell you what it is to me. I came here as a diversion, to see the miraculous icon. I will travel a great distance to see a miracle; I like to see how people's lives can change. But the miracle I found was unexpected; I found the genuine article gone, and a lot of people paying homage to a piece of art worth no more than this table. No, I am being unfair. As a piece of work, the copy has great merit."

"Copy? What are you talking about?"

"Were you not in the know, Agiris? I'm sorry, but I don't believe that. Nothing happens in the bishop's house that you don't know about. Well, whether you knew it or not, the icon hanging in the church has for some time been a fake. Weeks, months or years, it doesn't matter. What matters is, your sister didn't know, but she found out, very recently. And she blamed the man who painted the fake icon for the lack of answers to her prayers."

"Sambeca? What does she have to do with a forged icon?"

"So you knew about the swap? I notice you are not questioning me closely."

He sighed.

"OK, yes, I knew about that. Father Linos wasn't likely to keep it from me. But he swore me to secrecy, and I didn't tell. On my life, I never told a soul."

"What else have you never told, Agiris? What is the secret you all share, in this house?"

"Secret? What secret?"

"Let me show you, if you won't tell me."

Again, he reached for the holdall, and took out the shoe-box, and laid it on the table.

"Have you any interest in mythology, Agiris?" he asked. "Well, whether you have or not, I'm going to tell you a story. It's a love story."

Agiris gave a cynical laugh.

"Often, men don't like love stories," said the fat man. "But for every man, there's a love story that resonates. Have you ever been in love, Agiris?"

"Why are you talking to me about love?"

"I'm going to tell you the story of a young woman called Canace—does her name mean anything to you?"

Agiris shook his head, and seemed more interested in his coffee.

"Well, Canace was a daughter of Aeolus, king of the winds, and she fell deeply in love with a young man named Macareus. Being unmarried, they kept their affair secret, but unfortunately Canace became pregnant and bore a child. When Aeolus found out—he heard the child cry as a nurse tried to smuggle the baby from the palace—he ordered the child to be exposed and so destroyed—"left in some lonely place to be eaten by dogs and birds," I believe is how it's phrased—and sent Canace a sword to commit suicide. Which Canace did. What happened to Macareus is less clear. Some say he too committed suicide, others that he survived and placed the baby in the same tomb as its dead mother. Are you thinking all this was a little extreme? That Aeolus was overreacting to a commonplace love affair?

Then that's because I omitted one important fact. Canace and Macareus were brother and sister."

Agiris froze.

"Here," said the fat man. "Take a look inside the box."

Agiris was reluctant, but curious. The fat man lifted the lid, releasing the strange smells of bones and dead roses, and Agiris peered inside.

"What is this?" he asked, quietly.

"You mean, who is this, of course," said the fat man. "And the answer is, this is your daughter."

Slowly, Agiris rose from the table; his ugly face was made uglier still by rage.

"Out!" he shouted. "Get out of this house!"

But the fat man remained seated at the table. Calmly, and with great care, he replaced the lid on the shoebox, and moved to replace the shoebox in the holdall.

"I knew you were trouble!" shouted Agiris. "Get out of here, or by God I'll throw you out with my bare hands!"

The fat man's expression was dangerous.

"That you will not do," he said, in measured tones. "You will force me to do nothing. I will leave this place when I am ready to do so, and I shall not be ready to do so until you and I have discussed this matter in full. So sit down, and I suggest you stop shouting, because if you shout, I shall shout too, and your neighbors will have the full story from my own lips, at full volume. Which would be a great pity, Agiris, after all these years of keeping it under the carpet."

Red-faced, livid, Agiris glared at him; when he spoke, his voice, though low and controlled, was filled with anger.

"You have no right to come here with this..." He wafted his hand over the shoebox, and shook his head. "This... object!"

"Object? Object? Did you not understand what I have said to you? This child was your own progeny, your flesh and blood."

"Why do you say that? How can that possibly be mine?"

"She is your child, Agiris; she is the child you fathered when you forced yourself on your sister. That was a base act, an abomination before all the gods, and you know it."

"Who are you?" he asked. "Why have you come?"

"My reasons for coming here were innocent enough. But your sister is not altogether well, Agiris. Her mind has been troubled for many years, and that trouble has allowed a seed of—I won't say madness, for she isn't mad; but she is struggling for her sanity at present. And you, my friend—you are the root of her trouble. How could she not be troubled—impregnated by her own brother, then spending years praying for the return of a child she believed to be the only good thing to come out of your damned union, only to discover that the child is long dead, and that her prayer is answered in this terrible way—by the revealing of her baby's bones. Are you so callous, man, that you feel nothing for her?" He shook his head. "Why did you do it? And why do you not see what you have done?"

Suddenly, Agiris slumped in his chair and, laying his head on his arms, began to sob: sobs from a broken heart, in gulps which choked him as if they had waited years to be released.

"I was a different man then!" he said. "I was hardly more

than a boy! Look at me, look at my ugliness! None of the girls would look at me! There was to be no marriage, no children for me, no family outside of here. But I was taunted by my need; I spent my days around Priapus, and he taunted me. She was the only one available. We shared a room; one night I had been dreaming of some woman, and I crossed to her bed, covered her mouth and had my way with her. I knew it was wrong. But she said nothing. She never complained. She just avoided me when I came near."

"So you're telling me it was once only? Just one slip?"

He shook his head.

"I cannot say that, in truth. I had a taste for it then. I forced her, several times; she accepted it dumbly, like the docile creature she is, like one born to serve. Then it became obvious she was pregnant, though she tried to hide it. Somehow Mother knew it was me; I suppose she heard more than I gave her credit for. We became tied in this secret, and thought perhaps we'd got away with it, when the gypsy took the baby away. But he came back, and there could be no Christian burial. Mother knew it would break Sambeca's heart. She put the baby in the catacombs, and then put out stories to keep people away. Not people: to keep Sambeca away. Sambeca cleans that house; if she had known what lay under her feet, she would have gone stark mad.

"My mother's rage at me was cold, and has grown colder; she's as angry now as she was the day she first found out. But cold anger is not the same as screaming rage. It's frozen her heart, so now her heart is chilled cold as the grave. My sister's indifference to me—there's no affection left, I killed all that—her indifference is hard enough to cope with, but my mother's rejection, I feel every day. From the day the gypsy returned, she's never spoken to me—not one single word. The last words she spoke to me, before she took that box away to hide it, were to tell me I must never tell Sambeca, and to tell me I was dead to her as the child she was burying. When we're alone, she treats me as if I don't exist. A million times I have begged her forgiveness, and every time she turns her face away. And so I am punished a million-fold for my crime. My crime was lust, and rape, and I accept that; but I would rather have done twenty years inside some state-run prison and come out having served my time, than live my whole life the way we're forced to—miserable in each other's company, but desperate for appearance's sake to keep our misery hidden. What are my animals but poor substitutes for the family I no longer have? They at least don't judge me. So take away the evidence of my transgression! I do not need reminding! If there were one thing, anything, I could do to correct the mistake I made, I would do it in an instant. I've thought of suicide, but that brings more disgrace. And so my punishment is to live it out, tied to them both and their unspoken reproaches. My own mother cannot stand the sight of me! What worse punishment can there be for a son? You have the word of one who knows, and suffers."

"I am sorry for you, Agiris." The fat man rose, and put away the box. "You're right, your punishment needs me to add no more. Your sister joins you now in guilty torment, having in an ill-judged moment given in to her own understandable but misdirected anger. And your mother has built her anger into high, high walls that no one, it seems, can penetrate. If I have advice for you, it is that you persist in trying to win your mother's forgiveness, because once she is gone you will feel yourself forever damned.

"Good luck to you, Agiris, and goodbye."

Outside, Nassia sat tight-lipped in her chair. The kitchen door stood open; it seemed probable she had listened to every word.

Again, the fat man stood before her.

"You have punished him enough, in my opinion," he said. She opened her mouth to speak, but he held up his hand to stop her. "Don't interrupt. I know the truth of your situation, and I shall keep it to myself. But I cannot condone, under any circumstances, three human beings living in such misery as this. This is not why you were put here on this earth! Speak one word to your son, and you will all begin to heal. Melt one drop of the anger which freezes your heart, and you may all yet have some better years together. I do not say your family will be happy; I have seen too much of what long-term unhappiness can do to hope for that. I do not lie to you, predicting happy endings. But you can make your lives less burdensome, and yourselves kinder to each other. I cannot force you; but whatever he has done, he is your son, and he loves you. He has given you gross offense, I know that, and he has done great wrong to Sambeca. As he has said, you would have done better to turn him over to the police, and let them deal with him in the courts. You have some fault in this, in that the guardianship of your family's name was paramount in your mind, more so, perhaps, than the wrong done to poor Sambeca. She needs you now to be a mother to her, to leave your grief for things that will never be—weddings and grandchildren—and form as best you may a family alliance. Don't let this box of bones be all there is. Be noble, if you can, and be forgiving."

Head bowed, she was silent, and after a few moments, he made his way down the path between the livestock pens.

But she called out to him.

"*Kyrie!* The little one—where are you taking her?"

He stopped, and turned.

"North," he said, "to a place where it is peaceful, where there are flowers in spring, and a view of the sea, and of the boats passing. There are other young souls like her there; she will not be alone. If you will do as I have asked, and start forgiving, you have my word she will be taken care of."

She followed him with tear-filled eyes, which blurred his image as he walked away.

# Seventeen

As evening fell, the fat man emerged from the master's cabin and climbed the stairs onto the rear deck, where Enrico was about to lay the table for dinner. On the water, the air was cool, and carried the scent of mountain oregano; the harbor lights were bright against a darkening sky, the church above striking in floodlights. Aboard the nearby boats, yellow lamps glowed; on the deck of a German yacht, a man laughed.

The fat man had dressed for the cooler evening in trousers of tan twill, and a cream shirt beneath a sweater of Italian cotton. On his feet, his shoes were newly whitened; he moved so quietly, he was behind Enrico without being heard, and made Enrico jump when he spoke.

"I'll have a cocktail before dinner," he said. "A gin and tonic. Be good enough to bring it to me up front, so I can watch the sunset. Tell Ilias after he's served dinner we'll get under way; we've lost far too much time here already. Tell him to steer for the south, and I'll eat as we travel."

With a bow of the head, Enrico left him, hiding a smile.

The fat man made his way to the prow, and leaned for a

while on the railing. He watched the dark water, where from time to time unseen creatures jumped and splashed, whilst at the horizon the lights of some northbound ship moved slowly by. Overhead, the first star, Venus, began to glint. Down below, in the galley, Ilias was whistling; on the German yacht, a woman laughed with the man.

Behind him, ice chinked against glass, and the fat man turned to take his drink.

Kara stood before him, a glass in each hand, and smiled.

"I hope you don't mind," she said. "I begged a lift. Enrico said you're heading in my direction."

He smiled.

"What direction is that?" he asked.

"Wherever you're going," she said. "As long as it has an airport. Drink?"

They knocked their glasses together.

"*Yammas,*" he said. "To us."

"*Yammas.*"

The cocktails were bitter with the tonic's quinine, sharp with a squeeze of lime, heady with juniper spirit. The fat man turned back to the sea, his arms resting on the railing. Kara leaned next to him, her forearm brushing his.

"What happened to that urgent work of yours?" he asked.

"There was something more important at this end. I knew if I didn't come back to find you now, years might go by before we met again."

"I'm pleased," he said. "But the chance of your being back at the office tomorrow is highly remote. You could be marooned aboard with us two days at least."

She smiled.

"Why so? This beautiful boat should make good time, wherever we're going."

"I'm thinking of a short detour," he said. "With a passenger aboard to entertain, it seems only courteous that we should take the prettier route."

On the rear deck, the table was laid with fine porcelain and cut glass. As he took his chair, the fat man's expression was quizzical.

"Is it my birthday?" he asked. "Is there something you're not telling me?"

"I told the boy he could lay it so, *kyrie*," said Enrico, pouring cold wine into the glasses. "I hope you don't object. He has something to celebrate."

The fat man raised his eyebrows.

"A woman?"

Enrico laughed.

"Not so special as that, no. But an event worth celebrating, nonetheless."

Ilias brought bread, and a salad of tomatoes and red onions.

"What's the occasion, young man?" asked the fat man, breaking off a piece of bread. "If it's not my birthday, it must be yours."

"It's no one's birthday, *kyrie*," said Ilias. "But I thought you would like to celebrate a change from aubergines."

"No aubergines? If there are no aubergines, what's on the menu? Please tell me this is not a return to Enrico's courgettes?"

"Let him show you," said Enrico. "Go on, boy, and bring out the food."

Ilias returned to the table carrying a silver platter, and on the platter was a fish: a large red snapper charred in dark stripes where it had rested on the barbecue grill, its eyes baked white, its fins and skin crisp. Arranged around it on the platter were four quarters of lemon.

The fat man stood up from his chair, clapped Ilias on the back and hugged him.

"Well done, indeed!" he said. "At last! Enrico, pour yourselves a glass of wine to celebrate, and let's have the story. Which bait did the trick, in the end? What time of day was it? I want to know the secret of your long-delayed success!"

"Stale bread," said Ilias, accepting a glass, "rolled tight into small pellets. In the end, that's all I used—a leftover slice of yesterday's bread. If there's a secret, it's not very polite. I made the balls tight by wetting the bread with spit."

Kara and the fat man laughed.

"Well, however you did it, here's a toast to you. And as usual, the simple ways are the best."

Ilias served the fish. The flesh was white and juicy; but as he squeezed lemon juice over his portion, the fat man stopped, and sniffed the lemon. Its tang was sharp and citrus, but quite commonplace.

"The mystery of the Lady's disappearance grew darker after you left," he said to Kara, "and its solution involved one fascinating aspect: an icon painter who developed a passion for lemons."

As they ate, he filled in all the details, of the death at sea and the gypsy, of the catacombs and the earthquake.

"As for the lemons," he said, "I had the answer from a doctor friend of mine." He poured more wine into their glasses. "The poison that the woman used was chemical: in short, a good measure of Brasso. It made no sense to me, at first, how any man not mad or suicidal could eat food tainted with the stuff; its smell is strong, and noxious. The people in fact did think him crazy for his sniffing of the lemons, but Dr. Dinos knew better. The answer lay in Parkinson's disease, which not only causes a palsied shaking, but has very strange effects on the sense of smell. Some things, the sufferer can still smell, lemons being one of them. Poor Sotiris probably comforted himself sniffing the fruit, since there was so little else left that he could smell. And one thing he couldn't smell was ammonia—the chemical which gives Brasso its potency. Without knowing it, the woman who caused his death used the perfect weapon—ammonia-laced avgolemono. When the good doctor mentioned Parkinson's, everything made sense. The old man had become eager to train his son-in-law to his craft; whatever Mercuris chose to do with the skill, whether he would use it honorably or not, Sotiris knew his painting days were over, and had little choice."

"There's something you haven't mentioned," said Kara. "What happened to the forged Lady?"

The fat man held up a finger to ask her to wait and, leaving the table, disappeared for a few moments below decks. When he returned, he carried a parcel, heavily wrapped in brown paper, sealed with tape and tied round several times with string.

He laid the parcel on the table, and held out his hands.

"Voilà," he said. "A Lady of Sorrows."

"Here?" asked Kara. "What is the Lady doing here, with you?"

"Ah, but which Lady is she? The last time I looked, we had two. Are you still convinced the Lady is a foreigner?"

"She's Russian," said Kara. "That was where she was painted, and her original home."

"I agree with you. And a piece of evidence the butcher showed me has persuaded me that, when she washed up here, it was because she had recently been kidnapped."

"What evidence?"

"A kopek coin, of little value, except to let us know that when that boat went down there was someone aboard who'd spent time in Russia. Whether they were leaving or returning, we'll never know. Perhaps it was some good soul who was taking the Lady back to her proper home. As I intend to do now."

"Hermes! What do you mean? Have you stolen the Kalkos icon?"

"Not at all. I told Father Linos of my intention to take a version of her with me. I am returning to Kiev a Lady they will venerate as she should be venerated. Perhaps it is time the Lady found her way home, as is the tradition with stolen icons."

"And in Kalkos?"

"They will venerate their Lady as they have always done."

"But which is which? Who has the copy, and who the original? Who has the miracle worker?"

"There is no reason they should not both be miracle workers, in their way. The miracle is always one of faith. The age of the work and its artist are not important."

"Will they not show her to experts, when she arrives in Kiev?"

"They may do. But if they were to discover her to be a forgery, they would suppress it, because the church will want to welcome the faithful, and their wallets."

"So they have the real Lady back in Kalkos?"

"Unless I decided the real Lady should go home, yes." He smiled, and raised his glass to her. "I will share everything I have, whilst I am with you, but there are always secrets I must keep from you. What I ask from you is silence in the matter, a promise to tell nothing of what you know. But don't ask me again, and I won't lie to you; because which one is the Lady, and which is the pretender, is something I shall never, ever divulge, not even to you."

# GLOSSARY OF GREEK LANGUAGE

*Bouzouki* – a musical instrument

*Kafebriko* – a traditional, long-handled coffeepot

*Kafenion* – café

*Kali mera (sas)* – good morning, good day (*sas* = polite/plural form)

*Kali nichta (sas)* – goodnight

*Kali orexi* – good digestion, used like the French *bon appétit*

*Kali spera (sas)* – good evening

*Kamari mou* – my pride, my son

*Kyria* – Madam

*Kyrie* – Sir

*Mou* – my, often used in the sense of "my dear"

*Panayia mou* – by the Virgin (exclamation, often of surprise)

*Papa* – Father

*Pappou* – Grandpa

*Peraste* – go ahead, after you

*Periptero* – a street-corner kiosk selling newspapers, cigarettes, etc.

*Sto kalo* – goodbye (literally, Go to the good)

*Vre, mikre!* – hey, little one!

*Yassou, Yassas* – common hello and goodbye greeting, singular/plural or informal/polite forms

*Yiatre* – Doctor

# *Acknowledgments*

My heartfelt thanks to Helen McIldowie-Jenkins for her guidance into the ancient and fascinating mysteries of the icon painter's art; a more patient and knowledgeable teacher would be hard indeed to find. My grateful thanks too to Captain A. Morton DSC RN for his careful reading and correction of the novel's opening. As always, thanks to the team at Bloomsbury, and—last but under no circumstances least—to all at Christopher Little.

# *About the Author*

Anne Zouroudi was born in England and has lived in the Greek islands. Her attachment to Greece remains strong, and the country is the inspiration for much of her writing. She now lives in the Derbyshire Peak District with her son. She is the author of three other Seven Deadly Sins Mysteries: *The Messenger of Athens* (shortlisted for the ITV3 Crime Thriller Award for Breakthrough Authors and long-listed for the Desmond Elliot Prize), *The Taint of Midas,* and *The Doctor of Thessaly.*